PRAISE FOR
Whiskey and Other Unusual Ghosts

"In these perfectly constructed, intimately detailed, and emotionally charged tales, Edwards isolates the silent horrors underscoring our lives and woven into our closest relationships, urging them to take psychological and physical form. In the cold hours before dawn his creatures rise, arch their backs, and begin the search for sustenance, feeding off of childhood fears and lifelong grievances. Hidden in memories, abandoned rooms, and forgotten trails, adorned with the fantasies we invent to conceal their nature, our monsters merely postpone the moment of revelation until we're far too vulnerable to escape." — S.P. Miskowski, author of *The Worst Is Yet to Come*

"*Whiskey and Other Unusual Ghosts* by S. L. Edwards is a startling debut collection whose author has unflinching insight into the political and the personal, into the human and the inhuman alike. A true standout among the new voices in modern Horror. Fans of Nadia Bulkin will find a lot to love here." — Matthew M. Bartlett, author of *Gateways to Abomination*

"S. L. Edwards is a natural storyteller, with a keen command of voice, a delightfully twisted imagination, and a wily, prodigious intellect. *Whiskey and Other Unusual Ghosts* lives up to its inventive title with tales of hauntings that are chilling, funny, moving, and—quite often— all three at once. I loved this collection." — Jon Padgett, author of *The Secret of Ventriloquism*

"S. L. Edwards' debut collection is a bonafide marvel. This criminally talented Son of Texas has crafted something incredibly special here, flavored with a singular and deeply affecting voice. Edwards deftly moves from weird fiction, scrawling his lore in the blood of historical horrors, dipping his fangs into unnerving psychodrama with a deftness so sly and slick it's hard to believe this is his first collection of terrors.

Wonderful and wily and essential." — Mer Whinery, author of *Trade Yer Coffin for a Gun*

"Armed with a taut understanding of power and the damage that power can do, Sam's stories are conscientious, unsparing, and a reflection of the world we've broken. A writer with a vision to watch." — Nadia Bulkin, author of *She Said Destroy*

"S. L. Edwards has crafted something truly special with *Whiskey and Other Unusual Ghosts*. Phantoms and monsters haunt these pages, but so do far greater demons: loneliness, addiction, lost love. In these stories, there's pain, there's beauty, and beyond it all, there's a profound humanity that will by turns unsettle you as well as break your heart. A sublime debut, and one that should jump to the top of your reading list immediately." — Gwendolyn Kiste, author of *The Rust Maidens* and *Pretty Marys All in a Row*

"Sam L. Edwards' prose is as sharp as it is haunting. Combining horror, pulp, noir, fantasy, and war drama, this debut collection displays a craft of narrative and a depth of emotional resonance that's exceedingly impressive. Not to be missed." — Sean M. Thompson, author of *The D3mon and Farmington Correction*

"This titillating debut fiction collection by S. L. Edwards takes the reader through haunting gem-filled caves in the southern forests to the harshest winter terrain of Siberia. Stories range from protagonists defeating evil cats to the lives of anti-heroic guerilla war leaders to fae who always get what they deserve, no matter what oaths are broken. Drink in the rich, sweetened slow-burn of *Whiskey and Other Unusual Ghosts*." — Ashley Dioses, author of *Diary of a Sorceress*

"In this powerful and memorable collection, Edwards' stories are haunted by otherworldy terrors and the ghosts of the past in equal measure. These are excellent character-driven, emotionally resonant, and memorable delves into the realms of the terribly fantastic and weird." — Jonathan Raab, author of *The Lesser Swamp Gods of Little Dixie* and *Camp Ghoul Mountain Part VI: The Official Novelization*

Whiskey and Other Unusual Ghosts

S. L. Edwards

JOURNALSTONE
YOUR LINK TO ARTIST TALENT

ISBN: 978-1-68510-055-1 (sc)
ISBN: 978-1-68510-056-8 (ebook)
Library of Congress Control Number: 2022951314

First printing edition: February 17, 2023
Printed by JournalStone Publishing in the United States of America.
Edited by Sean Leonard
Proofreading and Interior Layout by Scarlett R. Algee
Cover Art and Interior Illustrations by Yves Tourigny

JournalStone Publishing
3205 Sassafras Trail
Carbondale, Illinois 62901

JournalStone books may be ordered through booksellers or by
contacting:
JournalStone | www.journalstone.com

For Mom, and all her scary books. I love you.

Contents

Introduction to the Second Edition
by Mer Whinery

THE FOLLOWING WORDS out of my mouth are sheer blasphemy. Fortunately, blasphemy has never been an issue for me, so here it is.

Draws in a deep breath...

I love Texas.

This might seem silly or perplexing to an East Coaster or a Californian. For an Okie, however, it's damn near profane to even say something like that out loud. The rivalry, a silly one to be honest, between Oklahoma and Texas is the brew of legends. How sad. We share so many similarities culturally, geographically, and ten thousand other ways in between. Good food. Country witticisms. Our often stubborn dedication to family ways and old blood tradition.

It's really all about sportsball, I think, this rivalry, and sportsball is stupid.

Sam and I have known one another for a good while. I am old now and forget just how many years, but it's getting on up there. We met via mutual friends and writers, signaling reciprocated respect and sharing trade secrets. I found him amusing and charming. Mostly the amusement was due to his complete deficiency of hubris about his talent. I mean, for real, Sam has no idea how much power he wields from that complex fortress of his heart. Zip. Not a clue. And he does write from his heart, however cerebral and meticulously orchestrated his unnerving narratives are. You can feel him actually *pulling* his memories from the deep and uncomfortable parts of himself. Dragging them out in spectral chains, commanding them to their knees, only to free them with a kiss upon the brow and a tender word. Reconstructing those dark moments into fiction of profound, penetrating terror. A lovely terror, but a terror, nevertheless.

I actually feel like tacking on the label of "horror writer" is a bit of a disservice to the man. This is, quite simply, just storytelling at its finest. Often, when reading Sam, I would forget this was horror. Not horror in a traditional way, as television and reading the fiction of other writers has been sold to us. This is the work of a conjurer of phantasms dipping into a whole new bag of tricks. Many of the tales seem to know one another. The kick to the already sore gut in the lonesome melancholy of "I've Been Here a Very Long Time" could be paired up perfectly in the hellish addiction rewire of "Maggie Was A Monster". Skewered childhoods and stained adolescence. Trauma bombs. The horror of having to be a grown-up in a world created to chew you up like chum in the water. Heavy things, my friends. But there is quirkiness and levity as well. Just try and read "And the Woman Loved Her Cats" without a shit-eating grin on your mug. "Movie Magic," to a lover of dilapidated small-town movie houses of the past such as myself, made me want to throw my arms around it and bear hug the hell out of it.

But it's not all spookshows and cheap thrills. There is also a certain specific bravery in Sam's work. He's not afraid to dip his mitts into the dreaded *P* territory. *P* as in political. Political horror is beyond tricky. You gotta work that tightrope act of getting it right and still be entertaining. Sam gets this, and gets it oh so perfectly sweet in the astounding "Cabras" and the crowning lynchpin of the collection, "Volver Al Monte". The latter, delightfully cinematic and intense as hell, will both get under your skin and make you beg for more of it. This is fiction that just *works*. Do you have any idea how tough that is? Do you?

So you see, this book you are reading here, whether it be by way of a dead tree copy or some electronic thingamabob, IS Texas. You can have its author, Mr. Sam L. Edwards (the L is for Leonardo, and I just made that up) to thank for that. It's *his* Texas. A distinctly southwestern flavor is cooked into every single page, seasoning each sentence with the palette of its author. As a provincial writer myself, I immediately identified with him. I understood it. That sort of connection, in my opinion, between an author and his audience is profoundly rare and beautiful.

Sam has no idea about this, of course. He would just mumble embarrassedly and try to change the subject to something else. Something other than him. Don't believe me? Try it with him sometime and watch him struggle to give you every little reason he's not something special. Something rare and singular.

Sorry, buddy, I'm in charge of this conversation and you get to be rightfully beloved here. Now, get back to work and give us more.

Mer Whinery
2/4/2023

Introduction to the First Edition
by Gwendolyn Kiste

ALLOW ME TO start right here by making a prediction: the book that you're holding at this moment is one you're going to remember for years to come. It's everything a reader could want in a collection of creepy short stories. At once a throwback to classic horror with monsters and spirits and all the usual trappings of the genre, it's also a brave and fascinating step forward in its exploration of the strange, the terrifying, and the deeply haunting.

S. L. Edwards—or just Sam to those of us who are fortunate enough to call him a friend—is a marvel to behold. Practically overnight, he's carved out an indelible niche for himself in the speculative community, and rightfully so. I can't quite remember now where I first encountered Sam or his writing. He's the kind of author who seemed to materialize mystically out of the ether, his work suddenly everywhere at once, in all the coolest anthologies and magazines.

There's a lot of heated discussion these days, in particular in the weird fiction and horror community, about separating the art from the artist, with many positing that you don't necessarily have to like a person to appreciate their work. Fortunately, an author like Sam makes it easy on all of us by being as awesome a human being as he is a writer. And this really matters, especially in the case of a collection like *Whiskey and Other Unusual Ghosts*, which relies on a keen sensitivity to the human condition. Only individuals with deep empathy and curiosity about the world around them—and the people in it—could put this much heart into their stories.

This book starts out with a punch to the gut in the chilling coming-of-age story, "Maggie Was a Monster." The prose is so beautiful yet terrifying, and the only thing that outdoes that stellar opening page is the tale's devastating ending. So many stories included here delve into this familiar yet undeniably meaningful territory: the pain of growing up, of being misunderstood, of losing the people you love and even losing yourself. This theme of loss and all the heartache that goes with it are explored expertly in "When the Trees Sing," "We Will Take Half," and "Whiskey and Memory," among several notable others. After the span of only a handful of paragraphs, you won't be able to shake these characters from your mind, even if you want to.

However, don't expect only melancholy in these pages. There's more to the human experience than just the downtrodden, and Sam proves how skilled he is at channeling a gamut of emotions here. If you want a wonderfully bizarre and humorous tale, for example, look no further than "And the Woman Loved Her Cats." As an affirmed cat lover myself, I find there are few joys quite so sweet as seeing felines incorporated into fiction in such a masterful yet deeply creepy way. (As a side note, "grotesque cat stories" needs to become a ubiquitous subgenre of horror immediately, and Sam can then lay claim to being among the modern trendsetters who inspired it all.)

Looking back over this table of contents that features so many truly incredible tales, it's strange and surprising to think this is only Sam's first book. No doubt it won't be his last. Still, a debut collection is no small moment for a writer, and this book is no small achievement. I initially read these stories months ago, and they've stuck with me ever since, haunting the edges of my life with both their honesty and their lingering intensity. The end result is the best possible kind of success for a relative writing newcomer: *Whiskey and Other Unusual Ghosts* is not only a unique literary triumph unto itself, but also a promise of great work to come.

So take my advice: read this book, relish each story in it, and then be on the lookout for everything S. L. Edwards writes from this moment on. If you love horror that plumbs the depths of the human experience as much as I do, then you won't be disappointed.

Gwendolyn Kiste
4/2/2019

Whiskey and Other Unusual Ghosts

Maggie Was a Monster

I T'S MAGGIE'S TURN to be the monster. You don't like being the monster, you hate the way your hands feel when they turn into claws and how your eyes glow in the dark when you look into the mirror. Sometimes you don't recognize your own smile and that makes you cry. When that happens, the sound you make scares you so much that you can barely breathe. But Maggie said that this is how the game is played, so you play along, being the monster when it's your turn to change and chase her around the house.

But, it's *Maggie's* turn.

It's been her turn for eight years.

You haven't seen daylight or a calendar since she trapped you. She was only eight then, when she caught you. You still don't understand how she did it, how you ran into the closet after her and have been there ever since. You can't move in the light, and the grownups must not be able to see you because when they open the door to Maggie's closet it's like they're looking right through you.

You've stopped speaking, because at first you used to plead with Maggie, *beg* her to let you out. At first you could hear her whimpering from the other side of the closet door as you threw your massive hands against it in thundering cracks. She would cry, sobbing so pathetically that you would eventually feel guilty and stop scaring her. Maybe you didn't understand the game after all, maybe you did something wrong. The grownups never seem to hear you anyway, so suddenly the ones that used to be the most important aren't important at all.

The nights are hardest. You know it's night because the little sliver of light on the bottom of the door becomes green, the color of the night light you and Maggie used to make shadow puppets around. At night you think about your own home, and you cry because you don't know if anyone thinks about you anymore. The only company you have is the mirror, and you remain the same ugly creature you are.

In daytime, you daydream about what life is like on the other side of the closet. You imagine Maggie as she goes to school, as she makes new friends and continues on with her life. Sometimes you hear people outside during the day. When you hear them in the day they are never nice. They scream, they shatter glass, and they howl out in a language that barely sounds human. Every part of you wants to leap out of the closet, to stop them from doing what they are doing so that you can go back to daydreaming about a life that is not yours.

But you can't. And those days when the people who can't see you are inside the house, howling at each other...those are the days that end with bad nights. The nights where Maggie cries into her pillow with choking, heaving sobs.

And you didn't even *say* anything.

As time goes on you begin to worry more about Maggie. You hear boys in her room, low people talking in sweet voices that always murmur so you can't hear them. One day, it sounds like a boy and Maggie are hurting each other and you begin to scream. She hears you, and she begins to scream too. The boy leaves, shouting at her like she did something wrong. And she cries again, and you imagine that she is sitting in a corner, hugging herself as she stares at your closet door.

The fights between the day people end. There are shrieks, and a door slams so hard that it shakes the floor beneath you. Maggie comes back into the room and she begins to cry. Another voice comes into the room, and for the first time in your life you hear a father cry.

You never hear Maggie's mother again.

And the boys come into her room more and more, torturing you with their *sounds*.

Maggie becomes a new screaming voice in the house. She fights with her dad a lot, though you don't know what about. It's quiet in the house for weeks, then through the muffling of the door you can make out coughs and splatters. She is somewhere in the house, moaning and coughing and laughing in a way that scares you more than any scream ever could. You push your way through the coats and shoes to find a corner in the dark closet where you can only barely see the mirror that has been your only company. Without sight, the laugh seems much less terrifying.

When Maggie's dad comes home he begins yelling at her. First, she shouts back, and then she begins to break down into tears. The process is more disturbing than anything you've ever seen in the mirror, and you grow more and more comfortable with your reflection. After a few more fights, you're not afraid of your reflection anymore.

You spend days just looking at yourself, realizing that you were never that scary at all.

The final days trapped inside your little prison you begin to make up for lost time, you reflect on *yourself* instead of Maggie. You notice when she opens the closet door, reaches for clothes and makeup, that she has grown thin and pale. The child who you watched grow up has become a pale, sickly woman. Her bones are poking out from every part of her skin and you think back to the zombie movies that used to give you two nightmares. Her eyes, which used to be so bright and happy, grow dimmer and dimmer each day. There are little marks on her body now, on her arms and between her toes, like bug bites that sometimes bleed even though they aren't scratched.

One day you hear Maggie shout.

A man screams back.

You wince, their crying and roaring rising, searing the inside of your ears.

Hours later, a door slams and it's louder than anything you've heard before.

You put your hand up to your ears and you don't feel your claws. You look in the mirror, and your eyes don't glow. You touch the closet door, and with just a gentle tap you are out in the blinding light of the bedroom.

Everything is so much bigger than you remembered it. Maggie's room isn't pink anymore, white and barren and covered in rumpled clothes and papers. There are notebooks thrown across the floor with depressing notes and though you want to stop and cry you know you have something to do. Down the hallway the pictures of Maggie grow larger and sadder, you only recognize the smile in one of them, back when she used to play "Monster" with you.

The house is quiet, worse than when it is empty. There is a dusty smell in the air that burns with each inhale. You are nervous and scared, stepping deliberately down the little stairs to the living room. There are stains everywhere on the carpet, different colors and shapes that let you know that the years have not been good to the house.

Downstairs, Maggie isn't crying. You know she is in the kitchen not because you can hear her but because you have *always* known where she is. In the living room you see a little red stain in the kitchen grow darker and larger, you smell something both rotten and fresh. You feel the tears well up in your eyes because you know what you are going to see before you duck through the kitchen archway. You dip your head and look into the soft-yellow-lit kitchen and see Maggie all alone.

She's sitting at the table, turned away from you. She grabs a dirty needle full of thick, yellow liquid and begins whistling as she plays with it. The song ends as the needle slides into her arm. Elegantly. Like a ballerina. Her body trembles at first then shakes violently so that the beautiful blonde hair you used to braid looks like a storm cloud. The whistling becomes a hum, lower and lower as her body moves against its own rhythm.

You cry out, run around the table and trip over a chair before you see her face. Her eyes are almost closed, but open wide when she looks up at you. You dread her scream more than anything in the world. You can only imagine what she sees, this fanged creature that hovers in eight-foot shadows that she put away for so long that she forgot you. Her scream would kill you, splinter your heart into a thousand pieces so you could never love again.

But she just smiles at you.

And it is the most beautiful thing you have ever seen.

Author's Notes: This story is about growing up. I've always been a fan of bildungsroman and wanted to try my hand at a condensed version.

Like many others, I've encountered addiction. This story is about too many true stories. This is its first time appearing in print.

I've Been Here a Very Long Time

CARL WAS CRYING in the closet. He held his favorite toy, a green teddy bear his father won for him at a carnival four years ago. Dark outlines of jackets and hanging shirts surrounded him with their empty, limp arms. Comforting rather than claustrophobic, the small closet was his only cradle from the world. He put his hand over his mouth, trying to muffle his thick sobs so his parents would not hear him, not that they could anyway. The sound of their fighting slid under the door with the low light of the living room lamp. There were words he did not understand, things that they had told him never to say, and indistinct roars of animal hatred. His face was stinging everywhere, wet with snot and tears that choked his anxiety with a heaving chest. He swallowed, rubbing his nose and trying to imagine that he was anywhere else but there. He put his face into his teddy bear, hugging it to the point of strangulation as he felt his own wetness soak into its fabric.

"Please stop crying."

He stopped crying. The voice was low and hollow, a beautiful chime dimmed by travel through a rusted metal pipe. It echoed into unseen corners hidden by clothes and toys. He looked around the closet, and seeing himself alone he could not breathe.

"I don't like it when you cry."

Carl blinked. In the absence of his crying the fight down the hall became louder, crescendoing in crashing footsteps and pounding.

Screams had replaced their words, the hard sound of flesh-hitting-flesh filled the noise like sprinkling in a howling storm.

A slow chill came from the floor and turned his breath to a thin mist. A light fog began to climb out from behind his jackets, enveloping him on all sides in a crawling hug. His lungs rattled cautiously, eyes darting around in the vain hope of seeing a friendly face. Soon, the unique curiosity which overtakes small children overpowered his more adult fear.

"Where are you?" he asked in a whisper.

"I am in here, with you."

The voice spoke quick and serene, as if the explanation was difficult but absolute. He could not find a direction that the voice came from, but he felt its vibrations of soft sound through every part of the mist. He thought slowly, formulating another question to ask his visitor.

"How long have you been here?"

"I've been here a very long time."

The quiet drowned out the fighting; he only heard his own breathing accompanied by his quick-beating heart.

"What is wrong?" the voice asked.

Carl sighed and told his story to the empty closet, how his mother and father had been fighting more and more recently; how at his birthday they had made horrible remarks about each other from the rims of their wineglasses. How his mother and father kept talking about someone named "Stacy" who Carl had never seen but apparently worked with his father. He told about how he had been sleeping at his grandparents' for a month now, how his parents had showed up at his grandparents' doorstep, hugging each other tightly and promising with wide smiles that everything would be different. Then he talked about dinner, how Dad had said something about the mashed potatoes that spiraled into a sniping, hateful conversation. How the name "Stacy" bubbled back into the house like tar from a bleeding earth.

His voice was fluttering. He made whining moans between sentences and was about to cry again when the voice spoke:

"Please don't cry. I'll give you whatever you want so long as you don't cry."

"What can you do?" he asked in earnest.

"Everything I can," the voice responded. "What is it that you want?"

"I just want them to stop fighting."

"Very well." The voice made it sound simple. "You must do one thing, however."

"What?" Quivering uncertainty leaked back into his voice. He thought back to the dark fairy tales his father had read him at Christmastime, ones where little boys made deals with creatures and were tricked into being food. He wondered if the voice would ask for a hand, or a finger, something to chew on while it sat in dark places underneath piles of clothes.

"I'll help you while you sleep...but you must promise me that you will not look at me when I leave this place. No matter what you hear...no matter what you feel."

For a moment he was desperately afraid. Then there was a shattering sound of glass and his mother's frantic sobs.

"Okay."

Though he could not see them, he imagined whoever the voice belonged to was smiling.

"Go to sleep."

He stood up and cracked the closet door, letting his nightlight fall on the jackets and toys. Hugging his teddy bear, he ran his arm through the rows of clothes and found only dry, hard wall. Braver, he pushed aside the clothes to reveal that he had been alone the entire time. Shuddering, he closed the door behind him and jumped under his covers.

He fell asleep to the sound of screaming.

At five in the morning his parents had stopped fighting.

Carl heard his closet doorknob twist, the door click and slowly swing wide open. Horrified, he closed his eyes and tried to remember the songs he had learned in Sunday school. There were heavy footsteps that shook his bed, the slopping of wet suction cups against the wooden floor. Another wet step and the pattering of fat spider legs. A second door opened, a door to the hallway where the sucking footsteps became softer and softer.

On the verge of panic, his eyes wide open under the covers, he strained his ears for any sound in the house. The door to his parents' room opened. He waited for screams, yelling anger. The silence was pregnant with horror. The footsteps pattered sloppily by his open bedroom door.

It hurt him to breathe.

When the footsteps came back again, his door clicked shut behind them. A moment of stillness passed before the steps came towards his bed, slow and deliberate. The air around him moved and he closed his eyes and pulled the covers around him tighter into a futile cocoon. Long, silky hair rubbed against the thin sheet above his face, the smell of something clean and cold filled his nose and mouth. The kiss on his forehead was freezing and dry. The footsteps ran back into the closet and slammed the door behind him.

At seven a.m. Carl sat up and looked at his closet door, closed completely.

He stared at it until nine a.m.

His mother appeared in his doorway, a look of concern on her face that found its way into lines and frowns. She was a pale, green-eyed woman with thick brown hair that rested just above her shoulders. In comically big pink pajamas, she walked across the room and rested her hand on Carl's forehead. Her words were indistinct, toned out by his sense of wonder. Her big, beautiful face had no bruises, no scratches. Her green eyes were not red but sparkling and well rested.

He said what came to his mind first: "I heard you and Daddy fighting last night."

She bit her lip with her upper row of teeth, frowning and confused.

"Sweetie..." She stroked his hair lovingly, calming him with a miraculous touch. "Daddy and I didn't fight last night. Did you have a nightmare?"

Relieved, he nodded sleepily. He must have had a nightmare after all, the worst one he had ever had in his life.

She gulped, her sparkling eyes for a moment watery and on the verge of tears. "Come on, Daddy is making breakfast." She stooped off from the bed, shaking the swinging legs of her pajama pants like she was a dancer. She smiled pitifully at him. "We made your favorite...we want you to be as happy to be home as we are."

In the living room Carl's dad whistled over a pan of frying bacon. A thick green robe around him, hair still messy from resting his head on one side for seven continuous hours, his smile was genuine and wonderful when he turned towards his son. His face was thin, pulled tight around a bony frame lined with thick glasses that made his brown eyes look owlish.

"Good morning, kiddo! Bacon, French toast, sunny side up, bit of salsa on the side?"

"He had a nightmare." Mom's voice sounded sad. "About us fighting."

The playful smile vanished from his father's face. He sighed, setting his greasy spatula down on the stovetop before walking over to Carl. Dropping to one knee, his skinny arms enveloped Carl and drew him deeply into the folds of the robe. There was a wet kiss on the top of his head.

"Kiddo, I'm so sorry. I'm so sorry that we ever gave you something to have a nightmare about. But you understand, we are better now..."

Carl looked into his father's face, seeing a tear roll out from under his glasses.

"We're a family again."

II

His childhood had been one without incident. Sometimes he wished for a little brother or sister, but other times he was too happy to ever consider being lonely. His parents were considered attentive, if not overbearing, by school officials. His father occupied a position in the PTA while his mother was renowned as a host to both adults and children alike. The house was full of family and friends, passing from childhood into adolescence.

Judy Carver became his whole world.

He fought his crush vehemently at first, responding to attraction with confusion and resentment. Refusing to acknowledge it, the love grew in a pit in his stomach which greeted him when he woke up and throbbed when he tried to sleep. His friends would make fun of him, laughing at him for staring too long when she walked by, bringing her up in normal conversations where girls had never intervened before. When she spoke to him, he responded with fumbling, panicking words that only elicited confused, awful looks from her.

When he saw her holding hands with a boy he had never seen before, he was crushed.

Throwing his backpack on the floor beside his bed, he bit his tongue and tried to avoid what he was told men did not do. Trying his hardest, the first tear rolled out of his eyes while he moaned. Feeling it, his resolve broke.

"Please do not do that."

He stopped.

The voice came from the open closet door. It had been light and distant, a gentle whisper from a long hallway. He walked cautiously to the closet, hoping and not hoping to find his mother inside, caught in an awkward situation and trying to hide from her son until she heard him cry.

It was empty.

"I hate it when you cry."

He stifled a scream. Falling to the floor, he trembled before the empty closet.

"Are—are you an *angel?*"

No response.

Gulping, he remembered the last scary movie he had seen.

"Are you...are you a *demon*?"

"Could you please explain the difference?" The voice sounded emotionless, uninterested but friendly.

He tried to stammer out a reply.

"What is it that you want?"

He thought hard, with all the concentration he could muster. "I guess..." He looked into the dark, open closet. "I guess I just want her to love me."

The closet did not respond.

"Hello?"

"After you sleep tonight, be sure you do not try to see me. If you look at me, I will take everything away."

With that, he ran out of the room, only re-entering it late that night, fully convinced that he had heard the voice under the influence of tremendous stress.

At five in the morning it crawled out of his open closet. With his eyes closed he heard its smacking footsteps, followed by the slithering sound of an open corpse being drug across a flat surface. Breathing heavily, cold sweat erupted all over his body as the door to his bedroom opened wide and shut with a quiet, tender touch. He heard the mechanical click of his front door. Throwing his sheets aside, he felt his stomach fall when confronted with a cavernous open closet.

He had closed it when he had gone to bed.

He turned on his lamp and walked towards the open door. Shaking, he peered inside the closet. The smell was overwhelming, clean and cold as frozen perfume or a bouquet of dying flowers. He covered his mouth with his hands, shivering as he stepped farther inside the closet.

For a horrible moment, he thought he heard wind.

Every reasoning part of his being told him that whatever this thing was, he should not be facing it alone; every rational part of his mind told him to give up and run to his parents, wake them up and tell them what was going on. But then another part of him, perhaps more rational than the others, whispered in his ear that he was crazy if he thought they would believe him. Another part, the part that became dominant and terrifying, told him that he *was* crazy, and that if he could not hide his growing insanity, he could at the very least postpone its revelation. Too often he heard rumors in the hallways of students who had gone crazy, overcome with depression and fear.

Jeremy Atkins had committed suicide not too long ago.

Down the hall, a door opened and closed.

He followed the smell of lavender. The dim, green hall light did little other than expose the darkness of the open bathroom, put there for his father whose eyesight had been deteriorating for years. He heard his parents snoring from behind their closed door, the clock ticking from its place above the living room mantel. Streetlamps poured light from behind the thin curtains, and the room was only populated by furniture.

He walked to the front door and pulled the knob.

Locked.

Sighing, Carl looked at the clock.

Five a.m.

He sat on the couch, looking at the front door. He knew that he heard it open, heard it shut. But there was no way to lock the door from the outside, not without a key. He decided he would wait, damn the voice in the closet. He would sit on the couch, waiting for it to come back.

At 5:30, the door opened.

He heard the footsteps, loud and fast as they slapped on the floor. In his mind he screamed commands at his body to turn around, to face the object of his torture and fear. From a primal part of his stomach, he found himself frozen against his will. The door closed, there was the hissing sound of a sigh through grated teeth.

"You really mustn't look." The voice was female now, lecturing and motherly. "I don't want to take everything away."

The footsteps came towards the couch, sending little tremors as Carl felt his organs shivering inside him. Never before had he been so aware of every nerve on his body as when those thick, cold limbs touched the back of his neck. A kiss like wet, heavy mushrooms. A scream died inside him as the footsteps rushed backward, as if in full sprint.

The closet door in his room slammed shut.

He did not sleep for two nights.

III

Sometimes Carl thought about Judy Carver. Mostly it was when he was sad, after he had a fight with Lilly or after he had too much whiskey. Sometimes he saw the glittering of her eyes as the sunlight peered through dying tree branches. When icicles formed on the front porch, he imagined the scene her parents came home to all those years ago. Their little daughter, hanging from a noose with a piece of notebook paper taped to her chest:

"I love you, Carl."

They hadn't spoken to him for years, and he blamed himself for her suicide. Judy had loved him, and though he had never been in love before, he loved her back. However, as the two matured Carl became increasingly annoyed in the little things that Judy did. Her laugh, the way she clicked her teeth. The little flaws in her chipped away at his love, and though his feelings changed, hers did not.

She killed herself the night he broke up with her. Two days after Christmas...so many years ago.

It was hard not to think about her now, after everything Lilly had told him. She had been cheating on him ever since their second son went to college. She explained that he was a cold, hurtful man who would make snide comments he thought were funny because he enjoyed hurting her, that he was so vain in his intelligence that everything he said only made his supposed brilliance unremarkable and rude. She told him that kind words were not in his vocabulary, that his touch made her shiver. That she only stayed because on some level she still cared for him, cared about the father of her children and about the young man she once married.

"A few awards and tenure though, and that happy young man is gone...swallowed up by a hateful, egotistical monster."

He hadn't been to the old house in a few years. His mother and father died twelve years ago, his mother shortly after his father. They had been like swans, so in love which each other that one could not live without the other. He was an only child, and there was such an intimidating amount of memory and junk in the old house that he only promised Lilly that he would empty the house *one day*.

When he had a chance.

He loved Lilly, no matter what she believed. He always loved her. Still did, even if she wanted to divorce him. He had to let her; he didn't want to hurt her any more than he already had.

He only hoped the next man would be better for her than he was.

Dust had settled into the atmosphere permanently, covering the surface of tables and photos of faces frozen in euphoric happiness. There were pictures of his parents in their later years, on trips to monuments and parks. There were weddings, grandchildren, and everywhere there were photos of Carl as he grew up.

They had been so proud of him.

There he was, holding the first copy of his first published book.

He walked up the stairs, glumly looking at the old photos of happier versions of himself.

Pushing the door to his old room, he only found his mother's study. There were pictures of him everywhere, along with his two sons when they were children. His mother was the best when she was around young children. As he aged, they had grown increasingly apart, to the point where he and his father would go on outings without her. She seemed sad that people grew up...one of the last things she had told him before she died was: *"You just seemed happier when you were younger, Carl."*

He didn't think she realized how much that comment hurt him.

The bottle of whiskey sloshed against his lips. Already his head was spinning, and he sat down at an empty desk to let the oak taste burn its way down his esophagus. By the time the sun had gone down, the bottle was almost gone.

He stood up from the desk and fell to the floor when the house moved. He cursed, screaming at himself to get up. When his body wouldn't move, he realized that nothing was the way he wanted. He began to sob the heaving sobs of a broken man.

"Please don't cry." The voice came from the vacant closet. "I hate it when you cry."

He rolled over on his back, heaving his chest. The door to the closet was open and visibly empty save for two cardboard boxes.

Beneath the whiskey he recalled the night when his parent's last fought, and the night when his premature love for Judy consumed him the way only a first love can. He remembered convincing himself that it was all a hallucination, something brought on by youthful stress. Now, he supposed the voice had come back.

"Where have you been?" Carl asked in a slurred, hateful voice.

"I've been here the whole time."

He didn't speak, waiting for the buzz to fade so he could formulate a coherent question. The voice did not wait:

"What do you need to be happy?"

"… That's all I want," he replied as sobs clogged his throat. "All I want is *to be happy*."

When he woke up everything was dark. There was a dull throbbing in his head and the feeling of a full, churning stomach. Groaning, he felt his way up from the hard, wooden floor. The thoughts in his head were swimming and disconnected. For a moment, Lilly was yelling at him, screaming at him with a red face of tears and sweat. Next, he saw his own eyes staring at him from a picture frame, tormenting him with their own joy. Finally, he heard the old voice from the closet.

Many times in his life he had thought himself mentally unstable, but he only truly believed it three times. He was too old and too alone to not have his mental health examined if he thought something was wrong. He would need to make an appointment with the psychiatrist in the morning.

He looked at his watch, balking that he had been passed out on the floor for so long.

He walked out of his room and towards the front door, laughing at himself to cover the sad realization that his dream of Lilly was no dream at all.

There were wet, smacking sounds on the steps below. Looking down, a scream escaped him before the enormity of what he was seeing truly struck him. Even with its hair thick and matted, white and swollen lips, he recognized his mother's face.

His mother's face opened wide to reveal rows of needle-like teeth.

Her face flew up the stairs.

Long, spider-like hands grabbed at his shoulders.

IV

Carl woke up that morning sleeping in his closet. He rubbed his eyes which stung from a whole night of uninterrupted tears. His chest hurt, and he moaned while he hugged the green teddy bear next to him. He was six, six and waking up from a nightmare of monsters and troubles. He looked around the closet, for a moment expecting a terrible face to poke out from behind the rows of jackets.

He was alone though.

Alone.

He heard soft footsteps outside his door. When it slid open, soft light flooded into the closet door. He put his hand above his eyes, blinded by the light. Initially a dark silhouette, his mother's bruised face came into focus.

"Hey, sweet man," she said. "We're going to go get breakfast, okay?"

Nodding and holding his teddy bear by the hand, Carl grabbed his mother's hand and did his best not to cry anymore.

Author's Notes: This one began with a simple premise: "the monster in the closet loves you." It loves you and it would do anything for you. That sort of unconditional, all-consuming love was only comparable to a mother's. The story was first published in a limited run in *Turn to Ash* vol. 0 and was my first published story.

When the Trees Sing

CHUCK, I'M CALLING because you're a *good* man. You're a good man and you *believe* people. Too many people don't believe me, and I've grown awfully tired of it.

Maybe, after we're done, you *won't* believe me. But as bad as it is, it feels good to talk about it.

It feels good to *confess*.

You're focused on government conspiracies, and though I can't speak much to aliens, I can tell you that some of the more sinister shit is more real than we would like it to be. I stopped believing in God the summer of 1967. That summer, I joined up with Tiger Force.

I was gonna be an English major, wanted to teach at some high school in Vienna...Vienna, *West Virginia*, but you were probably guessing that. That was the plan, until Martha got pregnant. Right after that, my number was called up.

It's true, I could've fought it. I could have protested, gone to college anyway. Hell, my family wanted me to. My dad, he fought in WWII, hopped around the Pacific and bled on every one of those goddamn islands. He told me he wouldn't think any less of me if I stayed home, that he knew that this was a war that wasn't gonna be worth fighting.

But I went. I went because I gobbled up that hometown narrative of a freedom worth fighting for. But that's not just it. No...no, Chuck, if I'm gonna be real honest with you, I left because I was *scared*. Scared of the child growing inside Martha, scared of seeing something with my own blood out there in the world. Scared of seeing something that I was responsible for. Scared of something new, and something unknown.

And in my mind, the child was far scarier than any war.

I was damn foolish.

How I got into Tiger Force is a longer story. I hopped around Vietnam a bit. By the time I met up with them I was already a veteran, drenched in every drop of blood those jungles could offer. But, Chuck...let's just say that you don't need any "extraterrestrials" to make the United States Government evil and mysterious. *Every story* about Tiger Force is true. Yeah, they cut off ears and wore 'em as necklaces. Yeah, they lined civilians up against walls and shot 'em to prove a point. The more gruesome things, the rapes, the mutilations of bodies...

Every single story is true.

I wasn't with them long, but it felt like a tour of Hell. And I won't lie to you, Chuck, I did some monstrous things. The first day, I couldn't stop vomiting, was just the sickest I'd ever been in my life. I tried to hide away, but that night three of them came into my tent. They pinned me down, hovered over me and made me bite down on one of those ears. I can't describe the taste enough. Dry, sour, flaked with copper and rough hair. I still taste it, a ghost overlaid on every meal I've eaten since.

Then they whispered, they told me that if I didn't participate, I wouldn't make it home: "We ain't stupid, Harv," one of them told me. "We *have* maps, we *know* where Vienna is."

So...so I started "participating."

I don't know how I didn't go crazy. Maybe I *am* crazy, maybe *that's* why I hear things.

I managed to get through those days though, by thinking about my wife and my little girl. Martha started sending me pictures after Ashley was born, and I'll tell you that I loved that little girl before I even met her. The anxiety, the fear that had sent me there, it went up in smoke immediately.

And my dad, God bless him, he gave me a book to read before I left. *The Divine Comedy*. He knew *Inferno* was my favorite, and he had tried *so hard* to convince me to not go. "Just remember," he said, "when it gets bad...it could get worse."

So, in the good times, I thought about Martha and my baby Ashley.

In the bad times, I got through daydreaming about *being* in Hell instead of *making* it.

The people we hurt, the people *I* hurt, they became nothing more than the sum of their parts, you know? They're nothing more than bits of bloody plumbing. They fall apart just like anything else does when you shoot it.

I stopped worryin' about souls, about fate, about morality. Our goal was to instill absolute terror into the enemy, to make ourselves seem so savage that they would stay down forever.

We probably would've done just that, too, if no one with a conscience stopped us.

My final week there, we were in a village. It wasn't too different from what happened in Mai Lai. Only we stayed. I think the leadership knew it wasn't going to have free rein much longer. They treated that place like a goddamn carnival of flesh and blood...I don't sleep much anymore, Chuck.

But I'll never forget one instance, one sound, of this poor mother howling and begging that they just leave her baby alone. That's all she wanted, you know? Just to be left alone. Her face, so tortured and red from screaming and crying, hair messed from what they had done to her...I never did forget that face.

I came back home, and everything was wonderful for a while. My Martha, boy did she look pretty holding my little girl's hand. You can't know how I happy I was. It was wonderful, being home with her...making love felt so right, so natural. And well, Ashley...

I'm sorry. I'm so sorry. It's hard not to cry.

But I'm gonna make it.

Ashley was the greatest little girl who ever lived, I'll tell ya. She would get back into our back yard and she would name each and every one of the squirrels that she saw. "Mr. Buttercake," "Princess Acorn," "Queen Prospera."

And then, you know, I've always wanted to be a writer. When she got old enough, I'd sit right out there with her, and I'd make up names and we would come up with stories together. Sure, I'd let her take the lead and the stories didn't make much sense, but they were *ours*.

At night when I tucked her in, I'd sing her a song. And she'd sing right along.

"You are my sunshine."

And she was.

Martha, though...as time went on something began to change.

I'd look at her at night, while she was asleep, and in that dim light I'd see something else. I'd see something pulled, stressed, anguished, with messed hair and tears running down its cheeks. I'd blink, and it would be gone. In the mornings I'd wake up with the feeling that somehow I didn't deserve my happiness.

That none of that life was really mine in the first place.

I lost my appetite for food. And for loving.

When she asked why I wouldn't touch her, what could I say? Was she not pretty enough? Good God, Chuck, I've never known a more beautiful woman in my life. Was it something she did? Every act of hers was as true a blessing as could ever exist.

Was there someone else?

What could I say, that when I saw her I saw the face of a mother that never lived? The *faces* of mothers who I had to kill?

There *was* someone else, lots of other people. So many ghosts standing between me and her.

So, my depression began to spread from me to my family. Martha took to drinking with me, in long periods of silence. We wouldn't look at each other, just sit up and sip while Ashley was asleep. I'd always managed to put up a front for Ashley, maybe on account of my training. But Martha, she couldn't do it.

She'd dip into rages, scream at everyone. Then she'd cry, hate herself even though she was the most perfect woman you ever knew.

It absolutely devastated me when they couldn't find her.

One day, as far as I could tell, she just up and left. Ashley woke me up, asked me where Mommy was. I was heartbroken, and we looked everywhere. The police brought the dogs out and we combed through every inch of those woods. We put up fliers, radio ads.

Nothing.

So the rumors started, as rumors usually do. More than any of it, that's what broke my heart the most.

Then I found the note.

It had been tucked away in my sock drawer, she folded it real neatly and small so that I wouldn't find it until she had been gone awhile...

I'm sorry. I promised you the story.

Point is, she blamed me. She said that the sadness, the depression which clung to me like a mist, was: "Contaminating the house and all its corners." She apologized by saying she "felt obligated to say goodbye. I love you...but you make me too sad."

It wasn't long after that that I found her in the woods. I don't know how we could've missed her, because there she was! Splayed underneath a pine tree, wrists open for all the world to see, face just as beautiful as when I last saw her. That face and the blood-crusted leaves under her said it all. They say that you can't blame yourself when something like that happens, but that's a load of crock.

The little voices inside of me that pulled since I got back from Vietnam were right. I didn't deserve any of what I had, so she left.

The town though, they *did* blame me. Maybe you remember the reports. There wasn't enough evidence for charges, but the court of public opinion sure as shit made its verdict. Martha's mom tried to take Ashley away from me, called me a killer on the steps of the county courthouse. That was enough to make me stop drinking forever. It doesn't do any good anymore, doesn't do *anything* to make the ghosts go away.

True, I didn't have to see the face of that mother sleeping next to me anymore, but I still heard her. When I turned on a water faucet, it would scream first. When I opened a door, it would squeal. Like a surprised animal, you know? I would move a pot or a pan to cook and there would be an explosion. And then sometimes I would wake up to the laughter...some of those bastards would just laugh as they...you don't wanna know.

You *don't.*

The laugh would come from all sorts of places. Open doors at night, television static during the day. It came from the cabinet where the unopened whiskey bottles lived, came from Ashley's bedroom when she slept. And I would stand there, looking at my little girl and wondering how she could be so peaceful when the room was so full of that noise.

And I came to accept that I lost my mind.

Then one day, Ashley said she saw Momma in the woods.

I took a look at the window where she was pointing. Nothing. But that old impulse took over me, that creative pull that you sometimes get with kids. They're so nice, so un-skeptical that you have to imagine the world is better as they see it.

So I asked, what was Momma wearing?

I expected something pretty, something fanciful. Ashley was a pretty thoughtful kid, naming squirrels and such. But no.

"She's wearing some sort of nighty. And Daddy...her hands are red."

I had tried to protect her from the news; Ashley didn't deserve to know what her momma had done. So at first I was horrified. But then I thought that somehow, someone had told her about what happened. I got mad. I told Ashley I didn't want her going in the yard at night anymore.

We didn't have much in the way of a fence, the woods just kinda begin at the end of the grass. I thought that maybe her grandmother was coming, visiting her at night and telling her about her momma.

I know, it was a crazy thought. But I already told you, Chuck, I wasn't well.

My new rule didn't do much good though.

It became a constant. "Daddy, Mommy is staring at me at night. She looks through the window and she has no eyes. Daddy, Mommy visited me today. She stood at the back door and smiled. She's *missing teeth*. Daddy, I don't think Mommy is really dead. Daddy, why can't you see her?"

I got angrier than I should have. But I was scared, I was worried. I screamed at her, and my little girl ran to her room and shut the door.

That was the last time I saw her.

Well, not the *last*.

Eventually I worked up the courage for an apology, something I had needed to do more and more in our last days together. I opened her door and she wasn't there. The window was wide open, with night air coming in.

I've never been more scared in my life. Not in the summer of 1967, not when Martha went missing. I was furious with fear. I ran out into the woods, screaming until I was out of breath, scraping myself and falling down over every root and fallen branch. I must have run for hours, pouring through every inch before I collapsed.

They combed the woods again that morning. Their looks were stabs, telling me without speaking that already they thought I had it in me to kill my little girl. My princess. My storyteller.

No good. No good at all.

This time, they tried to make evidence stick. Martha's parents made me into a monster. My own brother stopped talking to me, just flat stopped taking my calls. I still don't blame them. It seems pretty obvious as to who a prime suspect would be. After all, I was alone with my daughter and I was clearly going crazy. They were justified in their assumptions.

Then, about two months later...she came back.

I looked up from the television, and there she was out the window, standing at the edge of the woods, smiling and waving at me. She moved her hands, saying, "Come in, Daddy, *come in.*"

I don't remember opening the door, I don't remember putting on shoes. I just remember being out there in the woods again, screaming her name over the hurt of my throat and heart. Sure, she looked *wrong*, and somewhere in the back of my mind that fact registered. I knew that she was too pale, too thin. But more importantly, it seemed, I knew that she was running away fast and that I didn't have long to catch her. I knew that I may never see her again. So I kept running.

I was in pretty thick when I saw Martha. First, she was distant in my periphery, a tall, spindly shadow that seemed to twist and contort behind each tree she could hide behind. Then she stalked between the trees, running and disappearing amongst them like some sort of soldier. I was frozen. Her face wasn't nearly as welcome as my daughter's. Where once a face had looked at me with love, and then with pity, now it only looked at me with contempt.

And though I never stopped moving, it seemed that each time she appeared in my periphery, she came closer and closer.

That was when the trees began to sing.

"You are my sunshine...my only sunshine."

My daughter's voice came from the trees like she was calling from the edge of a lake, as if some great distance separated us and made her voice echo. Her song came from every direction, the way winds do in a storm.

Mesmerized and confused, I stopped running. That's when Martha fully revealed herself, stepping away from my periphery and into full view.

She watched me, confused and furious. Taller in death than she had ever been in life, craning her back so she could look down on me. Her eyes were sunken in, her mouth fluttering with the remnants of teeth and ragged breath. I tried to scream but all that came out was a scraping sigh. She walked towards me, slowly, deliberately, long arms swinging at her side. From behind her I saw my little girl's head peeking. And smiling. Like it was all a *game*, Chuck!

Her red hands came at me. I looked in her eyes and I knew what she wanted. I knew what I should do.

But I didn't. I ran.

I didn't stay, didn't pay my debt. I should've let her kill me out there, I really should've. And for all these years, for each breath I take, I can't forgive myself.

I was too scared.

I ran until I got to the house. I locked the bathroom door and I fell asleep clutching a gun. Then I woke up with a shame that hasn't left me since.

You know, Chuck, Dante has a bit in *Inferno* about the "woods of the suicides." I wonder if my little girl died a natural death. I also wonder, for that matter, if there was anything *natural* about my Martha's death.

I'm looking out in the back yard right now, and there's nobody there. There hasn't been in years. I don't think they're coming back. But I hope, sometimes, that they will. That they'll come and offer me my chance again, and I won't be such a coward as to not take it.

I don't have it in me to believe in God, not anymore. I just don't think the world's good enough, that *I'm* good enough. But I think, and I wonder, maybe there is some balancing of the scales, you know? Maybe something...some force, had to make me suffer for the rest of my life for what I did over there.

Maybe it's coming for all of us.

Thanks for listening...I don't have it in me to talk anymore.

Goodnight. Keep up the good work.

Author's notes: It'd be easy to scapegoat the events of this story on mental illness. On PTSD. On depression. But the uncomfortable truth of things like this is that horror can happen concurrently to depression. Horror doesn't need PTSD. Certainly that's true of the horrors of war. The narrator is unwell, but that's not the horror. The horror is Tiger Force. The horror is the true story. This story was written for the second volume of *Turn to Ash*, written as a phone call to a *Coast-to-Coast*, Art Bell-style radio show. It's as true a horror story as I can think of.

And the Woman Loved Her Cats

"We *own* a dog—he is with us as a slave and inferior because we wish him to be. But we *entertain* a cat."—H.P. Lovecraft

BEHEMOTH HAD BECOME God of the house.

The cat had made the house a hell as soon as Madame adopted him. Madame, with her big heart and even bigger heartache, took the cat almost immediately after her husband's death. Perhaps if she had picked a different animal, things would have been different. As it was, she had been intrigued by Behemoth's size and his odd smile. The cat had been taking advantage of her ever since.

However big Behemoth had been, he was not big enough to fill the hole that her husband left behind. She began adopting other animals, each of them a pretty little kitten that had its own personality and quirks during the car rides to their new home. However, almost immediately upon encountering their new master they transformed entirely.

Joe had seen it countless times, the cruel ritual which Behemoth performed with new initiates into the household. The little cats would sniff and play at Behemoth's paws with the typical adoration which children give adults. Without making a sound, Behemoth would leap up and crush the seized kitten under his paw. The kittens made a terrible mewling when they were choking, a half mouse squeak and bird twitter that rasped out from their miniature chests. Behemoth would wait for their eyes to shut, for their limbs to stop thrashing. Then he would lean in and slowly, methodically lick them. Right before they died, as their limbs became more still, he would leave them.

After that, they were broken.

The first cat to submit to Behemoth did not abate Madame's grief. Neither did the next. None of the eventual twenty cats which came to live under the roof alleviated her constant pain, nor soothed her choking night-sobs. And though she named and loved each of them, Joe believed their sycophantic fawning at Madame's feet was just a hollow, meaningless gesture. Their true master was and always would be Behemoth.

Behemoth had a will all of his own, a vampire charisma that bent the other creatures to his absolute will. The cats would stop at their food bowls and wait for Behemoth to eat. They would not drink until after he left and looked to him as they learned how to follow in his abhorrent footsteps. They sacrificed rats, squirrels, and birds to Behemoth, who would accept these tributes and bury them deep within the walls of the house. The smell of their tiny corpses began to decay into something both rancid and sugary, a nauseating candy-and-egg smell that permeated through the hallways as an unholy humid presence.

Though he had never seen them do so, Joe assumed that the cats allowed their kills to ripen before eating them. When a staff member did discover a little-feathered carcass or furry remnant eaten by white, stringy worms, the cats would hiss as if throwing the bones away was a transgression against their sovereignty. More often than not, the bodies were discovered later; after gorging themselves on dead flesh, the animals would walk into plain sight and begin convulsing until they vomited. They looked the staff in the eye as they did so, never blinking as a black-red mass piled out of their mouths while their bodies painfully heaved and contorted.

Behemoth also taught the cats to terrorize the staff mentally and physically. Through demonstration, each little kitten learned from either Behemoth or another cat to hide. From behind locked doors, cabinets, drawn curtains, and hidden corners, the cats would scream like dying, tortured children. Then they would bite and paw at their larger prey until finally the staff would hit the cats back. The animals would hiss and run away, only to repeat their assault a few days later. It had been worse when they had claws, but after Behemoth had torn apart some unfortunate woman's face, Madame's children demanded she have the animals declawed.

One by one, the cats drove away the staff with their yowling, their salty-tang smell, and their absolute worship of human misery. Over the years they turned the sprawling mansion into a claustrophobic nightmare. Only Joe, ever loyal, stayed on while the cats choked the life out of everything they touched.

The halls he maintained were once clean and stately, but now relinquished themselves to the primal decay that so often reigned in haunted houses. Cobwebs and dust produced fat, dry spiders for the cats to kill. Their corpses, tarantula in size and girth, were placed ceremonially at the entry of each hallway for Joe to stoop and pick up. They looked like withered, eight-fingered mummy hands covered with some fur that belonged to them and some that belonged to the cat that devoured them. The hairballs which littered the house as fungal growths were speckled with discarded limbs from the bugs, along with the red meat of whatever living mammals the cats could catch from outside.

Silence was now king, only to be broken with screeching or hissing. Joe was the only human presence in the house other than Madame. Though no other ghosts had made themselves known, Behemoth and his legion had the presence of a demonic force. Amidst all of the ruin, the dirtied carpets, fur-covered couches, and dusty picture frames, Joe was now sworn to serve the animals just as much as he was his dear Madame.

He was sixty now, only ten years younger than Madame, and worried that the cats would make his last years on earth a glimpse into Hell.

Madame's husband, Joseph Higgins, had been the one who built everything. Complete with gardens, a swimming pool, and fifteen acres of land, the house had been built for his wife and two youngest children. Henry and Jessie, the two oldest children, had only visited the house when they were in college, shortly after construction was completed. With grey-white rocks that looked exactly like riverbed limestone and wide, birthing windows which poured sunlight into the house during day hours and darkness at night, the home was luxury that Mr. Higgins had ever wanted for his family. Max and Wendy, the younger two children, treated it as their playground, and Madame uneasily slipped into the life of a pampered empress.

She had been reluctant to hire a large staff. She had cleaned, cooked, and maintained house and home while Mr. Higgins had struggled through school and saw no reason for her to be unable to do so in her new home. The gardens, however, had proved too much for her, and she finally consented to her husband hiring a groundskeeper.

Joe had been the very first staff member at the Higgins household. He had left a mutually disappointing marriage ending in an equally depressing divorce the year before and looked at the gardening job as an opportunity to work outdoors. He had missed the physical labor the military had asked of him, and though his belly had begun to haunch he maintained the large physique of a fighting man. The gardening job then, no matter the size of the garden itself, was easy enough for Joe.

If one good thing had come out of his marriage, it had been his son, Ely. Two years prior, Ely had joined the military to follow in his father's footsteps. The Air Force, but whatever, not everyone had to join the Marines, and Ely told Joe he better accept that. Joe must have bragged about Ely at one point, because it seemed like every day Mr. Higgins would ask him, "*How is that boy of yours, Joe?*"

"*Makin' me proud, Mr. Higgins.*"

"*Very good to hear.*"

While Joe worked in the garden, sometimes Max and Wendy would watch him. Other times Mrs. Higgins would come offer him a glass of water. When she told him that she never expected to be "some grand-Madame-type," Joe began jokingly referring to her as "Madame." Home more often than her husband, she would ask Joe about Ely and laugh dryly at jokes at her expense.

Then, Joe received the letter. He learned that bad news, whenever it came, did not always come with an omen or storm. It did not have a special black sigil or come in the mouth of a crow. One plain white, once-stamped envelope from the United States Armed Forces delivered the news that destroyed his whole world.

It had been Madame who asked that day, "How is that boy of yours, Joe?"

He had been part of the Higgins family ever since.

Mr. Higgins and Madame made sure he was invited to New Year's Eve, Thanksgiving, Easter Mass, birthdays, graduations, and all other family parties. His first Christmas with the Higgins family, his present had been a framed picture. In it, a younger Joe with military sunglasses held a chunky, bouncing baby Ely on his knee. It had been summer in the day of the picture, and as a tear rolled down his face Joe recalled the fresh-cut grass smell of his son's hair. The younger children hugged Joe, while Madame explained that it was going up in their hall so that Ely and Joe would always be part of their family.

Other staff members would come and go, Wendy and Max grew, but Joe was a mainstay in the house. Having no surviving parents and only a distant older brother who lived in Ontario, he had nowhere better to be. The gardens became his territory of the house, and the family placed their faith in him to maintain it without their input.

Then suddenly, Mr. Higgins died. It was before Wendy's wedding, and in an unusually tragic alignment of events the two ceremonies took place a week apart from each other in the same church. Walking Wendy down the aisle, Joe whispered to her, "*Your daddy always talked about how pretty you were,*" and though Wendy and everyone else cried, there was an unspoken happiness in the air.

But in the week after her daughter's wedding, it became apparent that Madame would never recover from her husband's death. And in her weakness, she brought Behemoth into her home.

If there was one comfort in Madame being sick, it was that she could not see what had happened around her. Her once great home had been transformed into a catacomb as her staff left one by one. Joe abandoned the garden, which had been invaded by some species of fungus that poisoned the soil so plants came up from the ground already rotten. That he was old did not help, because no matter how hard he tried he did not have the energy to keep up with the cats who so fervently destroyed what others had built.

Without care, the house itself aged rapidly. Wooden surfaces lost their gleam and grayed with each passing day. The spiders seemed to learn from the carcasses on the floor, and now large clusters of cobwebs thick as cotton hung in each of the house's difficult-to-reach spots. The lights that were not essential Joe did not bother replacing.

No one visited anymore. Not even the children.

Only Madame, consigned to her fate.

And Joe, consigned to see her to it.

He carried the tray of bland, milky-white potato soup with him through the halls. The woman who had once delighted in her husband's gifts of beautifully painted silverware now ate from plastic and paper, which one did not have to wash or replace. Doctors had advised Joe that the bold, spicy flavors which she once so enjoyed would only upset her stomach. Every meal was tasteless, lifeless, and Joe felt a little of him die as Madame enjoyed life less with each bite she forced herself to take.

He smelled the room before he saw the door. Before he had left for his first tour, Joe had taken his son spelunking as a surprise birthday present. There had been a terrible, nauseating stink coming out of one of the caverns. Some less experienced, less fortified people had to leave the tour, a guide taking them out while the other explained with a shrug, "*Bats.*" The smell that came out of that cold, damp cave had none of the sweetness, none of the death that permeated the corridor outside of Madame's room. It had all of the fur-and-shit wetness of that bat cave with humidity and a sweet, putrefying smell of a rotting cake.

Joe gagged, maneuvering so he could cough into his shoulder and still maintain control of the tray in his hands. Madame's room smelt no worse than normal yesterday. The little plastic cat-door flapped lazily, and Joe realized with no uncertainty that Behemoth would be behind the smell.

"Madame?"

Joe opened the door to a wave of stench and heat.

The floor was littered with body parts. Feathers, beaks, and feet from birds; fat legs from tarantulas; carcasses of crickets melting into mounds of brown mulch only identifiable by the antennas and legs which jutted out. Flies, hovering safely over certain piles of carnage, feasted slowly, buzzing in content as they added their microscopic acids and vomits to air. Shit, urine, and hairballs pock-marked the room's refuse as evidence to the presence of cats. Joe recoiled, running back to the kitchen with his tray before re-entering the room.

The cats had been killing her, poisoning her!

Joe was going to remove her from the room, from the house! He would call Max and Wendy, implore them that it was time to kill the animals and send their mother to a nursing home, no matter how sad it would make her!

He stormed back into the room, his feet crunching and squishing the thick layer beneath him. With only her face showing from above the covers, Madame would have seemed to be peacefully sleeping had she been twenty years older. As it were, her white skin was pulled too tightly over her skull, her face too scrunched and silver hair too sparse to be considered healthy. She coughed, moaning as Joe approached her.

"Madame."

She mumbled something.

"Madame, I'm going to move you to another room."

He went to move her covers when he heard a growl at the end of the bed.

The cat was a statue of Bast and the image of death. Sitting, the cat was over a foot tall, with a serpentine tale swaying behind him; he looked like a witch's familiar. With his ears pointed up like horns, Behemoth was the devil himself.

His eyes were not like the other cats'. They were orange, almost red, and did not move as he growled at Joe. The growl was low, loud, and pervasive. Joe thought again of the caves, the way that a sound could bounce off of so many walls in the dark and create a force out of the echo of a whisper.

"Get out of here!" Joe spat out from barred teeth.

Behemoth defiantly moved closer, slithering nearer to Joe and Madame. The hatred in his eyes had a physical force, making skin crawl and stomachs jump. Joe stared back, getting his hand ready to strike the cat. Behemoth looked to Joe's curled fist and back to his face. The cat had taken notice but was not amused, moving closer as it opened its mouth, showing the same yellow teeth that had already countless times before tasted the human flesh of the servants he could rend into. Behemoth was famous as a biter, and Joe was prepared to kill the cat out of nothing but spite.

Behemoth jumped, paws reaching to seize whatever appendage they could grip. Joe's fist arched, slamming into the hard muscle of Behemoth's chest and sending the cat from the middle of the air to slam against the wall. He cried out, more in surprise than in pain, as Joe turned his attention away from the cat and back to Madame.

He put his arms under her blue nightgown, ready to carry her out if he had to.

He stopped when Behemoth began to shriek.

There was something particularly human in his cry, an anger that made Joe freeze as his blood went cold. He coughed wetly, spurting out blood as he howled with rancor and disgust at the man who had struck him. One by one, the other cats filed in with all of the ceremony and apathy of a firing squad. Blocking the door, huddling together like a swarm, the other cats joined their weaker cries to Behemoth's.

Joe had never been afraid of the cats before. They had always been animals, and no matter how cruel they could be, he took small comfort in the fact that he could hit them away when he needed to. For the first time, he knew what had compelled the staff to leave.

"Joe, leave."

The howls stopped.

Madame's voice was dry, fluttering and brittle.

"Joe, leave."

She repeated herself, wincing as she strained to be louder.

Shocked, Joe pulled the covers back over her.

"Madame, I—"

"Leave."

As he stepped away from the bed, the cats parted to make him an exit. He turned around one last time, seeing Madame lying stiffly in her bed with closed eyes as she whispered the same phrase over and over.

"Good kitties...good kitties..."

Madame's health seemed to be improving, although Joe had not seen her in a week. He had moved her into a new room, one without a cat door. The cleaner air had done wonders for her; she was up and moving around, thumping around the room while Joe cleaned the house. She still did not want to be seen though, and asked Joe to stop bringing her food, claiming that she would feed herself when he left.

"I've been sick for a very long time," she explained from behind the door. "I'm afraid I don't look very healthy at all...I'm embarrassed. Let me regain a bit of my color and I will come back outside."

As easy as he had found this request, it had not been her only one. One day ago, she had asked Joe to start mixing raw hamburger meat into the wet cat food. He had said no, but she insisted. Encouraged by her show of strength, he acceded to her will if for no other reason than to make her happier.

He found the labor disgusting. Up to his elbows in fish-smelling brown fluid, he plunged the raw hamburger into the sink in bloody pink handfuls. Bright red currents ebbed to the surface, making the sink a mess of muddy scabs that made the sound of wet putty.

He looked up from the sink, finding a yellow-white cat staring at him from a perch on the kitchen counter. There was a perversity in the cat's eyes, hunger mixed with the same delight from which kittens maimed and tortured mice. A pink tongue darted on an orange face, sliding across exposed teeth. Joe grimaced.

"Go away."

The cat did not move, did not blink while Joe stared back.

Giving up on the contest of wills, Joe returned to the sink.

"Joseph...Joseph."

Responding to Madame's call, he pulled his gloves off and left them to coalesce in the filthy sink. The cats had been quieter, absent from the halls and corridors. He had managed to clean, to remove some of the bigger cobwebs from the hallway and dispose of what he guessed were most of the animal corpses. Behemoth had not been seen for the entire week, and Joe hoped that the animal had finally run away. He hoped even more that it was eaten by wild dogs, hit by a car, or that it met some equally gruesome end. The cats who did show themselves were silent, passive creatures, such as Jonesy, who only watched and followed while Joe moved from one part of the house to another.

He knocked outside of Madame's door.

"Yes, Madame?"

"Joseph...I would like you to put the meat in their milk dishes too."

Joe felt his hope sink. The cat food was repulsive, but already his mind was dredging up images of the new concoction. Pink, thick liquid with chunks of brain-matter hamburger floating on the top and filling the house with the same rot smell he had been straining himself to vanquish. He would not allow it; he would stand his ground against the cats.

"Madame, no."

There was a silence behind the door. A long, incredible quiet in which he heard the rustling of sheets and the scratching of a wooden surface.

"Come again?"

"I won't do it."

"Joseph..." Her voice was growling, anger rising up from somewhere in her benevolent soul. She had to know that he knew best for her, she had to know that after all these years he would only look out for her!

"It's not sanitary!"

"Joseph, you *listen* to me." Her command was a hiss.

"No, Madame, you listen to *me!*"

He opened the door.

He screamed, fell to his knees and pulled at his hair.

Madame's bones were bright white, covered with tiny indents of bite marks and scratches. No flesh was left, no organs in her stomach and no heart in her ribs. Pieces were missing or scattered around the bed as if something had taken it away to examine or gnaw on it in privacy. Bits of hair clumped to her ribs in red, bloody hairballs.

At the remnants of her feet, where only the largest bones were left, sat Behemoth.

The cat smiled, with something raw and pink between his teeth.

"I wonder if you'll taste any different."

Author's Notes: I couldn't have been older than five or six when the white cat showed up in our neighborhood. I love animals, despite a horrible fur allergy which in and of itself was part of the inspiration for this story. I always tried to make friends with animals, and still do. But that cat was just awful. And when my friend's mom told us the cat was "possessed by the devil," I became very afraid. It would shred the grates around houses, crawling under them at night. I had nightmares about it whispering to me.

This story began as a haunted house story about animal hoarding, and still has many of the motifs of the traditional haunted house. A decay. A wealthy family, closed doors, and horrible transformations. It also originally entailed many more cats from across horror fiction, though in the final draft only Behemoth was named. Behemoth is, of course, the talking cat from Mikhail Bulgakov's *The Master and Margarita*. He is much more malevolent in this incarnation than he is when wielding a gun or drinking vodka.

The story was originally published in *The Third Spectral Book of Horror Stories* and remains one of my personal favorites.

Golden Girl

I

ZACK'S FAVORITE PUPPET was the one covered in gold. Kevin, however, found the thing distinctly unsettling. It had a bulbous, uneven head. Caved-in in some places, perfectly round in others, its only normal feature was its little chiseled nose which looked just like a baby's. Its small mouth was full of glinting tooth-fragments, some jagged and some square but all of them yellow and rotten looking. Its absurdly round cheeks were painted gold to match its shimmering medieval clothes, face and clothing alike adorned with glittering, swirling patterns. Its eyes, however, were what transfixed Kevin.

They were a light brown, flecked with varying shades of light and dark greens. The milky whites around the green were lined with red, silk-thin veins that seemed to have just the right amount of blood in them. The eyes darted irrationally up and down as the marionette bounced on the stage in jerking, animated-cartoon motions. They did not seem painted on; more like the puppeteer had stuck glass eyes into the hollow wooden head and let them hang loose. While the puppet was small, the eyes were human-sized and gave the creature a haunting, diabolical look. Kevin thought the puppet belonged in a ghost town pawn shop, not in a children's show.

The stage was small, a three-foot-long, four-foot-tall structure with the jet-black curtain of a morbid kissing booth. Behind it, just poking above the edge of the curtain, were the head and shoulders of the puppeteer. Their shoulders were covered in something that looked like snow, while their face was covered in a mask just as disturbing the puppet's face.

The mask had, at one time, almost certainly been blank. Now it was covered in black and green glitter splotches, purple, pink, and red heart stickers, and streaks of yellow paint. It looked like a first-grade art project, made with all the unreasoning recklessness of a child just discovering its own creativity. There was a thin red fabric that covered the mask's eyes and gave the puppeteer a bloody, feral look.

The puppeteer, in their strange regalia, gave each of their puppets a variation of the same awful, screeching voice:

"I can do whatever I *want!* I am the Golden King and I am more powerful than *anyone* in the world."

The gold puppet's voice was grating, two pieces of shipwreck metal rubbing together along the bottom of an ocean chasm. Kevin was absolutely lost in the spectacle of the grotesque, nonsensical puppet show. Maybe that is all it was supposed to be, a *spectacle* for the kids. The juvenile audience sat around in a horde, a thick semicircle of folded hands in laps covered in jackets of all shades and textures. On all sides the vast semicircle was watched by a periphery of cautious, nervous adults.

Zack laughed and howled and pointed with all the other kids as more disturbing, distorted puppet figures leapt and danced on the black stage. There was a red dragon with centipede feet, a purple woman whose white face was painted with all the chaos of the puppeteer itself, along with various children and animals who gave stupid, irreverent lines that only contributed to the macabre insanity of the show. Each puppet had an unsettling mix of realism and absurdity that made Kevin cringe: human ears with all the fleshy irregularities, noses with nostrils of believable and unexaggerated curves, cheeks that looked like smooth little bee stings. Innocence, a certain cherubic happiness was carved into the glistening tooth-smiles of each of the little puppets.

He looked up at the other parents, moms, dads, and grandparents who also smiled uncomfortably at the stage. The plot, if there was any to speak of, was written in the magic of a madman who understood what it took to gain and hold the mesmerized attention of children. Adults, however, looked at the play, with its eerie dolls and black curtains, and saw only the deranged absurdity that existed on the fringes of unrestrained art. Their smiles were pulled tight across their faces as they hissed in winter air between locked jaws. Their hands fiddled with hidden keys in pockets, and occasionally one would turn to the other and give an uncertain shrug and a half-smile.

Kevin heard his little brother's laugh louder than the rest and smiled. He was happy he brought Zack to this thing.

Neither Kevin nor his mother had heard Zack laugh for months. When their dad died, Kevin had transferred to the local college. He planned to stay here a year and then transfer back. But Mom couldn't give up work, couldn't be there as often as Kevin to help out with groceries, cleaning, and making sure that Zack was happy. Everything had been good until some little shit at Zack's school started picking on him out of the blue. Like a kid with autism and a dead dad didn't have enough problems. Kevin took a breath in, once again suppressing the fantasy of going down to Zack's kindergarten and telling his brother's teacher to cut the crap and do their job.

Bullying, coupled with the loss of their dad, pushed Zack into a morose silence that made him listless and unable to enjoy any aspect of life. Zack could spend days without saying anything, and whole nights crying without words. Kevin hated the familiarity of his brother's crying, the half-angry, half-tortured screams of a child who *feels* cruelty but does not *understand* it.

The gold puppet, Zack's favorite, held up a sign: *The End.*

Kevin sighed with the rest of the parents. The boys and girls clapped, chattered, and yelled out in excitement as the puppeteer held up each puppet one at a time so it could take a slow, unseemly bow. Lastly, the puppeteer stepped out from behind the curtain and took a bow themselves.

Herself.

The snow-colored shoulders revealed themselves to be part of a shining, pearl-colored dress that gleamed in the grey December sunlight. It was almost a gown, with little ribbons of different colors attached to it like ridiculous homecoming mums. The multi-colored streamers were matched by a gigantic multi-colored necklace that hung around her neck like a Mardi Gras trophy. Kevin felt an involuntary nervous smile as he realized the metallic orbs around her neck were a rainbow of metal shrunken heads. The expressions on the heads were tight, dry and sour, as if they had been lifted straight from the pickle jar, dipped in acrylic paint, and placed around her neck.

Despite the awful mask, the random streamers, and the ghastly inappropriate head-necklace, Kevin could not stop the butterflies in his stomach. The kids seemed to like her too. She was short, but clearly built for the strange, over-the-top dress. *Any* dress actually, Kevin mused to himself. It cut off just above her knees, revealing thin little swan-legs that probably once belonged to a little ballerina.

She took off her mask.

Kevin felt the blood numb the spot just behind his face, smiling out of reflex and surprise. She smiled too, with bright red lipstick and long, curly blonde hair that probably reached the V between her shoulder blades. Her smile...completely happy, so absorbed in a joyful moment that even the skeptical and grouchy grandparents smiled back at her. How young could she be, to be so unrestrained and strange? He clapped too, hoping not to get her attention, but simply caught up in the euphoria of the children.

But he clapped louder than he meant.

She looked into him and he felt something slide through his chest. Her eyes were blue, the color of the sky seen through a sheet of ice on a frozen lake. The kind of blue the fish must see in the winter: mesmerizing, freezing cold, and alluring all at the same time. Her eyes could have gone on forever. Kevin reached up with his hand, scratched his head and pretended not to notice.

When he looked up, she smiled slyly with her red lipstick and perfect teeth, then looked down with unbridled enthusiasm at her adoring crowd. They were clamoring for her. She turned her attention to the kids, and Kevin breathed a sigh of relief.

He wasn't sure if he wanted to talk to any girl, he didn't want a reason to linger in town any longer than his family needed or wanted him there.

There were too many ghosts.

So as soon as he could, he persuaded Zack that they needed to go home. But he looked behind him as they left the park.

The puppeteer smiled at him, and he picked up his speed.

II

His nightmare was an uneven hell and paradise.

He could not see his own feet in the foggy, half-formed landscape that he dreamed in. He was walking on hills of grey gravel that he couldn't see, but he felt and heard tiny little rocks sliding under his feet. Fog wisped and curled around his feet like smoke snakes, ethereal tentacles reaching out from the darkness-soiled earth and licking him for just a taste. However, he was only disoriented, not frightened.

He walked forward, slowly and unsurely, towards some unknown goal out there in the black. There was something in his flesh and in every joint that compelled him to move forward despite every rational inclination to do otherwise. He knew there was danger on this path, in this eerie dreamscape that was horrifying in how dismal and how *big* it was. There was something comforting in it too, like he was taking a walk somewhere in his past, or that this was the walk that he had been working for his whole life.

It was a walk that could end all his troubles.

Then the fog cleared, and Kevin stood face to face with the Gold King.

The puppet loomed over him, its bulbous eyes replaced by normal little brown ones lined on a pulsing, beating face. Its entire head was throbbing like a purple, oversaturated heart. There was a wet sloshing sound as a mouth opened wide to show fragmented, broken teeth that grinned against fat, gold-painted lips. Clawed, wooden-raked arms reached out and grabbed his shoulders.

A long, throbbing tongue lulled out of its mouth and he could feel hot breath inches away from his face. He felt something scraping in his lungs, the ghost of a scream he was too paralyzed to make. There was a snake crushing his windpipe, his body shut down in a reflexive reaction against mortal fear.

He closed his eyes.

The hot breath went away. The long claws stopped tearing at his shoulders.

He opened his eyes. The puppeteer was there.

And her mask was her face.

III

Kevin's second time seeing the puppet show wasn't any less disturbing than his first. The day was windy, knife-biting cold rushing from miles away shaking black-bone trees while maple brown leaves fell like rain onto grey, dirtied pavement. The kids bundled up in heavier, puffier jackets and sat and rioted in laughter around the dreadful black stage.

The puppeteer wore the mask again, the crazy hodgepodge of color and morbidity that had made a strong enough impression to leak into Kevin's dreams. He wondered though; her face was pretty, one of the prettiest he had seen in months. Why couldn't he dream of *that* instead of her mask? He shrugged the thought off, happy enough that Zack wanted to go again. It was hard to find things his little brother liked, and if the consequence was that Kevin was a little unsettled, so be it.

There were more puppets that day. There was a little boy in blue overalls and a feather hat, freckles painted on with a mix of orange-brown-red. There was woman in a long black dress that melded into the curtain. Her mouth was wider than the others, the teeth more jagged, like rough rocks swept by a tormented ocean. Her hair was taped on.

Then came the Gold King.

He seemed bigger this time; his crown had grown longer and more pointed, like a stove-pipe hat with little bead-jewels on the tip. In some way that he couldn't define, Kevin thought the puppet looked *older*. The texture of the wood seemed marked with darker lines; his mouth seemed narrower and his clothes greyer than when Kevin had seen it the day before.

Then the puppet looked at him.

The Gold King looked Kevin in the eye the entire time it was on stage. The eyes did not bounce and jostle like they did the day before, but stayed focused and level with inanimate curiosity and hatred. Kevin looked around—none of the nervous parents or bewitched children saw the intensity, the canine-hunger in those eyes. They were redder than before, and as he observed this Kevin saw the little black centers get smaller. He shivered, unable to look away or even think while those dark, blood-brown eyes were fixated so rigidly on him.

Somewhere in the quiet outside of Kevin's existence, the play had ended. Snapping back to awareness, he watched each of the puppets take a bow. The red-faced children laughed and chortled while parents forced themselves to shrug off the uneasiness the play so easily inspired. Zack was slapping his hands together over a crossed lap and laughing in the almost forgotten chaos of childhood abandon.

Kevin looked to the stage.

Her mask was off, and her icy eyes were staring at him with the same intensity that her puppet had. He stood again, for all of the world feeling like he was crumbling apart. Nervousness, attraction, and a bit of fear boiled right beneath his throat. Her eyes weren't like the puppet's. They were the smiling, amused razors of someone playing with their food; something which knew, beyond the shadow of a doubt, that her funny little prey would never be able to get away.

Zack was loud, howling his sentences because he had trouble controlling his voice (especially when he was excited). He was practically jumping up and down, reveling in the special attention that the puppeteer was giving him, asking all sorts of questions about where the puppets came from and what their lives were like off the stage.

She leaned against her stage relaxed, looking attentively at Zack for intervals and sneaking glances and smiles at Kevin when she could. Zack's questions had more than once ventured into the realm of ridiculously childish. But she had fantastic answers like, "They live in castles," and, "Oh yes, they are married." Each puppet had a story and life off the stage like any other actor. The puppeteer clearly had an unbounded imagination, and it was this that must have echoed so well with the children when they watched her show. Restrained, stunted, and worn by life, Kevin and the other adults could apparently only see a fraction of what she called "Art for children."

Finally, Zack asked a question that could be answered in grounded reality:

"How do you make them so real? The noses and stuff?"

The puppeteer grinned. Her lips were sweet-apple red, her teeth wickedly white, waiting to tear and rend between those soft, shining lips. Her mouth was half-cruel, half-playful as she put a hand on Zack's shoulder and answered: "They're real. I use spare people parts."

Her voice was serious but soft, a mother calmly lecturing her child to sleep.

Zack looked up at her, a little paler and a little quieter. "You hurt people?"

She laughed. "No, the people don't even miss them. It's like getting your appendix taken out." She poked at his stomach and his eyes lit up in terror, glinting over to a glazed embarrassment.

"Oh."

She lost his attention as he suddenly spun off through the crowd, shaking some kid in a black-puffy coat on his shoulders until the boy turned around. Zack talking to other kids...that was good.

"Thank you for talking to him. Zack is..." Kevin struggled, not wanting people to unduly pity his little brother before they even gave him a chance, "a little different from other kids. It's been hard for us to get him laughing. So, thank you."

She quirked her head a little, a puppy confused at a new noise. "*Every* kid is different, but they all laugh at the same things."

Kevin was sure there was something profoundly artistic in that statement, but he did not want to look like an idiot trying to figure it out. He felt that instinctual, desperate pride a boy feels when he wants to impress a woman who is only half-interested, the desire to be as concise and intelligent as possible in fear of creating a conversational stumbling block that could bring him down.

"That was a cool trick," Kevin changed the subject. "Making the eyes follow me the entire time. How did you do that?"

Her smile got a little wider, as if it couldn't get more genuine and happy. "The Gold King doesn't like me looking at other boys...especially when they have prettier eyes than he does."

Kevin was caught off guard.

"My eyes?"

"Yes..." She stared into them, and even though she did not raise a hand he felt a soft, warm palm against his cheek, drawing him in and forcing him to look back into the star-scattered lights of her blue eyes. He felt weaker, using everything in him not to move an inch while she kept speaking. "They're this beautiful grey-green...like aged jade...a very rare, very beautiful color of eye...one I haven't seen many times before...you must get that a lot."

Women liked his eyes, but rarely had they made him feel this unsure about them. He didn't know what to say; somehow her description sounded like the most poetic thing he had ever heard.

"Umm...thanks...you must be a good judge of eyes then, having such a good pair yourself." This, he felt, was the single *stupidest* thing that he had ever said.

He felt all the discomfort, jitteriness, and anxiety that ended a long time ago with puberty. Primal adolescence was clawing at the back of his mind, and he hated every moment of it. Silently, mentally, he began hoping that God or Nature would intervene before he made a fool of himself.

Luckily, she didn't give him an opportunity. "You're a student?"

"Yeah, how did you know?"

"The only people in this town my age are students...the rest of them just apparently disappeared, an entire generation." Before he could fumble with another observation, she added, "Because of this, I really don't have anyone to show me around my last night here."

"You're leaving?" There was only a little dismay and surprise in his voice.

"Two days from now, the morning after next."

"Well, I know there's a great Chinese restaurant—"

"Great, I'll be ready at 8 p.m. tomorrow night!" She said it with the mild enthusiasm of someone masking deeper, stronger emotions.

"Umm...great, see you then."

She did not turn around to acknowledge his last remark. Instead, she turned away and began packing up her stage and puppets as if her sentence ended the matter conclusively. He liked that. While he chatted with the parents of whatever kid Zack talked to, he watched her carefully, lovingly put away her puppets into their little cases and folded stages.

She picked up the Gold King. The puppet's head dropped, tilted, and glared back at Kevin. She seemed surprised, putting a hand to her mouth and jumping a little before turning her own head to smile playfully at Kevin.

One wink and she turned back away.

His face was tingling.

If he had looked in a mirror, he would have looked just like one of her puppets.

He didn't even realize that he didn't know her name.

IV

He couldn't sleep.

Kevin hadn't really had a relationship of any sort since his dad died. That had been eight months ago. He had thrown himself back into helping his family, taking Zack to kindergarten, finding part-time yard work on weekends to put a little money back into Christmas or doctor funds. He didn't want to take the time to think about himself, to worry about himself. It was easier to worry about others than for him to face the fact that *he* may be having a harder time than his little brother. After all, he had known Dad longer than Zack had.

He was aware that he had regressed, turned back to a younger age when a girl would flutter her eyelashes and his insides would flutter back. He at once liked and hated this, not wanting to be a fool but also liking how innocent...no...how *happy* feeling this way made him. He wished he could have just had the date tonight, gotten it over with and taken whatever poisons or pleasures it would incur. Instead, he was restless in his bed at 2 a.m.

So he would wait. He would wait until finally, *somehow* he managed to sleep. He would try to think of anything *but* her. Anything *but* the next day.

It felt like there were little hooks in his joints. He felt a burning pull behind his knees, in his shoulders and elbows as his arms laconically dragged beside him. Something held his eyelids open, peeled them all the way back so he could not miss a moment. He had gotten up from his bed, accepting that he was in a dream and not second-guessing his impulses, and half-dressed himself in boxers and a t-shirt. With minimal movement, he padded softly down the wooden stairs, opened the doorknob slowly, and went out into the hours between night and dawn.

The world was different, vast and clouded so that he could only see a few feet in front of him. The ground was wet beneath his feet, grass and soil spotted with moisture that slid along under his soles like so many crushed night crawlers. He was cold, but not bothered. There was something for him at the end of this dream, something that would keep him warm.

Through the glinting of streetlights, he saw little stream-lines that walked and moved with him in the mist. They were fateful, tiny strings that moved next to him like all the friendly ghosts he so desperately missed. He felt hooks at his mouth and let a smile be pulled out of him. The painful hooks, the strings, he had accepted these things as good in his half-formed dream logic.

The mist was gone, and Kevin was in the park.

There was a trailer, a small and dingy white-and-brown compartment from the 1980s attached to a red truck that kept on going despite all the age holding it back. There were smiling cat stickers on the trailer door, little rainbow puppies that said, "Come in, come in," as Kevin went up the rough carpet stairs, pulled the door handle, and walked through the bright threshold.

So many people were there. A woman in purple with a big smile, a little boy with freckles, another woman with a long black dress. They all were so welcoming; Kevin felt a pull at his wrist as his hand waved at them. A voice that was not his own fluttered from his lungs, "My name is Kevin, I am most pleased to help."

"Hi Kevin," the audience said back. "We are so glad to have you."

His head turned to the side, and Kevin saw the Gold King.

He was tall and gaunt now, head craned down close to his face so that the King's unwieldy crown would not scrape against the top of the trailer. The King's face was frowning and empty, with tar-bleeding eyeholes that wanted to swallow Kevin whole. The happiness, the easiness of the dream suddenly left him as the King craned away from the darkness that surrounded him, rattling and snapping with each lifeless movement it made. The light of the trailer became darker, more dimmed and subdued as the King's face contorted into a vengeful torturer's.

A cruel, evil smile hurt worse than any bite ever could.

Kevin fell down, backing away from the smiling faces of the onlookers as the King came closer and closer. He wanted to scream, but there was no string at his lungs to help the air escape. He felt warm all over, blood leaking from every part of him as the dream became worse and worse.

Without strings, he turned his neck around to see if there was any way out.

There was a dark, cavernous room. She was in there. Her white face was covered in glitter, hearts, and streaks of ceremonial paint. She held something vaguely x-shaped in each of her two hands. Her arms were impossibly long. Her eyes were shadows.

Kevin managed to scream before something crushed his throat.

When Zack's mom took him to the puppet show the next day, she didn't seem too concerned about Kevin. She thought he "finally went out" and said, "He'll be back when we get home. He's just at school," and because she was confident about it, so was he. After all, she had the day off and really wanted to see what all the fuss was about. He had been frantically telling her about the show all this time, and he was happy to have his mother by his side. Not that he didn't love his brother, but Zack knew he was sad.

He could just tell.

Zack waited, static blood running through him and jolting his nerves to hyper-awareness while his mom sat with him, stroking his back lazily with her gloved hands. It was even colder today, but Zack didn't care that his nose was already numb.

He wanted to see the Gold King.

When the puppet came out, his mother stopped stroking his back. She was just like Kevin, he guessed, and couldn't understand why the play was happening to begin with.

But there was something different about the puppet today. Its clothes were brighter, paint more glowing and crown more regal than it had ever been before. There was something else too, a change that was lurking just behind the new paint and clothes that Zack didn't see but *felt.*

Until the Gold King looked at him.

Until it looked at him with sharp, grey-green eyes.

Author's Notes: It's a weird thing, falling in love. First your stomach starts to go, then the stupidest things crawl their way from the back of your throat and somehow find their way out of your mouth. And it's not exactly as if you can *control* the damn thing. And though it's fun and though you feel good and though there may be a new song you're whistling, you've *changed.* Your friends notice, mostly with a smile, but some are no doubt at least a *little* uneasy around this new you.

This story was originally written with the King in Yellow Mythos in mind. But as I expanded the characters of Kevin and the puppeteer it didn't seem necessary to include Carcosa. Some elements are still there, namely the play itself. It went through a few versions over the years before ultimately being published in Planet X's first volume of *Test Patterns.*

Movie Magic

THE HAUNTED PALACE Cinema was plagued with premature ghosts. Urban legends clung to the building like remoras, sucking out business only to bring in cult followings. The theater was in an old district of town, a part of the world where businesses died and buildings stayed empty forever. Whether they remained empty out of respect, or out of a viral desolation, was impossible to tell. The Haunted Palace attracted devoted fans whom flocked from all over the county to see obscure and wonderful movies of the horror variety. The fans fed it and the theater stood open, wearing its decay as ritual costume.

Peter had been obsessed with horror ever since he was little. He had grown up with R. L. Stine, transitioned to Lovecraft in his teens, and fallen upon Stephen King in adulthood. Horror had brought him together with Camilla, who had off-handedly mentioned Thomas Ligotti at a party within his earshot. His infatuation was instantaneous. Camilla was a strange girl who demonstrated powerful, daunting and lovely insights Her conversations were of a deep and meaningful level while so many of his other friends only conversed at the shallow-pleasantry level which always made him smile but never made him think.

They had been on one date, this was their second.

The lobby was full of smells, but not of popcorn, butter, or sugar like other theater lobbies. The smells were of dust and mothball sterility, smells that lovingly slowed decay in the back of closets. The walls, covered in black-grey carpet, radiated age and bleakness. The marbled floor was decorated in the stone pattern of graveyard rocks. Behind the concessions counter was a bar, lit dimly from beneath to give the colorful liquors a phosphorous, fungal glow.

"You can't order food here. But you should drink," Camilla spoke in an instructional voice. "You can't get the same experience if you don't."

Peter was wary of this place. He had never been, but he had heard stories and rave reviews from friends who had gone to see special screenings of *The Exorcist* and *Halloween*. In these special screenings, the cups of moviegoers would start to bleed something that looked like blood, stairs would crack, and shadows would move along the orange floorlights as images of monsters flitted randomly onto the screen. It was making scary movies scarier, the idea of bringing the most sophisticated and real horror to even the banal sequels of *A Nightmare on Elm Street*, when a razor-gloved hand would scuttle across the auditorium.

The staff had taken the same vow of magicians, and never told the secrets of chairs that shook furiously, or monsters that appeared in the aisles for only an instant.

The man behind the counter was characteristic of the theater. He wore the Victorian, drab black and white uniform of a ghastly butler, a young man seemingly drained of light with shadow makeup to transform into a hollow wraith of skeleton skin. His voice was low, monotonous.

"I'll have a Jack and Coke, I guess?"

"We don't have that here," the man responded.

"Just ask for the House Special," Camilla prompted.

The man handed him a wine glass, filled with something scarlet red and fizzing with club soda. Peter took a sip, found it to be rather enjoyable, and asked how much he owed.

"The House is paying for it, sir."

Peter smiled at the reference and nodded.

There were two types of people in the lobby.

There were those who *loved* horror, bespectacled people with clothing of varying degrees of sophistication. They wore nice jackets full of pockets and buttoned shirts with wide collars. They were well trimmed or not, men and women of beauty or plainness that stood around and talked about the popular demand for a Lovecraft-inspired movie. Peter heard comparisons of *The Exorcist* and *The Conjuring,* and disgust at the idea of a remake of *Rosemary's Baby.* Peter was one of these people.

Then there were those who *lived* horror. These people wore only shades of black that made them pale no matter how dark their skin was. In the languid red light of the lobby they, with their gothic Lolita dresses and turn-of-the century vests, could be guests at Prospero's party or serial killers behind Masquerade costumes. They could be plainclothes demons, ghosts, vampires, or any other of the alluring monsters that lived in the pages of books and rolls of film.

Camilla told him that these were the more regular patrons of the Haunted Palace. They came as much as four nights a week for the independent and classic screenings, lived on the fringes of the genre where dolls and people were the same and statues spouted fountains of blood each midnight. For the most part, they disowned the mainstream advancements of horror and held on to the past, hoping for a revival that would never come as long as anyone would pay money for a slasher movie.

"What are we seeing again?"

"There is a special screening of Gordon Smithson's *Ceremony.*" Camilla smiled vaguely, half-serious and half-thrilled at the prospect.

He ventured the conversation. "I think I read an article about this one. It was the inspiration behind the 'lost movie' meme, right?"

She nodded. "It's a very rare movie, I'm not sure what it's about, you know? The DVD rights are lost in limbo, the director's dead, and it's the only film he made. The actors were all amateurs who worked under fake screen names. The makeup artist must have been good; nobody's been able to track any of the cast down for an interview after all these years."

Peter remembered the article that he had read one night, as a more entertaining alternative to actually working on a paper. The reviewer had said that the movie was a masterpiece of sorts, but only of sorts. It was described as lost somewhere between *Eraserhead* and a 1950s educational film, with only vague hints of a story that connected the few characters and settings together. The narrator's voice, sometimes another, told the story in lieu of dialogue. Ultimately, the reviewer concluded, though *Ceremony* was a piece of art, it would certainly never be a piece of *popular* art. Its success had no doubt been fueled by its infamy and rarity.

"The screening is starting." The voice was empty of emotion, a female staff member in a white nun's habit. She spoke from behind a plastic Michael Meyers mask, sewing into the theater's atmosphere of unease and terror. "Please follow me."

The crowds dimmed their talk and followed the usher. The hallway behind her was long, with red carpets and hanging chandeliers speckled in fake cobwebs. The lamps on either side were made to look like torches, flickering on and off. A new scent hung in the air as the lovers and livers of horror forced themselves closer and closer, the rot smell of insect carcasses, tiny deaths coming together to form one consuming, animal stink. Peter looked around nervously, turning to Camilla as she wore the same nervous smile.

"Is this normal?" he asked.

She shrugged. "Not much about this is normal."

Two wide red doors, no windows, opened wide, and the crowd piled into its assigned seating. Each person sat down at their chair, old antique-looking things covered in butcher-room plastic that made no noise. The audience put their House Specials on the little tables in front of them.

"Our kitchen is closed," the hostess explained listlessly, "but if you need a drink, please press the little red button on your tables."

There was no "Enjoy" or "Thank you for choosing the Haunted Palace."

Instead, the lights went off and the movie abruptly began.

The screen faded from black to a soft grey. Before the picture became clear there was a sound, a crunching, slurping, shattering sound that was wet and long. Moans started to bubble out from the speakers, along with ragged breathing and restrained sobbing. Red streaks bubbled down the screen, streaks of blood trailing like rain outside a window as the smacking and licking sounds continued. Then a picture came from behind the red and grey film, a hunched shadow colored in hazy outlines. The picture began to clear; fuzz swept away to reveal an uncanny Bella Lugosi look-a-like.

With his cape, jeweled neck, and combed back hair he seemed straight out of the *Dracula* set. With his hand up to his wrist in this throat, he looked like something else entirely.

The camera moved up to his face, revealing trails of tears and desperately scared eyes as the hand continued moving up his mouth. Blood streamed from his lips, little bits of gore fell to the floor as Dracula continued eating himself.

"There has only ever been one monster."

Fingers dug themselves out from the other side of Dracula's head.

Peter was nauseous; he looked over to Camilla, who did not notice him. Her eyes were fixated on the screen, hands still in her lap while her mouth hung open into a soft, entranced O. He turned back to the screen, gulping as quietly as he could so she wouldn't hear him.

The fingers pointed together, a bleeding point through which teeth grew. Eyes popped out where there had been knuckles, angry yellow things that snarled as the form grew hairier and hairier, larger and larger. The form bubbled with new skin and gore until a soaked werewolf emerged in full form from Dracula's open skull.

"It's been with us since the beginning. As long as we've had fingers to paint its likeness on cave walls, the monster has had power over us...over our imagination."

The werewolf howled, revealing a long bloody tongue behind curved teeth.

There was a shuffling behind Peter. He could hear someone walking in the back aisles, sliding along the floor with big feet that never lifted from the ground. There was a soft banging, like a knock on the door. A scream came from behind a hand. Silence, save for the crackling of the film. A sucking sound.

The atmosphere leaked from the screen into the seats. Some people (the lovers of horror) in front of him shifted uncomfortably as the ghost sounds shuffled behind them in the very back of the theater. The livers of horror, however, sat still and entranced by the spectacle in front of them.

He looked back to the screen, the Orson Welles voice of the narrator continuing past the carnage.

"*We put as much significance in our monster as we do ourselves, perhaps even more.*" A man ran through a catacomb, chased by paper-skinned skeletons with curved arms that flailed like the headless bodies of dying chickens. The man was panting, refusing to look back as the arms seized him and drew him back into the shadows.

"*It has defined us, labeled our fears so that we did not have to bear the burden of responsibility. Like a primordial god, we have given our monster many faces, dividing up its power. With all the magic we could muster, in written words and otherwise, we have severed and scattered our monster.*"

An old, wrong-shaped city rose out of the sea. The water was littered with the scaled bodies of pre-human monsters. The city's towers were spinning, blasphemous corruptions, monoliths covered in blinking eyes. A miasmic cloud hung over the scene, a black scab in the sky that boiled tar down to the earth. Something rose out of the city, tearing it apart with sharp limbs and knife fingers. It danced under the tar rain, singing and screaming a song that compelled the sky-wound to bleed more.

The creature opened its eyes, drinking in the sky with a long mouth that swallowed the cloud whole. The black form split open, spilling out over the architecture of the city. The city became covered by the dark. Then the sea. Then the screen.

"*But like all gods, our monster needed a following.*"

There was a shifting sound on the floor. Peter looked down from the screen to see someone moving in the aisles. They must have been in costume, though what they were supposed to be was masked by the dimness of the auditorium, where the darkness was only accentuated with the light from the movie screen. They moved slowly, selectively, pausing in front of each seat to look down on whoever was in front of them. Peter smiled, knowing that this was yet another part of the "experience," an elaborate routine of the staff to conjure an atmosphere that could exist nowhere else.

"*There are certain practices we give our monster.*"

Rooms in abandoned houses flickered on the screen. Places without furniture, only carpet and dust with moldy walls. In one room, in one corner, sat a woman in a white dress. She faced the wall, her head banging against it as the sounds of faucets gurgled and flowed. A black liquid filled the room, and the woman floated, letting the current take her body until her face drifted toward the camera.

"Its face is always the same."

When he saw the woman's face, Peter jumped.

He was the only one who did so.

The form in the aisles below was gone, and the whole row now sat mesmerized as the woman's face spun slowly on the screen. It was marked with raw flesh, strips of meat that blossomed from pale skin. Her milky eyes looked blind, but Peter could feel the pressure of her stare. Her mouth opened to reveal row after row of suckers, each pulsating and bleeding with a life of its own. She smiled now, laughing with total freedom as the camera thrust itself into her mouth and anatomy.

"Its face is always the same."

He saw it again, the vague costume. It was hanging low to the floor, completely blackened by the darkness and made a living outline by the orange stair lights. It was a mass of shifting rags, human limbs popping out and moving in the contorting angles of a slow, deliberate spider. There was a gnashing sound as it slid past him, a thud as something shifted along the changing shadow and fell on the floor. The black outline of the thing grew larger. Peter watched with careful interest as the floor around the thing got damper, listening intently to the shadow contraption that went along the floor.

The larger shadow slowly moved away from whatever it had dropped. He was transfixed, feeling the burning heat of eyes from the thing that moved upwards into the auditorium. He turned to Camilla, willing to disrupt her concentration so that she would not miss the horribly intense spectacle unfolding on the stairs. He stopped. Her face was languid, pale and expressionless. She no longer seemed interested in the movie, merely looking at it because there was nothing else to look at. Her eyes were black, pupils devouring the whites of her eyes. The darkness of the screen reflected back and forced Peter's transfixion.

"Its face has always been powerful."

The haunted woman's face was gone now. The screen began to pulsate, become darker with the low, almost inaudible beat of a drum. Next came the slurping sounds, so loud and distinct that they might as well have been coming from the seat next to him. He could *feel* the sounds, the little quivers in his clothes and nerves as the air tugged and hissed with the small noises. He turned back to the stairs, hoping to catch a glimpse of the crawling slow horror.

The object it had dropped was bleeding, the red carpet soaked scarlet and damp in the orange light revealing the sickly remnants of a human arm. The darkness of the screen cleared, in full color a bonfire in the woods painted the entire auditorium in pagan colors. Pines split open, little embers floated like spirits as naked forms covered in the rot-green blotches of corrupted age danced in the same unholy revelry as the tar-eating god. The forms were covered in blood, their own or others'. The camera showed circles of dancing stars, pupils dilated and swallowing the whites of eyes, transfixed and hypnotized countenances gazing into something that was engulfing their souls.

"The face may be redecorated. Redone and repackaged by men who do not know what they are summoning. But it will always be the same. Our monster, our master, will never change."

A face came onto the screen. Peter cried like a child, screaming and pleading for someone to shut the projector off. He could not look away, his neck had frozen and his eyes had been cemented tightly open. His hands remained dead on the armrests as the theater lights came to life and revealed the wreckage of the screening. The face faded into the dull yellow-grey of blank canvas, the arm on the stairs revealed itself to be covered in hair and decorated with a glinting wedding ring. A tilted head with gnawed eye sockets gaped at him from one of the front rows, and beside him the smacking sounds continued.

The screen was empty now, but the face would never leave.

Peter knew what sat beside him.

Author's Notes: I've always been fascinated by stories of things that occurred during screenings of *The Exorcist*. From there came the idea of a theater with "interactive" screenings of old horror movies. Coupled with the "lost film" meme, the story came together rather quickly. It remains my love letter to horror cinema, with some subtle and not-so-subtle nods to the genre.

The "horror lovers" and "horror livers" dichotomy of the story is inspired by the all-too-common refrain of "*Really? You write horror stories?*" I smile a lot, I don't wear black. I'm a horror lover, not a liver. But people in both groups are often the kindest, most caring people you will ever meet.

This story was originally published in the debut issue of *Ravenwood Quarterly*, accepted by a very patient Travis Niesler. It came out around the same time as "I've Been Here a Very Long Time," and opened a wide door for me.

We Will Take Half

I

MIGUEL HELD THE sad, pale remains of his second child in his hands. With gentle tears he put her cold, still heart next to his beating one in the hope that somehow the life would pass between them. Emilia was screaming in the corner, holding her arms tight around her shoulders and shaking her head violently as her cheeks swelled with blood and denial. There was absolutely no hope in the village, where there were no doctors for miles and no money to bring one in. Children were born in the mud and were destined to return to it. The last two daughters of Miguel Rosas were examples of children who returned too quickly to the mire. Though he so desperately wished otherwise, it seemed that God did not want Miguel and Emilia to have children.

However, he was desperate enough and sad enough to defy that God.

And so, he sat up with Emilia, rubbing her back until she collapsed from heaving sobs and sadness and gave in to unwilling sleep. He kissed her cheek, brushed her messed hair from her face, and lifted her into the bed. He was not as young as he used to be, his muscles worn with the wears of the world. She was not as light as she had been on their wedding night, she now burdened with the same sadness which so choked them both.

He stepped quietly out the door, looking at her one last time before he left his wife behind and went into the jungle, armed only with a cross around his neck and a lamp swinging at his side.

The overhead canopy of overlapping trees only allowed starlight to poke desperately through, the wet soil beneath his heavy sandals squelched with each step. The scent of flowers and the thick fog did little to persuade Miguel away from his superstitions that this forest was an evil place; that the moist soil had been wetted from the blood of men and demons alike, and that their skeletons fed the gnarled roots of the ravenous trees.

The smell slowly morphed from the sweetness of flowers to that of a charnel table, a morbid feast of sticky and warm flesh. Somewhere, a bird fluttered its wings and took flight with a mocking laugh, indicating that even *it* knew how foolish Miguel was being. He stepped into the realm of the shadow people, the fair-blue folk.

The fair-blue folk had lived within the jungle and its dark sanctuary while men dirtied themselves in trees and fought wars with rocks. The fair-blue folk were monstrous scavengers who had never truly been seen, except for the monstrous infants which they left behind in exchange for a human child. With soundless crawls they would travel amongst houses and steal children in the night. Soundlessly, they left their own mewling offspring in return. The children were always the same, covered in dry blue scales of moldy sapphires and patches of furled white hair. They waved about in their cribs with long, yellow claws and looked upon the mothers of stolen children with their corrupted eyes. The eyes of the children giant and bulbous, glowing mushroom caps sprouting from misshapen, uneven heads. But the worst part was their screams...

As long as he lived, Miguel could not forget the crying of a blue child.

It was suspected that if the children lived long enough they would grow into human copies. However, the process was usually long, and while some parents tried to conceal the abominations that grew less blue with age, most were discovered by their crying. It could only be described as multiple sounds, a chorus of tortured animals coming from the gape of one open mouth.

These monsters were usually killed quickly, violently, out of the view of those poor parents of the unwanted gift, and then thrown back into the jungle. Their corpses served to warn the fair-blue folk of what fate awaited the children they so callously traded for precious human lives in the hopes that they would stop. But the fair-blue folk never *did* stop.

Miguel pushed aside a wet branch and began to sing the song of the fair-blue folk into the calm, foggy air:

"Upon the stairs I left my boy
Upon the stairs they leave a ploy.
A monster, evil and new
Skin blotched and blue.
Take care your children
Lest they come back again."

There was the sound of worms moving beneath the dirt, and suddenly the shadows were upon Miguel.

They remained out of sight, their outlines clinging upon branches with one or two arms like a large, perverse chimp. Their darkness only revealed the shapes of hunchbacks over two bright yellow orbs gleaming with inquisition. Their raspy breathing sounded like the rain, torrential and merciless as wave upon wave began to eclipse the noises of the jungle. Then the insect chirpings ceased too, and the choruses of birds and dogs were obliterated as one of the shadows moved down the trees. Its long arms propelled and pulled it forward, crawling downwards on the bark of a barely visible tree trunk with claws that made dry scraping sounds. It landed softly against the jungle dirt, using its arms and legs to walk only a few feet away from Miguel.

Miguel held to his cross to hold back his tears.

"You are foolish to seek the changing people!"

It spoke with an unrivaled authority, a deep booming voice that echoed through the jungle's twisted halls and rippled in every puddle. It came closer, revealing that it was far larger than he originally thought. Somehow the shadow defied every expectation of sight and light alike, becoming impossibly taller to the point where it towered above Miguel as it moved only a little closer to him.

Miguel gulped, certain now that the legends had not readied him for the entire truth of the fair-blue folk. Fear stripped away the muscles from his legs, and he fell to the wet earth and averted his eyes from the monster. "Please, I mean no harm and ask only for help!"

"Help?" The light of the eyes left Miguel, and darted around to their fellows. "Help after you split open our children, throw them into this jungle for wild dogs to tear apart?" The voice was roaring now. The shadow's indistinct face came close to his own, cold breath with a scent of pine breathing slowly into his face. He imagined he heard the clacking of long teeth which he could not see.

"What is it which you think to gain from us?"

Miguel's voice dropped, fluttering and wet. "You have never taken...either of my children. I thank you for that, but...if you give me one of your children, I will make sure it is never harmed."

The breathing stopped. The moon seamed to pass over and leave the earth covered in white light.

Miguel looked upward to the shadow and immediately wished he had not.

He could not look away again, but was transfixed in eye contact with the monster.

"Why do you want a changing child? What purpose does it serve you?"

"None. My own children die...I just want a child to love, to inherit my estate and take care of my wife after I am gone...I just want an end to our loneliness."

"And," the voice was firm and hollow, "how do you propose to hide this child?"

"It would eventually become a human, right?"

"No! But *he* would become so close that you would forget you ever made this bargain, and instead come to believe that he is truly yours. How do you propose to hide his crying?"

Miguel stared, dumbfounded. A cloud of fog moved, partially allowing the moon and stars to illuminate the scene in glittering white. The face before him was covered in blue light and various shades of jungle rot. Violet saliva dripped from its curved crescent jaw and soaked into the contaminated soil in a serious, deadly expression. Miguel could not think of a thing to say.

The nightmare voice responded. "The key...is to not fear the child."

"I will only love him!" Miguel responded.

"There is one part of the bargain not met."

"I will give you everything I have!" Miguel shouted, and threw his hands up in supplication. "Please...just give me a child who lives!"

"Your...son, will be one who will never die. He will live, as long as he remembers the bargain *you* made for *him*."

"Anything," Miguel whispered again.

"Anything the child will ever make or own...we will take half."

Miguel balked. But then, his wife had looked so lonely as she stared into the fire for days while their first daughter had died coughing up blood in the next room.

"He will remember," Miguel whispered.

"Leave our jungle, and in a few days' time you shall have your new child."

Miguel watched the monstrosities retreat, mixing and melding within the jungle until they cast no outline and left no footprints.

II

Alfonso Rosas was born blue and kept hidden from the world as his scales peeled away in a matter of days, exposing soft pink-purple flesh which reddened beneath light. His jagged yellow fangs fell out, and in their stead grew teeth which were not so yellow and not so pointed. His tongue become more round and less slanted, and within a week of his arrival in the house, the yellow had left his eyes and been replaced by a natural and beautiful green.

His father had never feared his son. But he kept him close, cradling him as he changed, wiping the white hair as it fell off and sweeping it away discretely.

At the age of five, Alfonso knew to leave half of his meals, which were twice as big as those of a normal child, on the porch at night. He knew when he received a gift from friends and relatives that he should split the object into two pieces and only keep one for himself. He certainly knew that, should he ever turn a profit doing some chore or labor, he was to toss half of it into the jungle. And though he had never known his mother, he always thought of her when he split what was his with the fair-blue folk.

Alfonso grew up very quickly, larger than his peers at a very early age and the focus of all the girls' attentions at a meek twelve years. Never forgetting his dedication to the fair-blue folk, he always paid his dues in quiet secrecy as his father had taught him, out of the sight of his fellow man but always within the sight of eyes unseen.

The changing people watched him from underneath every house, above every alley, and from within every shadow. They watched as he shed his blue scales and adorned the skin and form of a human, and they smiled upon their most successful and prosperous child. The fair-blue folk took care of Alfonso, secretly and lovingly, and it was through their indirect interference that he married at the age of twenty-two.

Katerina was a lithe beauty made strong by toiling in the jungle loam. She was one of the growers of vibrant fruits and vegetables from the insect-and-contagion clogged black soil. Like Alfonso, her eyes were the clearest green, and like Alfonso she was a desire of many young hearts and a sweet, panging remainder for older ones. It was the general consensus in the village that the couple's children would be more beautiful than the two of them combined.

The birth of his twin daughters was the happiest day of Alfonso's life. As his smiling, shaking father stood behind him and touched his shoulder with a withered trembling hand, Alfonso could not help but think that God himself was smiling.

It was only the morning after that Alfonso lost his faith.

In a terror, he had gazed into his daughters' room and discovered an empty cradle. The remaining little angel, lightly sleeping in her bundle, had slept through the night without waking once.

He ran across the village, heart thumping as he pounded upon every door asking what had been seen. Had strangers come into the village? Had the army been through? Had anyone seen his daughter?

When he ran out of doors, he finally looked into the shadows of the jungle. He tore across the dirt, cutting himself on tree limbs and thorns. Crying, he finally accepted that he would never see his daughter again.

A few days later, Katerina died of a sickness which she contracted during childbirth. Or perhaps, Alfonso began to suspect, it was something else. In mute horror, Alfonso attempted to nurse his wife, whose mouth would not move to eat and whose throat would not open to take water. In the end she left without a sound, a blank stare still present in her emerald eyes as she prodded the world of the dead for answers surrounding the whereabouts of their poor lost daughter.

Alfonso could no longer stand the sight of the jungle, with its primeval vegetation that leered out at him in broad daylight and whispered vague curses to him in the night. His dreams were plagued by a terrible crying which seemed lodged between the most intimate memories of his childhood, hidden under so many people and places that it was only a faint echo. And yet, that echo tormented him.

When the army at last came to the village, looking for young men to become valiant martyrs on the battlefield, Alfonso joined to escape the jungle. Leaving his last remaining daughter in the arms of his aged father, Alfonso was given a rifle.

Miguel Rosas cried for his son, but as Alfonso marched away from the jungle, each step gave him more peace. And with that peace came a new, clear conviction.

III

Wherever the army went, a trail of fire followed. Amidst the whistling of mortars, the thunderous rain of bullets, and the screeching final words of the young and old alike, Alfonso could not forget the wrong which the fair-blue folk had done to him. When he burned jungles to the ground in the name of fighting armies which were far too human to be the object of hatred, he made new ash memorials for the daughter and wife the changing people had stolen from him.

He no longer left his meals out for the changing people, as he needed the full nourishment of the foul army rations lest he come to rely on his hatred alone. He no longer threw money into the jungle, but instead kept all of his property within arm's reach whenever he slept.

But Alfonso quickly learned that he must become an exceptional soldier above all others. Each morning, no matter how tightly he hugged his ammunition the night before, half the copper war trinkets would be missing. Half of his water would be gone, and when he slept with his shoes on (one had gone missing once and he had been severely berated by his commanding officer), his knife was taken.

So, upon confirming his losses every morning, Alfonso would solemnly swear revenge against the changing people for the wrongs against his family. He would promise himself, the fair-blue folk, and God that once he had achieved a high enough office he would use his power to wipe out the monsters who had taken so much from him.

There were stories that circulated within Alfonso's ranks about the quiet green-eyed soldier who believed in changelings and fairies. Some said he was driven fever-crazy and joined the army in order to fight off his own fate at the hands of starvation. Some suggested he was a foreign mercenary in employ of the army who was so ruthless at the authority of a Northern government. Other rumors were far more sinister and suggested he was nothing short of Satan himself.

Frantic, sweating gossip quickly told that there were shadows which followed Alfonso during nocturnal battles. In the heat of gunfire, bodies were taken from the field of battle without the crunching of grass or sloshing of blood. Occasionally bodies of soldiers killed by Alfonso were found split in half, as if torn apart by two arms of incredible strength. Sometimes the torsos were left, and sometimes the legs.

However, these stories held firm that there were *never* any trails of blood.

Despite these rumors, Alfonso had trained himself to be more careful with half of his ammunition, and it was due to this cautiousness that he quickly ascended wartime ranks. When he made general after only five years of scorching his quiet hatred across the jungles, his ammunition stopped disappearing each morning.

Finally, he thought the fair-blue folk were in retreat. Surely they feared the new power which his office provided and knew that their annihilation was soon coming.

Three months into his new career, Alfonso was to engage the enemy army in one final assault. After five years of fierce fighting, the war finally seemed to be over. The government which Alfonso fought for held most of the major cities and virtually all the bargaining points, but some rebel groups refused to give in to the pressures of submission. These zealous final holdouts would rather welcome their own slaughter than defeat.

It was to be a bloodbath, but one which would put a permanent end to the fighting.

Moonlight overpowered the stars as only the brightest celestial bodies were visible in the slate sky that peered through the dark canopy of the jungle limbs. One hundred men were at his command, young officers who had, like himself, proven to be careful and potent soldiers. They hid under moldy logs, disappeared into tangles of vines, and buried themselves within the mud while slowly slinking toward a village on the fringe of civilization. This was the last stronghold of a particularly violent guerrilla group. Through the veil of vegetation, faint yellow lights began to appear inch by dreadful inch, faded windows behind which hostages and troops alike slept uneasily.

Alfonso's troops were now 20 yards from the edge of the jungle, so close that they could smell the rank, salty odor of pigs and poultry that wafted with a gentle breeze into the perfumed jungle. He held up his hand. When it dropped, a mortar leapt through the jungle roof, exploding into orange brilliance which for a moment showed the entire village in the form of slowly rising shadows.

There was a brief cracking hiss as the explosion sucked in all the air, and then the troops moved out of the jungle and into the light of the flaming village. Bullets burst through the air and lodged themselves quickly into the bodies of those foolish enough to wear their uniforms while they slept. The screaming of hostages and families were matched by the retorts of troops from both sides in a swelling chaos.

Alfonso's government soldiers solemnly broke down doors and executed their targets without mercy or mirth. Mechanically and ruthlessly, they carried out their duty of execution.

Alfonso, in his looming victory, thought that perhaps he had destroyed enough jungle in this hollow crusade against his fellow man to finally deter the fair-blue folk. Perhaps the changing people would finally quit the bargain which his father had made so long ago.

The screams which followed his thought were those of tortured cats with human tongues. The cry rose as the village was shattered and torn apart by something other than mortar fire. A tittering laugh rose above the sounds of bullets as soldiers ran with fright-contorted faces back into the jungle and away from the shadows which twisted themselves around the flames. Above the fires, figures rode the smoke, swooping down and snatching people at random, taking them back into the black night sky.

Alfonso stood in desperate awe; the defeat in his stomach grew heavy as some crying child begged not to be taken by the demons. The child's pleas grew into a bestial, rattling death cry which only grew fainter as some ghoulish laughter came over the village air. The throats produced calls of glee and amusement that were large and hollow, base sounds which made the birds of the jungle take off at once in imminent fear of horrible cataclysm.

Alfonso, however, did not flee. He fell to his knees, hands pressing so hard into his head that it was being crushed by physical rather than emotional stress. He cried out, "Will you never leave me?!"

The silence was so quick and absolute that Alfonso thought he was within a nightmare. But then some crawling voice responded with a faint reptilian tenor. "We will never leave you...our *most favorite* child."

IV

The government never truly learned what exactly happened to the troops who vanished from that faint rim of the nation. The guerilla population had been entirely wiped out, and hostages who survived the conflict did not speak a word. Likewise, the troops who lived swore that Alfonso acted as a hero and did what he could to stave off a surprise attack which wiped out half of their ranks almost immediately.

Alfonso himself insisted upon this story. That he *was* a hero. And from the position of war hero, he began a political career.

Spurred on by the new atrocity of the changing people, Alfonso sought positions more and more powerful so that he could use all of the nation's resources to destroy the fair-blue folk once and for all. With mounting charisma and passion fueled by his secret hatred, Alfonso sought to offer a solution to the people who had lost more and more to forces unknown as he climbed to the top of government.

On the eve of achieving the presidency, Alfonso mobilized the military to secure his nation's borders under the obscure threat of some imminent crisis from abroad. He truly believed that if the military slowly searched the country (in the guise of looking for spies), the changing people would be forced to permanently depart to their unknown world of rot and timelessness.

His coup was swift, and coincided with a public mandate in the form of a poorly monitored plebiscite vote. Comfortable with the mandate of the people, he slept quietly on the night of his greatest and final victory.

In the morning, his nation's borders were shrouded by darkness even in the light of day. The army had been swallowed whole by the engulfing clouds, and no word came from abroad. Mothers and fathers had woken up to find their children, or each other, missing without blue monstrosities to replace them. Proud, old cities were dismantled brick by brick; their remaining people were left baffled and desolate after the incomprehensible theft.

The chaos was immediate, and ideas both preposterous and desperate sprang up from the mouths of the panicked populace. Had they been ransacked by some unknown foreign enemy? Had God himself come down amongst them and placed upon the nation the plagues of Egypt? Some insisted that it was Alfonso's doing, that the green-eyed president was the devil in a suit who had claimed the lives of his people in some unholy rite.

However, after this destruction, Alfonso could not be found. The presidential chambers were empty, and many assumed that the president himself had been some sort of casualty in the unknown conflict.

In truth, Alfonso had accepted that he could no longer fight the fair-blue folk, who had been promised half of his life upon his birth and who rightfully owned half of his property. In quiet defeat, Alfonso withdrew from his office and disappeared into the cast of refugees who owned nothing...

Without owning anything, or caring for anyone, he finally was safe from the demands of the changing people. However, he still left half of whatever food he could find for his eternal masters, in fear of some greater reprisal.

Author's Notes: On the referral of a long-time friend, I began looking up information on the changeling myth. This came about the same time I was taking classes in Latin American history. The professor was a former guerilla fighter themselves and would go on impassioned sidenotes about Che Guevara in Cuba and the Tupamarus in Uruguay. All of these influences congealed in "We Will Take Half."

This was one of my first attempts to publish a story, and though the intended outlet shuttered its doors before the story was finished, I came back to it over the years. Any aspiring writers should know that this story took a *long* time to place. There were rewrites upon rewrites upon even more damn rewrites. Markets opened and closed; editors accepted it but unfortunately had to reject it upon not having enough money to move forward. That's what happens. Just part of the business.

The story found the perfect home in *Hinnom Magazine.* I honestly thought it was a long shot, because the market seemed more oriented towards horror than fantasy and I feel that "We Will Take Half" leans towards fantasy. But editor Charles P. Dunphey happily snatched it up and liked it so much he asked me if I had plans for a fiction collection.

A final note to aspiring writers: don't kill *all* your darlings.

The Case of Yuri Zaystev

DAYS WERE MEASURED in piling snow, lives in black-rotting cells, and time in final breaths. The white-washed landscape was the endless world. To walk there, in that terrible and featureless place, was to take one more step toward heaven or hell. To stay there was to consign fate to the primal elements that were both God and the Devil. The tundra existed before man walked, before reptiles crawled on the ocean floor, and would be there when the sun blotted out and the earth became silent.

The only refuge from the cold, constant, and unchanging place was even worse than the vast frozen desert. Death was written into the architecture of the outpost of humanity before the endless night-world, a prison where men were sent to rot and disappear in fog and ice. It was more secret than Kolyma, built in a place where no men, nomadic nor civilized, had ever visited before. Here, spit froze before it fell to the ground while blood turned solid in two months' time. Deprived of food and sunlight, men became slower and slower until they ceased to move at all.

Then, comrade Yuri Zaystev would do his job.

Yuri would drive, by himself, the bodies of overworked and starved corpses into the wasteland. Steam rising from his breath and feet numbing from cold, he would dump the bodies from the bed of his truck to form a pile in the snow. There was no need for burying corpses, no need to cover up bodies or hide transgressions against human life.

The tundra winds would claim human refuse, sweep it back into its cold folds, and take the bodies far away from human eyes and memories. Through its own waves and motions it would revert back to the clean, untouched state it had always been in. There would be no records. The men condemned to this eternal exile had been marked dead before they even marched through the overbearing graveyard gates of the prison.

He had never found bodies or tracks in the arctic snow.

It was sunless, the night sky hung over Yuri as he listened to the desperate hum of a coughing motor. Through his foggy cab window, Yuri could see the countless stars and heavenly bodies watching him, shining more brightly and more beautifully than they did anywhere else in the world. The only joy in his work was being with the quiet sky. Gone was the nervousness of Moscow, the fear of being called a dissident or traitor by some hungry neighbor. Gone was the fear of his mother being taken away, of joining his father in some deathcamp on some other island of the Gulag Archipelago. Out there, alone, he could breathe freely and easily despite the frigid air that choked out all other life.

Ice cracked and crunched under his tires as he went farther into the Arctic Circle. The feeling of being in a vehicle created the sensation of false warmth, something he could not even dredge up from a flask of vodka. The alcohol hit his stomach like gasoline and made him moan in unwelcome discomfort. There was a difference between *burning* and heat. Cold could *burn*. The vodka had been a bad idea, but monotony was the eternal enemy of the Gulag gravedigger.

He stopped his truck.

This spot was as good as any other.

The moon was brilliant, but in the featureless landscape the light did little for Yuri. He huffed, leaving the cab of his truck and bracing for the beastly winter that lived only in the Arctic Circle. He laughed, cursed, and left the cab. His boots met the snow, and beneath his many layers of fur and fat his skeleton felt a chill that no amount of tendon or blood could stop.

In the tundra, he was no longer the young foot soldier. He was not the hero of Stalingrad, the boy who read to his little sister on her deathbed, or the man who stood quietly by and said nothing when they took away his father from his howling mother. He was not culpable for what he was under the latitudes of the true north, not out there. Under the moonlight and the watchful eyes of Heaven, Yuri Zaystev was only flesh and bone.

The truck was large, given the number of passengers he was ferrying that night. Recently, the camp had opened its mouth even wider to gluttonous portions of useless flesh. Whereas before there had been a trickle of people, now there was a torrential flow of traitors and criminals. Starvation was spreading from man to man, prisoners were now walking skeletons that did not have the will or strength to strangle each other for food as they did in warmer parts of Siberia. So Yuri guessed he probably had twenty "people" in the back of his truck.

As he went to open the bed, Yuri had a drunken, evil thought. Part of him envied these men, who would be given a burial unlike any other. They died in this place, so far away from man and so close to God, where it was far too cold for their bodies to decay. If they were not eaten by polar bears, the winds would be kind to them and strip them of their useless skin until their bones were as white and gleaming as snow. When they became cracked-bone dust, they would be indistinguishable from the endless world around them and become part of something much bigger than themselves.

He swung open the canvas-covered cab.

The thoughts came slowly. Yuri looked dumbly at the empty bed of the truck, expecting to blink back the bodies that had disappeared. The alcohol seemed to be sucked from his blood and plummet into his intestines, leaving him nauseous and still in front of the gigantic, empty coffin-truck. He swallowed, completely sobered.

There were never any bumps, no way for the bodies to be jostled out. He breathed heavily, remembering that he and Fyodor had loaded the corpses into the truck meticulously, carefully, with the sacred silence of broken men. He laughed stupidly, remembering that they had first taken off the clothes of each corpse so that the worn garments could be recycled and given to a lucky few in the horde of new unfortunate prisoners. They had found food, knives, and silverware in the pockets of rags and tatters.

He touched his forehead, covered though it was, and looked around him. There was nothing, not in the whole world.

He ran back to his cab, stumbling and struggling for the radio between gulping, wet breaths. Finding it, he removed his glove into the biting-knife cold and pushed the black button to speak.

"This is Private First-Class Yuri Zaystev. I am without cargo. Has something happened?"

He kept the radio on, ready for the voice of the Gulag to hiss back. The little red eye blinked, and blinked, and blinked. Static sparked, crackled, and flared. A noise came through, something like a trumpet filled with water gurgling out of the speaker. Yuri remembered thundering mortars and flaring grenades and the noise rose to a shattering crescendo. It seemed as if there was one incoherent, inhuman voice that spoke along with the gibberish of the radio static. He could hear it crying as he pressed his hands to cover his ears and protect himself from the unwelcome, unwholesome sound. The speaker cracked, and once again silence reigned supreme.

He looked outside nervously. The black outside was absolute, unintelligible, and without answer. Everything was still; even the stars had stopped shining and maintained a constant, somehow feebler light. There was no sound of weather, faint or otherwise. For a ponderous moment Yuri gained a new understanding of the word "quiet." It was more dreadful than screaming, moaning, or pleas for help. It was far more unsettling and haunting to be perfectly and pristinely clean of noise, than to hear a man speak through a bloody mouth and confess to crimes both horrendous and false.

In the Gulag, people had been killed for less than failing in their duty to the State. Yuri recalled (suddenly Yuri again and not the mechanical flesh-and-bone creature that soullessly deposited humans into the cold wastes) that he and other soldiers had cruelly stripped another, prettier officer and put him in a prison uniform for bragging about his lovers. No one in high command had said a word when they saw the man, suddenly quartered with the enemies of the state, screaming at them that he was a good and loyal communist. They did not bat an eyebrow, nor even acknowledge his presence. It had only been a week before the pretty, experienced former officer was a corpse to be ferried in Yuri's truck, and Yuri had no particularly mirth or glee when he dumped the body alongside the other prisoners in a sacrificial pile.

Now Yuri wanted to go back and die at the barrel of the gun rather than at the canine fangs of frostbite. He would rather become part of the unspeakable corpse foundation than be alone in the tundra. He gulped, started his truck, and began to steer back towards the prison.

It was easy enough to navigate his return when he went on his grave runs. He was not careless; he did not drive for hours or ever put himself in danger of running out of gas. He had no delusions; no one would look for him if he did not come back. A notice may be sent out, his face sent to various train stations and an execution order placed on his name in case he turned up anywhere he shouldn't, but no rescue party would be sent. More effort was put into the creation rather than recovery of corpses, and every hand was needed in the prisons.

This night, however, the frantic attempt to escape back south seemed to go on forever. He went for hours, looking desperately outside as the lights of the stars and moon became dimmer and the landscape began to glow like cadaverous, phosphorous fungus. Tonight there was something unusual in the snow, which became increasingly incandescent and bright as the night went darker and darker. The cab of the car became smaller with every moment, and beneath his layers of wool and fur Yuri could feel the damp chill of sweat sliding over him.

Something in him was about to explode. There was a sort of premonition and hyper-awareness which crawled along the wrinkles of his brain and whispered that something horrible was about to extend its claws into his bleeding heart. His teeth clamored as he heard a frantic throbbing not in his heart but in his head, veins pumping blood to his brain in an attempt to make him superhumanly alert.

Then the world went wrong.

There was a moment of deafening noise, the roar of a gigantic monster out in the darkness that rocked the car and sent Yuri into shocks of spinal tremors. The wind began to pick up and howl, slamming sheets of glowing snow against the truck. There was a scream in the wind, the oscillating cry of a cat with human lips being skinned with a rusted knife. Yuri panicked, about to scream Orthodox prayers that he had not uttered since he was a child. He cried out for his father when a shadow smashed against the windshield.

The glass splintered and shattered as reality broke apart for a moment. The truck sputtered, cranked, and exploded into smoke in front of him. He could not see the thick fog that choked him, but he felt the exhaust and smoke pour like poison into his lungs. He could taste the fire. Panic swelled up in him as he thrust the door of the truck open, ignoring any wounds he may have suffered in the crash. It did not occur to Yuri that there was nothing to crash into in the empty expanse.

The fatal, frigid air was on him again.

He cried out, but could not hear himself over the pitch of the wind. The car was making a rattling noise, whining and squeaking like a little bird. Through the wind he could detect only the faintest hint of smoke. Blinking and near the point of nature-induced blindness, Yuri walked toward the front of his truck, aware that at any point it could explode. Any attempt on his part to understand or rationalize what had happened would sooth him, calm him. Perhaps with a clearer mind, he could fix his vehicle and get back to the prison.

He tripped, falling face-forward onto the hard ice.

He was on top of something, something large and...*warm*. With a Herculean effort, Yuri pushed himself off the ice floor and shifted himself to crouch over the object that had tripped him. The ice was fighting him at every turn, the snow picking up more speed as its glowing white surface came to engulf the night. Yet it was because of this unnatural, strange snow-light that Yuri could clearly see the cause of his fall.

He reeled at first, unable to comprehend what had happened.

Then he laughed.

He had tripped over one of his corpses, discarded from the truck by some bump that Yuri had been too drunk to detect. The bump, whatever it was, had somehow jostled the engine and radio. Salty tears came down his face and left burning streaks where they froze. He would have to look at the engine again, try to fix it and get back. He thanked God that the radio was broken. His call to the Gulag, even if it had been an honest mistake, could have become a death sentence.

The snow stopped for a moment, and the land seemed to revert back to its natural tranquility. Yuri saw the body in full form, and a glacial terror receded from his eyes all the way down the base of his spine. It was a man; his skin was a sanguine red, full of more blood than men were supposed to be. He looked...*ripe*, a very *ripe* and red corpse that had let loose little streams of steam. There was not a patch of blue or black over the man, impossible since all starving prisoners died and decayed prematurely from the cold.

The man was unnaturally *healthy*.

He was lean but not skeletal; his closed eyes not hallowed cavities but instead normal and even handsome. He almost seemed a little *plump*. There was something oddly grotesque in the uncharacteristic *plumpness* of this character, the bulge of a stomach that had been fed to its full and then only a little bit more. There were no stomachs like that in the Gulag, and the only fat existed in the trash-meat soup they fed the officers who maintained watch over barbed-wire walls and ramshackle wooden mausoleums.

Yuri, not in courage but in that reflexive curiosity which makes children touch stoves, went to the body to stoop over it. He could not recognize the face or any other distinguishable thing about it. There was nothing about the shape of the nose, the sculpting of the chin, or any sort of scars or hair that would have caused Yuri to recognize the man. He was part of an endless, unremarkable crowd, only remarkable because he stood out against the decrepit wreckage of what is left in the human frame after its humanity has been forcefully removed.

The heat was radiating in an invisible cloud. There was an *aura* of warmth in the air next to the corpse that was perversely not comfortable like other warmth. It was unnatural, musky and humid in a place where water was dry. Every nerve on Yuri was creeping, every inch of him humming with tense electricity as he reached down to touch the man's forehead.

He felt the heat through his glove.

The eyes of the body opened.

This time Yuri heard his own scream. The eyes were glazed over and grey, the ornament eyes of a troglodyte creature to which light is useless. Bulbous and blind though they were, Yuri could feel them following him as he ran stupidly and desperately away from the corpse and his truck. The eyes followed him like the bead of a gun, and Yuri felt that he was in a line of sight far more dangerous than any armed soldier.

The wind stirred up again, into a maelstrom of glowing white snow that blotted out the night. The storm was an assault on his senses, where sight became muddled with the booming cacophony of the blizzard and his sense of touch became as dull and blunted as his eyes. There was an undercurrent of exhaustion and electricity under Yuri's skin as his breathing became more ragged with each croaking gasp. He moved slowly, encumbered by his clothing, and tripped over something again. Shivering, screaming, the reflexive realization rushed to Yuri's mind before his subconscious could try to repress it:

Warm.

Yuri could feel the tears and snot on his face, dementia and panic binding him as much as the storm around him. He felt the softness of flesh through his glove as he lifted himself from the thing he could not see. His mind recited all the prayers he had ever been taught into incoherent syllables, streaming together chants and songs that he had forgotten until he needed them. Everything in him was alert, stumbling and crying through the blizzard. He fell over five times in what only seemed like a few minutes. Each time he felt the awful, steady warmth beneath him, and each time he pushed himself off of something other than hard ice.

The flurry must have masked the graveyard, the unholy place where corpses were still warm and opened their eyes to watch their gravedigger at work. A creature seemed to scream out in the wind, a demonic laughing cry that came through the whipping white and the night blackness. It was not far from him, he imagined only a few yards away and getting closer with each shrill call that matched the tempo and torrent of the storm. The place was littered with these warm bodies, and he could feel the weight of their blind eyes laughing malevolently as he stumbled and tripped over them.

He was not a bad man! No worse than the men he worked with! But he had been a hero! He had been a hero of Stalingrad! Stalin had *personally* thanked him! This alone should have been the ticket for his salvation, *something* to save him from whatever cruel trick the snows and winds were playing on him now! He screamed out his life, that it was not his fault men were killed! He was not the one who decided to leave their corpses unhallowed in the Tundra; he was not the one who gave the order to pollute Siberia with the litter of executions!

The wind lifted him off the ground and tossed him onto another warm body. Screaming, thrashing against the loose arms that softly wrapped around him like a mother, Yuri pulled free and began running again. There was no destination in his mind; even if he had cleared his head for a moment and thought rationally, the Gulag was no longer open to him. The tundra had exposed itself to him, the casualties of war and cold had been revealed to him and he knew he could never work in snow again. He would leave Siberia; he would run across the Arctic Circle into Canada. He would keep running until he never saw snow or ice again!

Something cold and strong grabbed at his ankle, pulling him down and dragging him along the endless floor. He clawed at the ground with all his force, making out red trails through the flurries, and he knew that the blood was from his own raw, ungloved fingers. Death was all around him now, the storm thundering and mixing with the songs and prayers in his head into a mocking sound. He flipped upright and exposed his cold throat.

Was he choking, or were there cold fingers thrusting themselves into his mouth? Was something laughing at him? Were there warm, red bodies standing around in the snow looking down on him? They must have been, he could see them, smiling stupidly with straight white teeth, staring with lifeless grey eyes unmeant for sunlight.

The grey eyes were unchanging and unmoving. They did not blink, but glinted and shifted with the patterns of shifting snow. He could not hear breath, moans, or any other sounds to indicate the existence of sentience in those eyes. Only the patience, the constancy and weight of the stares crushed Yuri into believing that he was being watched. He was dying, he was mad and he was dying while the lifeless world watched without mirth or remorse.

The cold was inside of him now, his throat dry and cut with shards of ice and fear. An arm covered in knives was tearing him apart from the inside, and he could feel the taste of wind-scarred blood running down his mouth. Every part of him seemed to bleed as numbness spread from his fingers to his arms. Slowly all motion became impossible as his nerves became unresponsive. The numbness entered his lungs and crept into his heart.

A new, mad thought entered into his head:

Breath, please, breath!

His lungs stopped heaving. The throbbing in his head soon became aware of the slowing of his heart, calming and stopping for intolerable intervals. All thought left him, and death entered Yuri Zaystev as one final, slithering breath.

The steam from Yuri's face rose up into the dark, stormless, calm air of the tundra night. The world around him watched content with another of countless bodies that had already been brought into its fold. Nothing blinked for centuries, and nothing changed for all eternity.

Yuri had been wrong in one regard. They had not sent a search party for him, but they sent one for his truck. After all, equipment was expensive and valuable. Yuri would be replaced after he was killed, and his replacement would drive his truck. The soldiers followed the tracks to a spot not far from the prison. Yuri lay on the ground next to the truck, eyes frozen permanently open on a green-blue face with an open mouth.

His mouth seemed to have been forming a word when he died, but no mention was made of that in the report. Yuri's name disappeared into records, and his body was left to disappear into the unknowable tundra winds. He was never found or remembered again.

Author's Notes: This story was written after reading Tim Tzouliadis' *The Forsaken: From the Great Depression to the Gulags*. It is also inspired by other works of Soviet-era literature, namely Vasily Grossman's *Life and Fate*. The Stalin regime was especially ruthless to its poets and writers.

I also wanted to write a piece of landscape horror, something in the vein of Algernon Blackwood. Being someone who has lived exclusively in warm places their entire life, I have a primal disdain for the cold. To me, the very *idea* of the tundra is alien and strange.

This work was first published in the Onyx Neon Press *Book of Horror Stories*.

A Certain Shade

IT BEGAN WITH the death of my brother.

Edward was something of a disappointment, to put it mildly. I believe it would have been good if our parents had outlived him. He always brought them such worry in his long disappearances. I did not hate him, probably because such feelings were always difficult for me. It is hard for me to find anything worth hating or loving in the vast majority of people, and Edward, though my older brother, was certainly not worth anything. He was an abusive wreck of a boy and a catastrophe of a man.

His wild and reckless behavior was probably what led our parents to approach me so radically different than how they approached him. Though Edward was given a normal childhood with rules and limits, my parents allowed me as much liberty as I desired should I keep my grades up and stay out of trouble.

I kept my grades up and, being a more cunning creature than my brother, managed to hide my trouble.

But such was my misfortune that Edward did not die before our parents. He did not even come to their funerals. I had tried to find him, to reach him by any way and means. Ultimately, my lack of faith in him was warranted.

I was not surprised, nor even upset, when I was called into a Charleston police station to survey my brother's body.

It was his to be sure, a recognizable face stretched over a drug-thinned skeleton. He had apparently given himself to the wrathful gods of ennui and addiction, chasing a euphoria through his veins that in turn had captured and bound him.

But the scene faded away from me. To my mind the low-hanging lamp, the darkness pulsing in waves from the walls, seemed unimportant and not even part of reality. The awkward, cobbled-together words of comfort by the police officers meant nothing to me. It was only in his *skin* that I recognized something important.

For it was in the skin, in the color of it, that I recognized the potential for inspiration.

The officers mistook my request to be alone with my brother for a desire to part with him, last words and all. This was possibly for the best, as they did not question the long moments I spent with his corpse. I surveyed all that remained of his body, pouring over every detail in the feeling and color.

It was the color that caught me, a thin mix of a decay-dirtied yellow and the milky color of stagnant cream. It brought to mind dying maggots, the encroachment of death that so punctured the air of our current social climate. It was in the uneasy sunrise of a dreaded day, the very color which one becomes as they make their ungraceful exit from this earth.

The color of our times.

My brother's flesh was cold, and his company only meant slightly more than when he had been alive.

I left him for my paints.

Hours at the easel proved worthless, mixing every shade of yellow and green and white I could to portray the wonderful awfulness that had wrought its way across my brother's skin. There was no sleeping as excitement and anger cross-pollinated into an adrenaline that kept me awake and sick.

My other pieces stood half-finished in my studio, untouched for weeks and then months. My other commissions became distant memories as I mixed eggs and mustard and even my own bile into my paints.

I feared that soon I would lose myself to my own zealous drive, that I would work myself into a fever which would either hospitalize or kill me. Worse still, I feared I might fail.

It was then that one of my patrons intruded upon me, curious to see his commission.

"My dear lad, you've adopted absolute squalor since we last met. Do you need money?"

In truth, I was not sure. I had not paid attention to my funds, but the electricity had not gone out and I had not showered enough to see if the hot-water heater still worked. I thanked him for his concern, feigning an attempt to beg forgiveness for my lateness in his work.

"Well then pray tell, what is it that has driven you so?"

There is a fascination that the art appreciators have with artists, an unawareness but desperate desire to learn where passions and inspirations come from, to discover the source of the font of creativity which they so envy but cannot partake in. Ultimately, it can be annoying. However, in this instance, I knew this particular patron was one who shared my more morbid tendencies.

"Hrm," was his only reply when I told him of my brother's corpse.

"Hrm?" I repeated, perhaps angrily and with too much hostility.

He met my eyes, reminding me of the wolves my art ran amongst. Powerful, hungry collectors who had enough money to translate the language of currency to that of power, men and women who could dispose of money and bodies alike. I feigned forgiveness again, repeating that I was more stressed than normal.

He nodded.

"You continue to work on your commissions. But I believe I have a route that will better enable you to channel your frustration. It will not be easy, but at the very least it will be an adventure. Perhaps in that, new inspiration even."

"What exactly do you mean?" I repressed my contempt for riddles.

"If it is all the same to you, I would rather not say."

It was not all the same to me, but I did not say so.

"Very good, I'll email you the details. Merely keep up your end of the work, and I will help you as best as I might."

He exited from my apartment, and shortly after, from my life.

After I finished this patron's commission, I was rewarded with a curt thank you and, as promised, an email. The links provided internet lore regarding a certain new urban legend called "The Matchmaker." The Matchmaker forums, as they were called, were a series of writings detailing rituals, maps, and even a few news articles which seemed to indicate unsolved murders that may or may not be attributed to the Matchmaker. Curiously, none of the testimonies ever mentioned *seeing* the Matchmaker, although every member of the forums was prepared to swear that the folklore was real.

However, the very premise of hiring someone to kill for me appalled me. I cannot say whether it was my morality, if I ever had such thing to begin with, or an innate elitism that made me believe that such acts were *beneath* me. But I closed those forums and attempted to think of other things.

But the nagging curiosity tormented me, keeping me awake at night and hounding my every waking thought. The hue of my brother's skin bled its way into every dim light, every flickering headlamp, and every growing stain. I could not keep living this way, and because of it I gave in and began carrying the ritual out.

It would be at the very least an adventure, exactly as my patron suggested.

So it began. Popping certain amounts of money into a trash bin, another into the mailbox of an abandoned house. All according to the particular times and dates suggested by the various internet forums regarding a Richmond summoning.

After the requisite three months, he reached out to me.

An unknown email address.

A simple subject line:

"Lunch?"

"What you are asking for is not all that uncommon."

That is all the Matchmaker said to me after I explained myself.

He chose a sandwich shop in the periphery of downtown for our meeting, a dimly lit and homely place where the woman at the counter smiled and waved to him after we came in.

To say he was not what I was expecting would be a gross understatement. After the months of dropping various amounts of money into random locations across the city, of tracing lines across maps of Richmond to make complex geometric patterns that at once resembled signs of divination and marks of wrath, I had expected a cold and calculating mercenary.

Instead, he seemed to pay more attention to his tuna fish sandwich than he did my story.

He couldn't have been older than twenty-five, thick brown hair combed in waves. He wore neat black clothing, a buttoned shirt and jeans that displayed a narrow and thin frame of a body. He was only slightly shorter than myself, with a wide smile of white teeth which immediately disarmed me. His hazel eyes were warm, far warmer than any killer I had ever imagined. The only unusual things about him, as far as I could tell, were the sideburns that framed his face and the enthusiasm he paid my testimony.

"What do you mean?" is all I could think to say.

He nodded, understanding that his response was not enough for someone uninitiated and unfamiliar to his world.

"What I mean to say is, that a certain curiosity about the subject of death is a natural part of being human. And you, being an artist, are acutely sensitive to what it means *to be* human. You, I have no doubt, have a certain..." He looked at the ceiling, trying to summon the words. He snapped his fingers, pointing at me and clapping his hands as if he were amused with his own intelligence, "'... *economy of feelings*,' that is to say, you do not necessarily feel *often*, but when you do, you do so *intensely*."

I was stunned. He was more aware of what being an artist was like than anyone I had ever met.

"Precisely!" I responded.

He snuck another bite of his sandwich, wiping his mouth with a napkin before continuing.

"Good. Well, I can arrange this service. It'll be no trouble at all. Give me three days and I'll find a good candidate."

I balked. Until this point, it had been merely a joke, an adventure. All of the money required for this "summoning" had been drawn from my various patrons, as I claimed I needed these funds to pursue a new and ambitious work. In this regard, I am not so sure that I lied. But I had not before contemplated...going through with it.

"I can tell you're not sure about this."

My fascination with this young man was growing. He was adept at reading people, uncanny at it. Looking at him, I wondered if he had a military background. There are plenty of horror stories about young men and women recruited into intelligence agencies, committing clandestine and brutal crimes across the world. Surely, underneath the wide smiles and friendly eyes there dwelled something more.

"I don't suppose," I found myself smiling meekly, "you could be persuaded to pose for a portrait?"

He did not change his smile as a chill entered his voice. "I find the less of my likeness is out there in the world, the better it is for me."

There it was.

"Ah," I ventured.

He swayed a hand in the air, dismissing any concern on my part, before he turned his attention back to his sandwich. "You have paid the final fee. You have time to think about withdrawing, in which case I will return all of the collected funds. But," and that same chill bubbled from his voice, "know that I am the only one who provides a service like mine. I don't have any competitors."

It was strange to me that he, offering me the chance to murder with no consequences, would think about competition. He envisioned himself an entrepreneur, or at the very least portrayed himself as such.

The Matchmaker finished his sandwich and payed for mine, leaving me with a wave and a charmingly innocent smile.

He told me how he would contact me when I made my decision, though I was sure he knew that I had made it shortly after he left.

I do not know the name of the man I killed. Nor did I ever even see his face. Perhaps out of spite of Edward I requested someone who had given themselves over to addiction, someone who would not be missed and (preferably) someone who had hurt their family.

I did not, however, want any face or scream haunting my nightmares and forcing my guilty conscience. So his face was kept covered, his arms bound. I only needed his rotting flesh.

The creeping yellow hue.

"Is there a way to end it quickly?" I asked the Matchmaker.

He nodded. He stood in a corner, allowing the majority of his form to be absorbed into dim shadows. He reached into the darkness of his coat and removed a needle. I held it up to the orange-yellow lamp, seeing something clear and thick coagulating inside.

"What is it?"

"You don't really care." He said it as an observation rather than a rebuke.

I found a vein. The man's flesh was cold and clammy. He must have been sedated beforehand, as he only grumbled lowly in confusion from beneath a burlap hood as I wove my palms across his bound arm. I was no doctor, but my father was, and he had told exactly where to hit the vein. I smiled then, remembering my father as I slid the needle in and allowed a thick bead of blood to bubble up.

I stood back, watching as his body began thrashing violently. Each part of him moved independently and sporadically, a disjointed electric toy attempting to tear itself apart but unable to overcome its own skeletal binding. He did not scream, perhaps because his teeth were so clenched together under the sack that no sound could escape his lips, or perhaps the pain was so intense that he could not even think to scream.

Luckily, it was over quickly. The trashing stopped, and the beating of his heart soon followed.

Poor soul.

I turned to the Matchmaker, seeing if he had left me.

He stood resolutely in the corner of the room. His friendly smile had been engulfed by a newfound gravity, a focus that cut through me and into the dead man on the floor. He was entirely motionless, his chest did not move and his arms did not sway.

As I opened my mouth to speak, his eyes fell on me. In a glint of unusual light, they flared red.

I gasped, turning away from him and back to the corpse.

I got to work, taking a scalpel-like tool which I had been provided to cut and peel what I needed. Rising blood, the ripping of sinew had no effect on me. Art is, of course, suffering, bleeding, tearing, and rending. It is not for the weak of heart or stomach, and anyone who tells you otherwise is a charlatan and fraud, feeble-minded souls feigning artistic talent to cover their absolute lack of talent or character, unwilling to sacrifice their sensitivities or selves to produce anything of worth.

No true artist is squeamish. And I am proud to say that as I carefully cut bleeding skin from an exposed rib cage, the careful hours taking pictures and mixing my paints rose no emotion in me, but only furthered my zeal. In the color I so rigorously worked for was the truth of life, the inevitable jaundice of both society and flesh. Already decay was everywhere. It had pierced the zeitgeist, heroes now far less popular than the monsters they fought. It was in the news, in our politics more overtly and proudly than it had ever been before. And as an artist, I had a duty to bring the public to the truth, to drag them screaming and begging to the only altar which truly matters.

I collected several fine pieces and set to immediate work. Mixing the paints was far easier with the inspiration directly before me. The color, rather than leaping out, seemed to leak in from my memory, slowly forming and rising as I first led my brush across the strips of slightly reddened-and-brown flesh and into my mixing bowl. I smiled, elated at my accomplishment and innovation.

I turned to thank the Matchmaker.

But he was gone, leaving me to a soundless and stinking room.

The flesh did not maintain its color, though I had by that point painted several new canvases. My new works consisted of a trifecta of scenes, all painted with the same unnerving color. The acts of violence were outlined in thin white lines, to make them murky and unsettling. A woman cradling a hateful infant child that grabbed greedily at her breast, the fear in her face coming from the knowledge that her child's generation would cannibalize her flesh. A man, alone with empty alcohol bottles that reflected his own face, each reflection hateful and cruel as the man tore at his hair and silently screamed. And then, a falling house, giving in to rot as it was overtaken by the malicious and oppressive nature that swirled around it.

But these paintings only inspired new nightmares, new zeal in me. I dreamt of the corpse of the universe, jaundicing and changing as the life-blood of stars left us. The sun, getting fatter and fatter until it hung so close to earth to wash it all in its seeping color.

I dreamt of some indistinct human form, bound and pulled apart.

I had developed a thirst which I had never felt before.

So I retread my old steps, unable to part with my works and scraping the various monetary requirements for the ritual by selling material possessions and lesser works of mine. My inheritance had run dry, I often went to bed hungry and observed my thinning stomach as I went through my customary evening showers. I could not sleep until biological imperatives took their hold, forcing sleep rather than giving in to it.

At the end of all these months, I only received one message:

"No repeat clients."

I then resolved to sell even more of my belongings to attempt a summoning in Norfolk. However, when I arrived at the first specified drop-off point, he was already there.

He frowned at me, those same red-brown eyes glinting in the sunlight of the ending day.

"I thought I made myself clear."

"I...I just need more."

"You don't *get* any more," he growled.

He walked toward me, looming over me as he placed a hand on my shoulder.

"I suggest you stop this. It won't be good for you."

"I won't." I surprised myself by the strength in my voice.

"You will." He walked away, leaving me in the empty Norfolk alley. Defiantly, I placed my monetary offering in the dumpster and continued on my way.

For a long time I could not tell if I was asleep or if I was awake. I was drowsily aware that I could not move, and that something rough snaked its way across my body. Breathing was difficult, both because I was too tired to do so and because something hot and thick covered my face. I attempted to move, to speak, but coordination seemed a far-removed possibility.

A mild euphoria calmed me in the darkness as I heard a voice permeate through the murky fog.

"And you are certain that there will be no consequences?"

"I pride myself on my professionalism," the cold, resolute voice of the Matchmaker responded.

"As I said, what you asked for is not uncommon. Pain is a natural part of art, and it's only natural that you as a sensitive artist be inclined and curious to observe pain long and closely."

The realization was beginning to reach me, though I could not scream.

"This man, he is an addict? He is dangerous?"

"Oh yes...a *dangerous* addict indeed."

There was a long silence.

The cold touch of a knife. Then fire, etched across my flesh.

Author's Notes: This story was originally written for *Ravenwood Quarterly's* fifth planned issue, "Yellow." Brian O'Connell, infuriatingly aspirational as he is, asked contributors for stories with themes of social decline and decadence. I have to say, the times sure seem different these days, and transplanting The Matchmaker into a story about the theme was easier than I thought.

The Matchmaker first appeared in another story, but I prefer this one. He is an autobiographical monster, written to look and act like me. This gives me an uneasy feeling when I write him, so I don't very often.

This is his first appearance in print.

I'm sure there will be more.

Cabras

WHEN THE SOLDIERS cut out his tongue, they forced Manuel into five years of silence. He came to appreciate the noise of the jungle around him, the songs of birds and bugs, the lulling night wind and the thunderous whispers of moth-clouds and bats. Moving away from his besieged city, deeper into the hills and closer to the sprawling rainforest, had given him time to think, to look inward on his life and thoughts. He now was forced to commit his words and thoughts to paper. Now everything was so much more deliberate and beautiful than when he had been confined to the spoken word. Sixty years old, a widower and a survivor of two civil wars, cut off from a larger world.

It was too late in life to discover he was a poet.

But he didn't care. In his mornings he would wake from his small bed, put his feet on the cold concrete, and slip into his rough sandals. He kept his breakfasts simple enough—bread, homemade cheese, and fruit, cutting everything into tiny pieces and sucking on them so that they were soft to swallow. Then, he was out into the wet and mild air of the tropical morning, spending the day lifting shovels, rakes, tending to his meager plot of land and the goats he kept. From them, he would draw his milk to make his cheese. Learning how had been a process—his first cheese had been sour and made him deathly sick. But now he made it safe enough to eat not only for himself, but for the neighbors who were kind to him.

When the third civil war erupted, only three years after the second had ended, he was unconcerned. *Were the rumors true?* his neighbors asked. *Was he once a guerilla, un insurgente?* And he would write that yes, ages ago, when he was young in body and mind, he had fought in the *first* civil war. But he gave up *la lucha* the moment he held his first daughter. Some things were bigger than ideas. Memory being one. Love, another. The government that emerged out of that first conflict had spies, archives and notes spanning across the entire nation and the past hundred years.

When the second civil war began, men in black uniforms and masks drug him from his bed. *You were a guerilla; you are still a guerilla.* No, no he wasn't. He knew nothing of the new group. *No, no you are lying.* And through the heavy padding of their uniforms, through the masks which covered everything but their eyes, Manuel recognized who and what those men were. Their signatures were in the deliberateness of their walk, the straightness of their stance, the methodology and precision of the places where the butts of their rifles and heels of their boots struck him. The way they moved about the pictures of his daughters and wife. The lupine coldness of their gaze.

After all that time, Manuel still recognized the eyes of men ready to kill.

It was their fondness for the pictures of Rita, his youngest daughter, which made him stay silent. He would have lied, sent them on a false trail and told them what they wanted to hear. Such were the tactics of his old group, whose leadership had known that anybody would give way under torture. But he feared what these men would do to her. Though he knew *his* disappearance would be of little consequence, he could not fathom his Rita, by then a young woman just beginning to enjoy her beauty, becoming an unnamed statistic like so many other victims.

So in the end, he clung to the truth. He did not know anything. And instead of killing him, the soldiers decided that if he was going to tell lies, he should not be able to say anything at all.

Five years of silence. Five years of the taste of cold iron and hot, coppery blood.

But two years of peace, of uprooting himself from his old home for a far humbler one. He had no illusions, he knew the men would find him again if they wanted to. It had been a selfish decision, to save the three daughters who loved him. Two were grown women and married now, happy. Shy, beautiful Rita remained in school. It was his desperate hope that they would live a life better than his despite the war. In the big cities, they would be safe. The government would maintain order there at any cost, keep the violence well outside those boundaries. But if they were to be visited by a man marked by the government...that would put them on a list. And those wolves were not above arresting a young woman based only on her looks.

So he had left without saying goodbye.

The day Rita showed up, unannounced, had been one that at once made his heart alive, and shattered it.

"*Papá?*"

He had been tending to his goats. By then he had six, which was a considerable rural wealth in the meager village. Her voice came through to him as a gentle wind-chime giggle, timid with all the uncertainty and heartbreak of a confused child. He turned and there she was. Every time he saw her, she reminded him more of her mother. Her bright brown hair was cut short so that it rested just above the nape of her neck as a gilded-copper crown. Her skin, dark and smooth, seemed unblemished by the wrong he had done her. Her deep brown eyes were where the burden rested, and looking into them he immediately felt the guilt he had so successfully staved off for so long.

She rushed to him and he was overwhelmed with the happiness that exists only in desperate, loving fathers. He smelled her hair and drowned in memories of stories, of trips to parks and zoos, of consolations and celebrations. Memories of her, and of the family he left behind.

"*Papá?* Why didn't you come back after the war ended? When things were peaceful again?"

And so, he took her inside and he wrote for her. Pages of the deepest, most heart-felt apology he could offer. And she accepted them, with gasps, tears, and laughter. Rita was always such a loving, sunny little child. Her sisters would have not been so easily swayed. He was old now, his bones too brittle and joints too thin to hike back to the city. But more importantly, he was scared. The new government had seemed too fragile, too much a congealed and desperate compromise that could not last. He believed it was built of angry children, not of men. And he knew all too well, that in the absence of mankind, wolves would rule. So he had opted to stay in the countryside, where he knew he could do no harm. He had instructed one of his neighbors to hold on to his documents, among them a will to be given to his daughters upon his death.

Quite frankly, he had not expected to live this long.

He spent the rest of that day showing her his world.

He began with his yard, a green little square of mostly grass and overripe, unfolding bushes. He brought pieces of bread, placing them in her hand as if she were a little girl. And, just as if she was a little girl, she laughed when the goats licked her hands. She laughed even harder when he pointed to the goat with a light brown head and handed her a note.

"*Mi Rubia.*"

"You did not *name* her after *mamá*! *Papá*, you are *terrible!*"

He smiled meekly. What more could he think to tell her, other than a man who is so alone takes whatever comfort he can in pleasant memories and cheap humor? The color of the goat's head reminded him of the playful nickname he had given his wife so many years ago, his arm over her after they had left some cheap Hollywood movie. Every man's eyes had been glued to the blonde woman on the screen, but not him...he had been completely entranced by the young woman next to him.

Mi Rubia.

He took her through the village, where houses of wood and mud stood the test of time and weather. Gárgola, the old black dog who lived in the village longer than he had, followed him from a distance, cautious of the new arrival. People in clothing smiled and waved, and little boys poked their heads from around corners and behind trees to get a look at the beautiful woman walking with Old Manuel.

He took her through the jungle paths, navigating over moss-covered roots and vines which flowed so copiously from their trees. The branches became thicker, winding over each other to form an emerald canopy through which the sun could only teasingly peak through. He was old, but the aches from his body seemed to dissipate as he listened to her talk, the sound of her voice reminding him that there were things to live for other than peace.

"*Papá*, I'm in love with a young man."

And suddenly, the sun was no longer there. He was at once happy and suspicious. Rita had always been a meek child when it came to delicate issues, the first to admit she had done wrong but often taking too long to stammer out her admissions between plaguing "ums" and "ohs." There was a reason that she was here then. A reason that she had tracked him down while his other daughters had not. The other girls were already married, to young men who, if he could not say he liked them, were at least good to his daughters. And there was a reason that she had waited to tell him out here in the jungle.

"I brought him with me." The timidity in her voice gave everything away. Old instincts and questions flared up in the back of his mind. How could she have brought him with her when he himself had seen no one new in village? How could this man hide from the village if he was already with one of them? Why could he not hear the chiming of the bugs anymore?

The shadows beyond the thick entanglement of plants became suddenly distinct.

They were surrounded.

Artemio and his "comrades" had been with them for over two months now. Manuel found him insufferable and horrifying, all of the bravado of youth with the arrogance of the well-read. Rita had told him that her father had been an *insurgente*, that he had fought with all of the dead men who Artemio so religiously read in his not-so-secret Marxist university book clubs. And because of this, Artemio would often come alone to Manuel's house, asking overzealously about what it had been like to work with "Comrade" Fuentes and "Comandante" Figuero.

And Manuel would try his best to answer some of his questions earnestly, but the boy was too well-read in his history. He knew the biographies of these men, their daily movements in their struggles and every word of every speech that Manuel had heard during that time. He suspected that Artemio's sunglasses were for more than show, that he had lost his eyesight in dark rooms with dusty pages.

But when he took them off, that is when Manuel became afraid. Not of Artemio, but of what he represented. These new children, the group which had fool-heartedly taken the name of Manuel's old fighting force, were nothing that their grandparents were. They were spoiled by peace, unfamiliar with the concept of a true struggle and the price one had to pay for that peace. The second civil war had only lasted two years, but the first had lasted ten. This one would last a matter of months. But Artemio and the acolytes who so desperately swallowed every word he gave them would convince themselves to stay here in the village, to use it as a base of operations after the government and more consequential groups negotiated a peace. They were after glory, and as of yet had not spilled blood. They had not yet learned the art of restraint. Their guns were toys, not weapons. And arms in the hands of idealistic and untrained minds...one way or another, Artemio was destined for an early grave.

If not by an *actual* soldier, then by his own hand.

But Manuel could see how in love Rita was. The way she looked after him as he walked away, the wide smile and weak eyes when they met. And for his own part, Artemio seemed to reciprocate, though he spent most of his time patrolling the village, plotting schemes with his "lieutenants" and bothering Manuel. He would have made a good enough accountant, or maybe even a decent pharmacist, had he not sought off to chase the little boy's dream of glorious conflict. But there was *so little* glory in conflict.

Manuel kept this to himself though, and wrote all of his frustrations down into a journal which he kept under his bed. After all, it is not as if he could tell Artemio to leave. A bullet was a bullet, and in the end one of these "soldiers" could fire one off into a villager to prove a point, a meaningless point though it would be.

Becoming bothered by his own powerlessness in the situation, Manuel deliberately began spending more time away from his house. Pieces of bread in hand, we would treat Gárgola and scratch her old black-grey head. She, like him, was distrustful of these new arrivals and seemed desperate for any chance to escape the bounds of her home. And like him, she seemed too old, or perhaps too comfortable, to leave entirely. So the two of them, with a sort of mutual understanding that only exists in unspoken language, herded the goats to the jungle periphery. There, Rubia and her friends ate at the weeds and grass.

There was a certain beauty in watching them, a simplicity that made Manuel feel as if he had earned some calm in his life. His goats lazily stood by, their slanted eyes and jaws hanging slackly and open. Every now and then, Gárgola would come up to them, growling and nipping with the instinctual motherliness of an old herding dog that could not betray its own nature. The goats would simply stare back, perplexed and a little angry that such an old thing could deign to boss them around. And Manuel would laugh, calling Gárgola back with a piece of bread. Begrudgingly, she came to learn that there was more reward in gentleness than cruelty.

Rita would come and find him sometimes, and he worked up the courage to ask her that the "*revoluccionarios*" not disturb him there. At first she seemed confused, and then sad.

"They admire you, *Papá*."

Manuel was skeptical of this, but did not tell her so. Whether they admired him or not, he needed his solitude. If he was as truly revered as Artemio suggested, then they would find it in their hearts to leave him be for a moment. There were other people in the village to trade with, to protect. Manuel did not want constant attention.

And so she would come and talk and he would only listen. It was good to hear her voice, but it was also good to hear what came in its absence. The birds sang and the gentle sounds of rural life floated up from below. Children playing, women talking, the guerillas laughing as they played soccer and made fanciful war plans, all made a medley with the sounds of the jungle itself. Branches shifted with slithers and cracks, things scuttled gently across its floor against the ever-present, almost silent, hiss of mist rising from the morning dew.

It was only a matter of time before he took to taking naps up there.

When he heard the scream, he thought it was in a nightmare.

He jarred himself awake. His heart was pounding, the early afternoon sun hung just above him. The goats were all there, still moving lazily around the end of the jungle. He nodded, resting his head again.

Then he heard Gárgola growling.

Turning over, he saw her standing on all fours, back arched and face towards the jungle. The fur along her spine was up, her eyes wide and mouth gritted to show a row of teeth both sharp and missing. She growled lowly, stiffly towards the jungle.

There were no bugs humming. No birds chirping.

Manuel leapt up from his sleep, grabbing the old rifle that Artemio had given him as a token of respect and protection. The weapon was familiar but inadequate. If there were soldiers out there in the jungle, he would be the first slaughtered.

The scream came again. It was high-pitched and shrill, both of surprise and of pain.

He thought of Rita, and the soldiers were suddenly not a concern.

He heard Gárgola barking, but the sound of her feet padding behind him was replaced by the drums in his chest and ears. He tore through the bush recklessly, scraping himself against vines and bark, only just barely dodging the tangles of roots with an instinctual expertness. With the rifle cradled in his arms, his eyes darted madly about for the sight of his daughter.

He heard her screaming again, this time closer and louder.

He did not cry out, knowing that if he did he would lose any element of surprise.

The jungle became deeper, darker around him. The heat of his body made him sweat, and through the stinging sight of his eyes the world became a green haze. The scream again, now sounding more unfamiliar yet more feminine. His heart became frantic, unaccustomed and unprepared for the vigorous sprint. His feet burned and bled against the jungle floor, his knees cracked and exploded with every reckless leap. Time and he both became slow together.

Fading against the green backdrop of the jungle, a woman's naked backside stalked only briefly through a wide wall of foliage. Pale, shadowed grey by the canopy around her, dark hair resting just above her lower back. She laughed playfully, without revealing her face.

Manuel fell to the jungle floor.

As he faded away, her laughter went farther away, only to be drowned out slowly by the panicked barking of Gárgola.

He woke up, dizzy and faded, in his own room. Pale moonlight flaked every surface, the concrete floor and bare wooden furniture marked him for the impoverished man he was. The sheets had been neatly tucked around him, lovingly and cleanly. The open window revealed a portal into the jungle, and all of the native noises which had been absent before gently lulled him towards calm.

He remembered his chase, and with that all of the aches he had earned assailed his body. His shins, knees, and ribs pulsated from foolishness. He must have heard some animal, he decided. There were only so many things men could come to know about the jungle, as it would not willingly give up all of its secrets even to the most faithful of followers. Someone had changed him, and he recalled the loving detail in neatness and cleanliness of the sheets.

Rita...*que preciosa*. She was a good woman, despite everything, she was still his little girl.

He shifted his back, sighing heavily as he reached for the jug of water on the floor.

That is when he heard the laughter.

Slowly, out of dread, his eyes shifted towards the open window.

The face there was framed by thick, matted black hair. In the moonlight he could only see the shape and some of its features. A soft, rounded chin with a thick smile, a little nose with two tiny nostrils resting under it. There was certainly a beauty in it, but it was surpassed by horror, as the figure was simply *too large*. The face, what he could see of it at least, belonged to a giantess.

And she laughed again, placing her arms against the window frame and carefully maneuvering her shoulders through. Placing her hands on the floor, she slid her whole body in carefully and quietly, taking up half the width of the room. She motioned to stand, but found herself unable to without her head touching the top of the roof. Finding that she had to duck her neck, she laughed again. The laugh set his blood on fire, and standing fully in front of him Manuel saw her in her full nakedness.

She was certainly beautiful, in a wild and natural way. And her skin was so pale, too pale to have ever seen much of the sun. Unshaven and unblemished, brimming with beauty from every curve. She looked upon Manuel and smiled. Her eyes remained covered by hair and darkness, but he could feel the crushing weight of her gaze.

He was frozen. Fear, arousal, he could not tell.

She leaned down on him, picking him up as if he were a doll. She cradled him and then...

He would not have called it "making love." Somehow, it was as if his mind were somewhere else, and he was watching events unfold through a television screen rather than through his body. Occasionally a sensation would cross the threshold, either of pain or pleasure. He felt wrong, as if he was *being* wronged. He watched his hands reach up to touch the crown of her head. When something hard and stony greeted his touch, she thrust him down onto his back, maybe in retaliation.

She scuttled away from him, growling perhaps. She stood there for whole minutes, watching him. When he could not move, she contorted her frame back through the window she had entered, leaving him alone to the night melodies.

He was not sure what to call his dream. A nightmare, for certain, but too vivid and potent to be compared to anything he had dreamed before.

Despite the disturbance of his dream, a whole night's sleep had somehow healed all of his pains. In the morning he felt spry, flexible, and limber. Rita had scorned him thoroughly, proving that when she wanted to she could be stronger than any man with a gun. A more naïve, younger fighter, undoubtedly loyal to Artemio and only incompletely aware of his greater context, tried to prevent Rita from confronting her father by standing between her and him.

The look in his daughter's eyes melted the young man.

It would have been funny, if he were not trying to fight a war.

What had Manuel been thinking? Why had he run off into the woods like that? Why was the bed so messy? Was he such a damn fool that he did not drink his water? Did he learn *nothing* from being so inconsiderate to his daughters? What would the other girls think, when he finally met them again?

This time, Manuel had no regrets and no guilt. He only laughed and fetched a notebook from his room. He explained that he must have heard another goat out there, screaming in the woods. They can sound so much like a screaming woman, especially when they are being hunted by jaguars. He had only thought he heard his daughter in trouble, and he was sorry for scaring her.

Rita only begrudgingly accepted his apology, tearing the page from his hand and storming out of the house. There was no doubt that she meant to report his recovery to Artemio, who increasingly was functioning less in the capacity of a guerilla leader and more as a tribal elder.

Walking outside, Manuel found his suspicions confirmed. The guerrillas walked more brazenly, more openly as they wove themselves into the life of the village. They stood against short wooden fences, teasing the old women who became red and blushing at the words of young men. They kicked worn soccer balls with village children, returned from the jungle with wood for fires and fruit for those too sick or too elderly to get it for themselves. Manuel prayed silently, thanking God that he was not so weak yet as to survive solely on the mercy of those with guns, men who were so uncomfortable standing on their own that they constantly leaned on their weapons for support.

Only Gárgola remained skeptical of the interlopers. From her spot on the corner of two dusty trails, she looked sternly on the unfolding scene and made no motion to join. As Manuel approached her, so did a young man with a gun. The man reached down to pet her and she growled, baring her row of mangled teeth. The young man laughed and withdrew his hand, rejoining his comrades, unaware of the scorn he had so grievously been dealt.

Manuel approached, his offer of bread in hand and his goats trailing behind him. Gárgola lapped up the bread from his palm, wagged her tail, and rose to follow him up to the summit of the jungle. He crossed a band of small children running through the road, pretending branches were guns and shooting each other. He bitterly ground his teeth together, angry that their innocence had been so suddenly and thoroughly polluted by violence.

The air seemed more still, the village sounds more subdued and the jungle more quiet. He decided on a change of scenery, taking a different trail from that which led up to his goat-perch. The goats followed behind him as the jungle grew around them, and Gárgola remained unfazed at his side as the shadows grew thicker on the dirt beneath her. The trail opened up into a small opening, surrounded by thick grass and vines, making a natural enclosure for his goats to graze in. He smiled to himself, noting that he could barely see beyond those green walls, and took this as a sign he would not be disturbed.

He laid down, threw his hands behind his neck, and remembered the woman of his nightmare. There had been a rawness in her beauty, a sort of attraction that he had never experienced before. And he recalled the force with which she removed his hands from her head, the strong impression of something cold beneath her hair.

A voice made him leap, grabbing his rifle and pointing at the trail he had entered.

"*Tranquilaté*, Don Manuel."

Two guerillas stood at the opening of the enclosure. Their neat, unsullied, dark green uniforms spoke to their inexperience, their black boots only barely caked with village dirt. The fuzz on their face had only been two days old at most, doing nothing to conceal the too-youthful features of boys. Their smiles showed the whites of their teeth, curved with condescension as if to suggest that they did not believe one as old as he was capable of properly using his weapon.

Nonetheless, he lowered it.

The guerillas kept their rifles slung behind their backs, but moved forward slowly with their hands swinging at their sides. One approached before the other, who hung back and placed his hand on the sheath of his machete.

"Our comrades, it has been so long since they have had meat. We have been trading with your neighbors, but they do not want to part with their meat. It is too precious, too great a commodity. So we have eaten fruit, vegetables. Granted, ours is not so bad a life, but we look at your goats every day and all we can think is that we want to help you. We know you must not be able to kill the animals yourself anymore. So we will do it for you, if of course you share with us a small portion of their meat?"

Manuel stared them down, trying to muster a force from an old part of his soul. He tried to recall the eyes that had killed men, those eyes which had so mercilessly and thoroughly slaughtered soldiers. He remembered the intensity of his hatred, his overwhelming conviction that men had to die by his hand. But the sharpness of his stare had been dulled with age and peace, so the young men merely smiled back, barely suppressing their laughter between quick breaths.

He shook his head slowly, mustering conviction in his motions.

"Don't be ridiculous, Don Manuel, let us help you. Here." The closest one motioned to the man behind him.

The second guerrilla laughed, unsheathing his machete as he walked up to Rubia. The soldier swung one leg on top of her and brought his weight down on her back. The goat buckled under his weight, legs folding in as her eyes widened. She reared her neck in a panic, whirling it around as her mouth hung open and screaming. The scream alerted her peers, and the goats turned their heads in horror to the sound. Gárgola growled, trying to make herself fearsome through her mangled teeth.

Manuel reacted quickly, bringing his fist down hard against the young man's face. All of his strength sent the boy back a few steps, cursing and holding his cheek as he coughed up blood and teeth into an open palm. A few staggering steps backward and he was standing again, looking at him with the same eyes he had so desperately tried to summon just moments ago.

"Bastard." The whisper was cold and pointed.

His comrade had released Rubia, and ran towards Manuel with machete drawn. Gárgola brought down her remaining teeth into his calf and the young man shrieked in surprise. He moved the machete upward above his shoulder, and for a terrible moment prepared to bring it down in a decapitating arc. For that second, the sun hung high above the enclosure.

Manuel raised his rifle to his shoulder.

The bleeding young man knocked Manuel down, pushing him into to the ground and sending a flaring pain across his back. The shot cracked out regardless, and the air filled with the sound of something wet and gasping. But the boy on top of Manuel did not care that his comrade was dying. He was consumed by an all-too familiar rage, ornamented with the eyes which he had always known he would die by.

His hearing and sight faded with the repeated blows to his head, forceful stones battering his mind and disorienting him with every second. Somewhere Gárgola was barking. Somewhere someone was laughing. A light, melodious giggle.

Then there was a second shot.

One which cut through the numbness and the sounds.

There was an indistinct roar, the sound of crying, the wet thwack of blunt objects against flesh. The grass slid around him, someone propped him up and put something cold to his lips. Minutes later a wet rag was on his forehead, cooling the pulsing heat rising from what would surely be horrible welts.

After what seemed like hours later, his sight returned.

There was an untrained fierceness in Artemio's features. His sharp face, the peak of his nose betrayed no emotion. Its leanness, and the matching leanness of his frame, suggested an animal quickness. His sunglass-hidden eyes only lent themselves to the gravity of his presence. The red beret on his head was ridiculous, however, a crown which made him the leader of an imagined yet still lethal army.

"Don Manuel, I apologize profusely. These...men," he hissed at the word as if to suggest he now thought them less-than-human, "will be punished. No one, you especially, is to be coerced into giving anything they would otherwise not give."

Two tall solemn soldiers stood behind him. The goats grazed lazily, as if they had already forgotten they had witnessed something unusual. Underneath their hooves, the grass was marked with dark-red blood. Gárgola's heavy breathing at his side filled him with relief. After all of this, he had a friend left.

"Come with us, I'll carry your weight on my shoulder."

Manuel shook his head, motioning weakly with his hands.

Artemio nodded, reaching into his uniform and pulling out a notepad and pencil. Holding the pencil was torture, but Manuel managed to scrawl out his crucial note.

Artemio held the note closely.

"If..." He paused, confused. "If that is what you want. But I will leave these men outside the clearing, on the path. They will help you come home when you are ready. And you should hurry, Don Manuel." Artemio changed his tone from the matter-of-fact imitation to that of a sincere man. "Your daughter will worry about you."

Alone with his thoughts, Gárgola, and his goats, Manuel was grateful. He was grateful that he was alive, though bleeding and hurt once more, and he was grateful that he was not a killer again. That the young man who knocked him over had intended to kill him, but had inadvertently saved his friend. And that the "soldier" saved a life rather than took one made Manuel laugh. It was a dry, wheezing one from between his broken ribs and bubbling in the blood in his mouth.

A light giggle answered him back.

From just beyond the green wall, shadows stood. Tall, long shadows which had a vague impression of curved torsos, strong arms, and too-tall legs.

He sat, paralyzed for hours, watching the shadows which only occasionally seemed to move their limbs.

A force kept him there, staring at them until they receded backwards into the jungle darkness.

Walking back from the jungle, arms leaning on one of Artemio's elite guard, he began to think that he was unfair. Injustice seemed so much more wrong, so much more daunting when youth burned the blood. He had been only a little older than Artemio when he joined the insurgency all those years ago. But that had been against a dictator, the son of a father who had also been a son in the tradition and bloodline of a tyrant. The enemy was so clearly oppressive, execution squads descended on the countryside and mutilated mothers to demonstrate their unquestionable power. Artemio's war, if it could be called that, was against a government which barely had time to bring itself together. And unlike Artemio, Manuel had been cautious about the fighting.

Until he killed. Then someone had unlocked the part of his soul where ruthlessness lived. Men became the sum of their limbs and parts, merely automated bags of blood whose execution was of no consequence. This was his way, he now supposed, of coping with it. Some men would tell jokes, others would take some pleasure in torture. But he merely considered his enemy soulless, and much like weeds being pulled from the garden, he pulled them from this world.

He did not yet know the kind of man Artemio would be when he first killed.

And that, more than anything else, scared Manuel.

As the jungle gave way to the village, the purple sky began to poke through the dark trees. The night wind began to gently move through the trees, and the night predators began stalking silently. The two tall men, imposing though they were, were not accustomed to the jungle sounds. Beyond the patting of Gárgola's feet and the calls of his goats, Manuel heard the soft padding of something following them.

He remembered the shadows who so oppressively watched him and wished he could move faster.

The village was a welcome sight, and his house even more welcome.

A soldier motioned for Gárgola to back away, but Manuel shook his head. He was afraid and he was hurt. He decided that Gárgola could spend the rest of her days as his pet, and as such was entitled to sleep at the foot of his bed. The old dog had rarely been inside a home, or at least it had been a long time. Her tail wagged harder than he had ever seen it before as she circled his kitchen, sniffing at corners and turning back to him in disbelief. She ran from one end of the room to the next, stopping briefly before Manuel so she could smile in thanks.

But she stopped at his closed bedroom door. Her stillness, her body poised as an arrow ready to leap through the door should she need to, made his blood run cold. She made no sound, merely preparing herself to spring on someone.

Or something.

Manuel looked outside his open window. The tall soldiers had gone.

He unslung his rifle, but it was heavy and shaking in his arms.

Cautiously, he turned the handle and pushed the door open.

In the dim, artificial light, Artemio leaned against a wall. In one hand, he had a pistol equipped with a long, dark silencer. In the other, he had Manuel's notepad.

"I wanted to change your sheets, Don Manuel," the boy's voice was encroaching on a dangerous tone, "as an apology for what those men did to you. To my surprise, when I flipped your mattress I found this notebook." His eyes turned from the notebook to Manuel. Manuel's stomach tightened; Artemio's eyes looked familiar now.

Artemio nodded, as if he knew that Manuel now understood the danger he was in.

He lazily flipped open a page of the notebook with his silencer. "Artemio is just a child, and an arrogant one at that. His soldiers quote Marx, but have no concept of cost. I doubt that they are ready to pay. They look back fondly on the past and mistake the color of blood for the color of roses."

His voice was unattached, unaffected by what he was reading. It was as if he was reading a manual rather than a scathing critique.

Manuel felt foolish. No matter how frustrating it had been, he should have kept those thoughts inside.

Gárgola made a desperate attempt to leap through the air. But her legs were old, and she only landed a foot away from Artemio.

Artemio, however, was far younger.

It was a motion of the wrist, a simple swaying motion which put the end of the silencer in line with Gárgola's head.

She didn't cry.

There was barely any noise at all.

In shock, Manuel fell to his knees.

Artemio approached him, gun still drawn. He put it away, lifting Manuel's chin to force him to look into his eyes. "Don Manuel, I regret what just happened. I do not enjoy killing. But I understand there are some instances in which there is no other option. Some dogs are too old, too set in their ways to survive and thrive in the new world. So they either die slowly in the bitterness of old age and cruel sickness, or they die swiftly. By the mercy of the gun. And whether it is old dogs, two young soldiers who torment an old man, or an old man turned traitor by age...some things shouldn't survive in the new world."

Artemio crouched down, putting his eyes on level with Manuel's.

"Don Manuel, I am taking this notebook, and I am burning it. I am sprinkling its ashes beneath the feet of the two soldiers whose necks will be in nooses by tomorrow morning. For good measure, I am going to add the dog to the pyre too. One message is for my men, and these villagers. The doctrine won't be betrayed, not by anyone. The other message is for you, Don Manuel. And for the sake of your daughter, whom I love. I hope you understand it."

Artemio picked up Gárgola's bleeding corpse irreverently, slinging her over his shoulder and letting her blood drip over Manuel's hung head. A sadness welled up from Manuel's stomach, and involuntarily he began to cry for the first time in years.

Artemio smiled, as if he were attempting to console a child.

"Don Manuel, I suggest you get your tears out tonight. The new world is often greeted in tears. Tears, and blood."

Manuel's stomach hurt from its heaving. He had to leave the room for an hour, vomiting loudly on the side of his house. When he finally worked up the courage to return to his room, he grabbed a rag wetted from well water. He felt sick and angry, cleaning up Gárgola's blood. He was angry not at Artemio, but at himself. He had been foolish, too foolish, and in doing so had awakened the very thing in Artemio that Manuel had quietly mocked him for not having. He understood that he had unleashed a monster not only on poor, loyal Gárgola, but on the world as well.

On his daughter.

His tears stung his eyes. He sat on his bed, choking back loud screams and wishing he still had a tongue to bite down on.

When he finally noticed her, he could not tell how long she had been there.

At this angle, the moonlight revealed more of her face than it had before. She leaned through the window, looking at him with the same beautiful, child-like smile she had the night before. This time, she made no motion to come into the room. She merely watched in a silence so complete that it was not clear if she was even breathing.

As before, the power of her stare enraptured him. The white moon made her skin even more pale, and with an unwelcome clarity he saw her eyes and could not even muster the power to scream.

Through the dark distance, he could see her long, black pupils. They made her lips darker, her hair more bestial.

She did not laugh this time, but merely sighed wistfully, regretfully. She placed a hand on the window frame and made a motion to draw herself closer.

For a horrible moment, Manuel thought she was going to climb through again.

But when three more faces made their way through the window frame, each armed with the same monstrous dimensions and inhuman eyes, Manuel fainted.

He woke to the sound of women screaming. The old, familiar stench of death wafted through the window and sunlight. Cries and prayers went up from the village. Questions burst into the air from the mouths of witnesses. *What was happening? Who did this? What in God's name?*

Through the window he could hear Artemio, commanding now, a deep voice which resonated through the crowd. A voice that needed no help in imposing itself.

"The soldiers here betrayed their mission, and tried to take from Don Manuel. No one will take anything from you, and none of you will take from each other. Now, more than ever before, we must be unified and trust one another." And he continued onward, not quoting Marx or Mao, but saturating the air with original words that stank of the power not of bullets, but of the minds that commanded them.

When the screams of the women became loud outside his window, Manuel placed his face in his hands.

They weren't women at all.

Artemio had commanded the slaughter of his goats.

The sound of an animal as it becomes aware of its own death is a sound that Manuel never forgot. Shrill, filled with a horror beyond regular frustration and terror. The goats bleated and shouted, raising their voices only for them to fade out through the gurgle of slit throats. The stink of fresh blood filled the air as Manuel's house became one of slaughter. He tried closing his ears tightly, squinting his eyes and imagining old songs. But the sounds of the knives carving at wet flesh, the snapping of bones and sinew overpowered him.

He covered himself in his sheet, and eventually forced himself to sleep through the day.

"*Papá.*"

Rita stood in the doorway. It was night now, and she carried an old lantern in her hand. Her hair was tied tightly, held under a green cap to match her uniform. He wanted to retch, seeing her in such clothes. Despite everything he had done, despite everything he had given up, violence had found his most innocent daughter. Her soft smile only served to make her beauty more tragic.

"*Papá*, I know you are not feeling well…but Artemio has declared a meeting. We've come to your house, hoping you would host it and be a guest of honor. It is the least we can do, for you agreeing to let us slaughter the goats."

He hated himself. But he knew now that he could not afford to deny Artemio.

He moved himself from his bed.

"*Papá?*"

He hugged her for longer than he wanted to. But he was so weak, and holding her close he recalled memories of when he was strong enough to protect what was his. He choked back a sob, and perhaps she realized what he was crying for.

"*Papá*, it is okay… You've guarded me for so long. Let *me* guard *you*."

He couldn't voice his objections even if he still had a tongue. He simply moved himself from her, nodded, and followed her into the kitchen.

Artemio and his two tall soldiers sat at the table, crude clay plates in front of them. The meat smelled savory and spiced, forcing a hunger that was instinctual rather than pleasurable. In the yellow-orange light of the lanterns he saw his place at the head of the table, brown and stringy meat cut up so thoroughly that he would almost be able to drink it. Artemio stood, offering his hand.

"Don Manuel, thank you for offering us your food. We have prepared a place for you at the head of our table."

Manuel nodded, sitting down in the chair. Artemio pushed it in, feigning all courtesies and respect, perhaps out of love for Rita, or perhaps out of a need for him to have *someone* to worship.

Artemio raised a glass of something red. How had he gotten wine? Manuel blinked, noticing that he had a glass as well. The soldiers followed, and then Rita. Manuel joined.

"To the struggle which Don Manuel and his peers began. We will continue it. And we will end it. *Por el causo!*"

The wine was sour in its insincerity, with a metallic aftertaste.

He took a bite of his meat, and it tasted bitter and unfamiliar.

"Now, the reason I have called you all—"

A scream made Artemio stop. Then another. A cascade was arising from the village. In the darkness it seemed as if someone was flaying cats alive, torturing them long before they killed them.

"It's the government," one of the soldiers muttered.

No, Manuel wanted to say. There were no shots, no clapping bullets, no profanity coming from the mouths of men who were animals. The government had never bothered with the village. Not in any of the two previous civil wars. It was too far off, too isolated from the rest of the country to be of any strategic concern. They would not be there now. Not for an army which had only just started to form.

Then he heard the laughter.

Artemio grabbed his rifle. The screams became those of men, terrified beyond belief. They were running now, shouting indistinct words and pleas. The soft laughter was rising above them, children plucking at flowers and frolicking in their debris.

He ran for the door, the two soldiers quickly following him.

There was a gasp of incomprehension, and the chirping of stalled guns.

"NO! NO! PLEASE, GOD!"

Something wet crunched, thudding softly against the ground.

"ARTEMIO!"

Rita ran for the door. Manuel lunged across the table, grabbing her arm and holding it as tightly as he could.

But it was not enough. Unthinkingly, she cast him aside and ran out the open door.

Her scream was the worst of all. It lasted for minutes, and with each soft plop on the ground it got weaker and weaker. Until finally, mercifully, it stopped.

Manuel watched the doorway, still frozen on top of the table. His breathing was the only sound in the village now.

Then a figure emerged in the doorway.

And the woman who bent down to crouch beneath the door frame, the thing which folded her neck so that she could walk through the house, the monster which held his daughter's head in her hand as if it were a fruit, stood above him.

And now, unprotected by the darkness, he could see her looking at him with the eyes of a goat and the smile of the devil.

Author's Notes: The French political journalist Jacques Mallet du Pan is often quoted for saying, "Like Saturn, the Revolution devours its children." Too often, revolutions give way to civil wars which in turn give way to new revolutions. This story is informed by "*La Violencia*" in Colombia, by the struggle against the Somoza regime in Nicaragua.

"Cabras" is inspired by *Dr. Zhivago* more than any other work. The book is often filed away as a love story, and it certainly has elements of pervading romance. But it's also a story of civil war and contains some of the most potent and soul-crushing imagery of violence in literature, in this author's humble opinion. I would also be remiss if I did not cite my fondness for Guillermo Del Toro's *Pan's Labyrinth*. I wrote the story almost exclusively to the theme of *Suspiria* and Johnny Cash's cover of "The Last Gunfighter Ballad."

This story came to me while I was stuck behind a train. Travis Neisler opened up subs for his "Goat Worship" issue of *Ravenwood Quarterly*, and I'll admit that I thought it was silly at first. I had no idea what sort of story I would write. Then, stuck behind that damn train, it came to me.

Though "Goat Worship" never came to fruition, "Cabras" found a home with Gehenna & Hinnom as a novelette. Then, regrettably, this project closed too. It remains my favorite thing I have written.

Volver Al Monte

GENERAL ALFONSÍN SANTOS looked down on the garden he helped grow. Every verdant tree was a gravestone, and every flower burst from black, corpse-fed soil. Between the hum of the helicopter blades, the general listened to the oblivious choir of the birds who soared above the sprawling, cultivated earth.

He had dreaded this return for so long, but nonetheless found himself smiling. For the first time in years, he was coming home.

In the highlands things were primal and familiar. General Alfonsín Santos was a director and the field of war was his theater. The general was a man who could play chess against three opponents at once, a man whose fist was rolled and ready should the contest flow from one of wits to one of strength. Under the light-devouring canopy of the tangled trees, the general had been a force of nature, a dreaded name whispered on the lips of insurgents and terrorists who ducked under the whistle of chopper blades and the screeching of mortar fire.

Several "human rights watchdogs" had brought shame to his name and his country, claiming that General Alfonsín Santos had "depopulated the earth" with his counter-insurgency campaigns. But such claims were far cries from the truth: the general had *filled* the earth, made its dirt ripe with the iron and nutrients that it needed to fuel its ever-growing beauty.

But he had grown tired. Looking across the helicopter cabin, he saw the faces of boys. Boys who fancied themselves men because perhaps they had shot weapons or perhaps because they had known the love of a woman, but who were boys nonetheless. Boys who were over-eager for war, boys who could see little beyond the possibility of a promotion. Boys who could recognize neither the hardship nor beauty of battle. Boys with thick hair and wild eyes, nervous smiles, and shoulder-clapping hands who grinned and made dirty jokes as they flew above the ground. Boys who were desperately trying to cope with the fact that they were a fat, sitting target in the sky. The rebels could renege on their deal at any time, all it would take was one rocket.

The *Tuta Puriq* had made a deal with the government. Paint a white flag on a black helicopter. Put General Alfonsín Santos on it. *He* could negotiate with them for the life of the vice president's daughter.

General Alfonsín Santos had not seen active duty for a matter of decades. Gone were the days when he had direct access to government and foreign intelligence, when he charted the movements of guerrillas and peasant bands with black x's on maps. A failed presidential campaign and several lecturing tours across a system of U.S. military colleges had made him fat. Years of inactivity put strain on his joints that the boys in the helicopter would only come to know if they were lucky enough to grow old.

What he did know of the *Tutas* scared him, not because they seemed ruthless, but because they seemed *directionless*. Santos had dismantled, demobilized, and destroyed his share of insurgent groups and believed he knew all types. He had fought violent groups before, groups so hated and evil that it was simply a matter of arming the peasants so they could fight back. Groups that waded into schools, executing children in front of their teachers to petrify the population into unequivocal submission. Guerrillas who hung thieving children along with their mothers, groups who executed onlookers for too long and too awkward stares.

But for all the violence he knew, the *Tutas* seemed different.

Even the groups who reveled the most in bloodshed would leave messages, signs of their presence and symbols of their power. They could not resist it, and breaking the authority of the state meant constructing an authority of their own. They *had* to plant their flag on their corpses.

But the *Tutas* were boogeymen, quiet highlands ghosts who moved through narrow mountain paths with such a silence that they were cast as an urban legend before they were discovered as an insurgency. Refugees from the countryside seeped slowly into the alleyways of the capital, wraith children claiming ghosts had killed their parents, that vampires had emerged from the mountain caves to feast upon the flesh of the barely living. By the time the government realized it was facing an insurgency, the countryside had been nearly emptied.

No one knew their demands. The military campaigns that captured *Tuta* foot soldiers revealed that they had cut out their own tongues so that they could not speak. If left alone, the captured *Tutas* would go so far as to break their own hands so that they could not write. They did not seem to mind pain, nor did they show fear of death.

The group had not named itself, and the general recalled his confusion when he first discovered what the journalists were calling them.

Tuta Puriq, an old Indian phrase which roughly translated to *those who walk at night*.

The general turned back to the jungle below, consumed with dread. The jungle had taught him that most beauty is superficial at best, that any joy was the punctuated break before returning to the mountains.

Before returning to the natural state of things.

The helicopter reached the landing site, a square space on a hill marked by felled trees and white spray paint. The blue sky seemed to explode overhead as they descended, the birds scattering up in wild panic. The helicopter roared as it hovered above the ground, kicking up wet dirt and the remnants of dry, yellow grass.

For a moment, it seemed as if they were alone.

Then the general saw them.

They came through the shadows between the trees, black-clad forms who covered their faces in thick bandanas. He gasped despite himself, surprised at how many of them there were. At least twenty, holding their rifles ready with both hands, moved towards the helicopter in a remarkable, tactical discipline. The general bit his lip for blood and composure. He unbuckled his seatbelt and stood, disembarking the helicopter and turning to the soldiers behind them.

Their eyes were white. Their faces were quivering.

"This is not how you greet death." Santos smiled weakly.

They snapped their attention toward him as the soft footsteps of the *Tutas* grew louder and faster.

"You greet death as a member of your family. If you are kind to her, she will be kind to you."

A meaningless platitude, but one which had calmed his troops as he sent them out to die. The boys smiled, fearfully and softly. They raised their weapons, following their general's lead as he walked out into the clearing to expose himself to the mercy of the *Tutas*.

He raised his hands, feeling for a moment the warm sun on his face.

The gentle kiss of a pre-monsoon wind.

Yes.

Yes, this would be as good a time to die as any. As good a way as any.

For a moment, he could feel the pang of a bullet as it entered his body, for a moment he let his world darken. But it was nothing more than a hopeful hallucination. Before him a young man, face shrouded by black cloth and hair concealed by a dark beret, extended a gloved hand. The general took it, finding that it burned with a dry-ice cold. He winced.

"General Santos." The young man spoke with a high-pitched voice behind his bandana. "We thank you for your attendance today. We invite you back to our camp, and there we may talk further."

"*Señor*." General Santos smiled. "And how am I to trust you? How can I be sure that you will not slaughter me when we arrive?"

"Frankly, General, we don't need you to trust us. Look behind you."

The young men from the helicopter had their backs to the general, rifles pointed to the jungle. Beneath the trees black uniforms seemed legion and shifting, writhing and twisting into the jungle shadows.

"Please appreciate your situation, General, and follow me."

The young man lifted his hand into the air and pointed backwards. The *Tutas* re-entered the jungle, folding back into that yawning, cavernous darkness. Santos found himself not afraid of dying, but of dying in captivity. For seconds that seemed like years, he did not move.

Finally, his feet lifted and he followed the shadows into their lair.

They had been hiking for longer than the general had anticipated. The insurgents were not being kind to him. He was an old man, one who had to stop often and lean against the slippery black bark of wet trees. He hissed the humid air in and out, clutching his chest amidst the hysterical chittering of monkeys and the quiet, knife-ended stares of the guerrillas. An attendant was at his side now, rubbing his ribs and looking nervously around.

The boys he had brought with him had divested themselves of their machismo. They no longer had anyone to impress, and absent the eyes of young women they became terrified, armed children.

"Thank you," he moaned, leaning against his attendant's shoulder as they continued.

Perhaps it was a tactic, to make him tired when he finally arrived at their camp, more prone to negotiate.

He had only hoped Katerina was okay.

Over his pain he recalled his friend Raul's baby girl, a little child who Alfonsín knew would be as close to a second daughter as he would ever come. Katerina Villalobos did not take well to her father's career, as he became a colonel, a general, a minister, and finally a vice president. She did not care for the elitism that her life demanded, and spent more time listening to the folktales of her Indian nannies than the demands of her father. She treated Alfonsín first as an uncle, and then as a friend.

The general welcomed having a friend so young, treasured knowing a young woman who reminded him so much of his own daughter.

"General." The high-pitched voice of the masked *Tuta* brought him back to reality.

Santos never failed to be in awe at the perseverance of guerilla groups.

They lived on thin, dirty blankets that rested just above the wet ground, under dark green tarps which barely kept the rain off them. They hung their clothes on stolen ropes, kept their cooking utensils fire-sterilized, and maintained everything in a way that would be ready to move at a moment's notice. Most of their shelters were twigs, lean-tos built with a carpenter's precision.

They moved him toward a large lean-to in the center of a camp, a great thing built around the trunk of a thick, sprawling black tree. Entering the opening, the general found that the ground was covered with ornate, dirtied rugs. A single kerosene lamp was lit, revealing a series of cross-legged figures whose faces were as shrouded as the foot soldiers' who surrounded them.

Outside, a low rumble of thunder growled through the jungle canopy.

"General." A cross-legged form bade him to sit. They were so covered that Santos could not tell if they were men or women, though he supposed that it would not matter either way. Women could be just as ruthless as men in the field of war, and just as noble as well. The gender of his hosts had no bearing on the lives of his men.

"Thank you for speaking with me," the general winced through the pain that came with sitting down.

"Thank *you* for accepting our invitation."

"Where is Katerina Villalobos?"

"She is with us. Tell us..." The figure leaned over the lamp, and for a moment it seemed as if its eyes were orange and yellow. "What is the girl to you?"

"A second daughter."

"And what happened to your *first* daughter, General Santos?"

The general did not speak, waiting for a full minute before the *Tuta* finally gave in and retreated over their lamp.

"No matter, we will have time to get to know you."

"Why am I here?" The general did not mind dying, but he did not enjoy being interrogated. He had conducted enough interrogations himself to know when he was being toyed with, for him to know that he was merely food for the cat to play with. Under their coverings, the *Tutas* were probably laughing at him.

"We simply wanted to get a look at you, at the famous General Alfonsín Santos."

The *Tuta* laughed then, a light chuckle laden with cold evil.

"I'm sure you have heard the joke about you, General, that if there was a Nobel Prize for war, you would have received it. But there isn't, so you had to settle for those little aluminum foil medals that presidents stuck on you."

"I'm content with the fruits of my labor, content with peace. I don't need recognition beyond that." Santos spoke through clenched teeth.

"Oh now, we don't believe *that.*"

"If you're going to kill me, you can get on with it."

"Now, General, we have no intention of killing you or your men."

The rain began to fall, pattering gently against the tightly bound wood. Outside the men began to pace in uneasy, wet plodding steps. The kerosene lamp flickered and the *Tutas* sat up straight, as if anticipating the storm themselves.

"We agree with you, General. The fruits of your labor *were* peace. But you did not go far enough in tending to your fruit. For all the talk of you *depopulating* the countryside, there are so many people still left living."

"So that's it then?" Santos smirked. "You're not some utopian Marxist group, you're just a death squad?"

"Our face may as well be yours, General."

"I've had enough of this." Santos stood. He did not travel all this way for riddles, to be laughed at. If they killed him on his way back to the helicopter, that would be fine; but he would *not* be laughed at.

Outside the rain began to pour, drowning all other sounds.

"What?" he heard one of his soldiers murmur.

Then there was a scream. The cracking sounds of an automatic rifle.

The general turned to his hosts, furious.

But they only sat impassively.

"What the hell are you doing?" Santos screamed.

"Not us, General, we are not alone out here."

The general ignored the pain in his joints and ran outside the lean-to. The air was grey, the water pouring over his eyes in a continuous wet veil. He held a hand over his forehead, drawing his pistol and narrowing his eyes. The guerrillas were gone, but the screams of his men filled the camp with an all-consuming panic. Over the beating of his heart he followed their screams, slowed down by the sucking wet dirt beneath him.

The bullets kept flowing, punctuated with the sounds of tearing flesh and spilling gore.

He called their names, which ones he could remember. But none called back.

His legs gave way to his weight and he fell to the dirt. His open palms slipped in the mud, black dirt covering his eyes and splashing into his mouth. His entire body ached, but he moved to raise himself.

Something warm and firm slowly sank onto his head, pinning him down. He froze, uncertain of what to do next. He moved his head up as far as he could, his blood going cold as he began to understand what was in front of him.

A giant foot, pale and white, with a big toe the size of his fist. The foot seemed as large as his torso, connected to an ankle as wide as a tree. The pressure holding him shifted across his back, the lingering touch of slow fingers.

He could not breathe.

The pressure increased, forcing him flat on the ground as his knees and elbows slipped from under him.

A human arm dropped next to him, ragged strands of wet red flesh where it used to connect to a shoulder.

There was a pinching at his neck and his body grew warm.

The world drifted away into blissful darkness.

II

The general woke to find himself dry.

He had been changed, out of his military uniform and into the black fatigues of the *Tuta* foot soldiers. He was sitting down, propped against a smooth rock wall. The cave ceiling was low, cool, and wet as fat, dirty drops of water fell on his forehead. He could hear the rain far away, pittering dimly against thick dirt and smooth rocks.

In the light of the dim kerosene lamp he could see the *Tutas*, still masked. They stood ready, as if they had anticipated his waking at the exact moment. They held long sticks, clubs and crudely made spears.

The general shifted, letting the shale and pebbles slide beneath him.

He knew guerrilla groups sometimes used the mountain caves to hide from government bombardments. They had taken him somewhere from the light, kept him alive for some unknown purpose and—

He remembered the foot. The severed arm.

"What is going on?"

"We are learning to trust you, General." The voice seemed to come from all sides, from the walls of the caves themselves. It was low and high at once, the sound of a distorted record and a gargling demon.

"Where are we?"

"Closer to the truth."

"What was that?" he asked, nausea and panic boiling in his burning throat. "What killed my men?"

"Not too much farther now," the voice answered.

Two of the *Tutas* broke their ranks, picking him up by his armpits. He gasped as electric needles dug into his knees and lower back. The hands shoved his shoulder blades and he fell to the earth once more. A stone cut his cheek and he bit back an indignant, angry tear.

"You're going to need to stand on your own, General, if you want to go any farther."

The same rough hands lifted him again and let him go. He took a breath in, keeping his unsteady balance and looking around slowly.

The cave was wide, and they were far from the mouth. Behind him the rain and wind were ghostly echoes, but he could not see any light to indicate an entrance. The tunnel walls were smooth and shimmering in the kerosene light, as if they had been deliberately paved by nature. There were five *Tutas* with him, all impassive and motionless until the same garbled voice spoke again.

"Forward, General."

He felt the butt of a spear at his back and moved forward as they commanded him. He resolved to not speak, to die with as much dignity as he could keep. The *Tutas* were little more than nihilistic madmen. Their annihilation would be the duty of some *other* general, some other poor, unhappy man set on a course he could not reverse. He maintained his silence, letting the walls come tighter and tighter until the *Tutas* and he were walking in a straight line between the cavern walls.

"These caves," the voice of the *Tuta* spoke after some time, "were only uncovered due to Spanish greed. The Indians knew the truth, and they implored the Spanish to leave the mountains be. The mountains were where the gods slept. They told the Spanish that they could have silver, but just *enough*. Only so much as they truly *needed*. The Indians begged the Spaniards to exercise moderation. But when," the voice became accusatory and amused, "when has power *ever* exercised moderation?"

The general would not respond to this provocation. He looked ahead, carefully and slowly moving one foot in front of the other. There was nowhere else to go, nothing else to do. Even if he escaped the *Tutas*, there was no way he would find his way out of the mines that fed into the caves.

"And so," the *Tuta* continued, "greed consumed the earth, filling it until even the Indians were its children. Then greed became violence, and the violence was eternal until *you* mastered it. Now, General...now we are all *your* children."

A little girl. Pig tails tied in bright blue bows. An innocent smile.

"Don't say that," the general hissed.

The *Tuta* laughed. "Why, General? Is there no better legacy for a man than a child? To imprint themselves onto future generations?"

"I have no children!" the general roared.

"Save for your *second child*, Katerina Villalobos."

The general halted. He had forgotten about Katerina. She was surely dead, or at the very least it was clear that she would not be returning to her family. They would not have gone to such great lengths with the general otherwise.

"Tell us, General, what happened to your *first* child?"

Santos bit his lip.

The butt of a spear came down on his back. He fell to the floor of the cave, his head crashing into the rocks. Overcome with pain and guilt, he let himself slip away.

Rosalinda Santos ruled her father.

Everyone in the capital knew that the general was subservient to his little daughter, who walked around the general's household as a princess in her palace. Perhaps it was because his wife died in childbirth, or perhaps because the general did not want to be the same man at home that he was in the battlefield. Dinner guests often smiled when Rosalinda ran up to her father with little slips of mandatos, *nonsensical commands such as* Daddy must read to me *or* Daddy must take me to the movies.

And in curiosity, they watched as the general bowed to his little daughter and followed her orders to the letter.

The general's head was buzzing. Heavy hands were lifting him up. He tasted sour, acrid vomit in his mouth. They leaned him against a wall and let the flickers of light fade from his sight.

He was still in the caves. Still alive.

"Just kill me, just be done with it!"

"General..." The distorted, scraping voice seemed sad. "We aren't going to kill you. But you *are* going to meet our gods. *Your* gods. And to meet them, you must be strong. You must unburden yourself of your sins."

"I don't have any regrets," Santos spat. He laughed madly, driven dizzy by torture and all the exhaustion it entailed. "I've *killed* before. I've killed so many, and every last one of them deserved to die. I don't care about them, so you may as well stop."

A spear shaft struck his ribs. There was a loud crack and the taste of stale blood at the back of his throat.

Rosalinda was a smart girl who became a brilliant young woman.

The general, it was said, was at once in awe of and exasperated by his daughter. He would laugh with his guests over cups of wine, explaining that it would have been easier had she simply been pretty rather than pretty and brilliant. But she got the best grades in her class, read everything she could get her hands on, and seemed to pierce the veils of higher meaning immediately. Metaphors, codes, and formulas. Nothing could escape her.

And there was no telling her no.

He wasn't sure where she began to read newspapers, or when she became interested in politics. Her first explanation to the general was that she was reading Marx in order to better understand what her father was fighting, so that she may guard herself against it. But it went from Marx to Lenin to Mao, and soon she dropped the pretense.

Heated discussions at dinner were routine as she changed from a girl to a woman. The general began hiding her from society, avoiding guests in his home lest some competitor within the government use her as a piece of gossip which would have her blacklisted.

He implored her to be careful, to be mindful. But she only looked at him with eyes that broke him. Eyes that knew him.

"Very few people in this world *matter*, General," the *Tuta* spoke softly, as if it were speaking to a child.

"We are not interested in the people who are unimportant to you. A man cares little for the bugs he kills by brushing off his shoulder or those he exterminates to save his crops. These are *not* sins. Tell us then, General, what bothers you? For you must leave it here before you meet your gods."

They weren't going to stop. They would not beat him to death, they would not let his heart give way to the strain. They would merely keep beating him, keep prodding him and hurting him. But they could not hurt him as much as he had already hurt himself.

He was tired. He breathed in slowly, his chest quivering between shattered ribs. The tears in his eyes were reflexive, but they burned just as they had on the day he learned about his daughter.

The day he consigned himself to hell.

"Very few people matter to me." Santos' voice was weak, surprising even himself in his temerity and reluctance.

"Understandable." The *Tutas* shifted the general, supporting him as two of them held their arms behind his back so he would not need to walk on his own. They moved slowly, gingerly. The walls of the cave were different now, shimmering with rich veins of salt-and-pepper crystals as wide as his arm.

In the kerosene light it was beautiful, the sort of shimmering stars that Rosalinda would watch with him. He would help her on the roof of their home and watch the sky with her. She would ask him the name of a star and he would say that they, too, were named Rosalinda.

Every star was named after her, he explained.

The crystals seemed to pulsate with the pounding of his head and the lurching of his stomach. He breathed in deeply, trying to stifle what could become a torrent of sobbing.

"People are burdens on the soul just as they are burdens on the earth, General. For one to move through life as far as you have, they cannot be held back. You are an important man, General. A *good* man."

"I am not a *good man*." The salt and snot fell into his mouth. He felt his sobs boiling into burning aches behind his mouth.

"Please." The voice was tender now. "Please tell us."

Rosalinda running away was inevitable.

She had been admitted into several universities, but her interest in education seemed to fade away faster each day. One evening, the general came to her room, a cup of coffee on a silver tray, as meager a peace offering as he could muster after their latest fight.

But she was gone. A window open and a backpack missing.

He called in every favor he could, his peers in the military and government horrified that their staunch killer could be reduced to a mewling baby. They acted urgently, combing the capital with sleek black cars and halting every bus so that armed men could walk down the aisles searching for her. Flyers were put up; a reward was offered and then raised. Five times.

The general no longer slept, and as the insurgency increased he readily threw himself into his work. He orchestrated elaborate, merciless campaigns from his office, mapping out small massacres in the faraway highlands. He could not secure his own household, so perhaps it would be enough to secure his nation.

But for all the maneuvers of his troops, the general became disinterested in regulating the minutia of operations. Paramilitary groups came from the shadows, offering to take up duties the general did not care to examine or discuss. Through backchannels he gave his authority with ambivalence, moving from one mission to the next and not caring to examine what was left in his wake. And in the darkness of the general's inattention, these groups divested themselves of the semblance of man and became animals.

"But I don't regret it," the general explained. The *Tutas* stood still, engrossed and reverent of the general's story.

"Are you ready to move forward?" The distorted voice seemed clearer now, booming and low.

The general chuckled, letting the bloody tang of his mucus fill his mouth.

"I cannot move on my own anymore."

"You may lean on us, General. You may *always* lean on us."

Gently, gloved hands came to his side and back. He rose slowly, carefully as two foot soldiers spread his arms over their shoulders. Gingerly moved forward.

"Thank you," the general whispered.

"General," the voice continued, "why do you *not* regret setting the *paramilitarios* loose on the countryside? As you said, they were animals. Not men."

He sighed. He had given this speech so many times. Over his bitter cups, over the gasps of his peers. It was a moment when he dropped a façade, when he opened himself up and let loose the demon which rested just behind the veil of his eyes.

He took a moment to notice the pale purple veins of crystals, pulsing with their own inner light. Large geodes burst open as luminous, amethyst fungi. The walls were narrowing, so the *Tutas* and he lowered their heads and moved softly around low-hanging rock formations. The kerosene lamp was dimming, and it seemed that with each step the general's pains were healing.

"There is no real difference between men and animals," he began.

The cave walls shimmered, a rich swirling vein that glowed with the falling and rising cadence of his voice.

"We were built for violence. Every man and woman is readily designed for murder the day they are born. Our arms were made for spears, our legs so that we could ride horses to better pursue each other. War is part of our natural evolution. It is nature at its most exposed.

"So we deserve it. And because we deserve it, it's only justice."

"Did your daughter deserve what happened to her, General?"

The question bore into his stomach deeper than any bullet ever could. The weight of the memories came down on his knees, but the

Tutas moved forward, not letting him stop to fall. The shimmering purple of the crystal-veined wall became shining beams of sapphire. It was the bright blue of the summer sky, and for a moment the general was beneath it, holding his daughter's hand. And the brief, temporary hallucination was crueler than any torture.

"No," he answered. "No, she didn't."

How many executions did he order that day?

The report came down slowly from the highlands, a trickle of information had fed a blossoming hope in the general's heart. If he could reach Rosalinda before anyone else, if he could only bring her home in secret, he could save her from the tomb she had built for herself. The guerillas wouldn't be able to protect themselves, much less her, when the weight of the state came down on them.

Vague rumors of a young woman fighter, someone who resembled his daughter.

Someone he could save, the only person who ever mattered.

How quickly did those reports silence? How fast did those vicious paramilitarios *turn inward, guard themselves to protect themselves from his wrath?*

Santos had been used to torturing for information, for a purpose. He had never hated his enemy until that day. That day, he became a more real devil than those men could ever know.

He was tired. He was hungry and he was afraid and good god, he was thirsty.

His howling sobs overtook the darkness around him. The caves were shimmering with the lights of a nascent, unfolding galaxy. Around him the darkness sang and hummed. The light became all-consuming and blinding.

Something cool and smooth came into his hands. Someone lifted the object to his mouth and he was overcome with an aching, sweet smell.

He bit into the unknown fruit and let the blinding light take his sight away.

III

The world was red.

The kaleidoscope cave ended in a single crimson portal.

The general walked through unafraid, escorted by a race of giants.

The red light poured from a miniature sun, a disc that hung low in the air and shined down on the expansive, obsidian city. He had seen Machu Picchu before, back when Rosalinda was fourteen and he was trying desperately to recreate a little girl who refused to stay the same. This was a darker, grander Machu Picchu of towering black pyramids, glistening walls, and roads unfolding in every direction. In the scarlet sky, leathery prehistoric birds cawed and cried out, preserved from the ravages of the world above them. Around them, tall trees broke towards the artificial sun, allowing some unseen, secret breeze to rustle them gently.

The *Tuta Puriq* abandoned their disguises, rising above him in long strides. They were pale, statuesque things made of tight, white sinew. Their black hair unfolded wildly to their lower backs, and when they smiled down on him it was with the horrifying kindness of beings who knew more than men ever could.

They spoke without moving their mouths, perhaps broadcasting from somewhere within his own mind.

"You knew, did you not, General?"

"Yes," he answered, giving up every defense he had.

"How sad," the voice answered.

Then it continued: "Our children are ourselves, miniature and wild. And it is always a terrifying thing to see yourself made wild. This is why you allowed the brutality of the war to escalate, although you knew perfectly well that your daughter was out there. Fighting. Just like her father."

The general made no protest as he walked through the city, nor did an objection even occur to him. The sacred nature of the place was boring into him, crushing him as the weight of the world above him.

"It's normal, the disdain for your progeny." Spires rose into the sky as twisting needles, glistening with the red light as the leathery birds of prey rested at their tips. The giant race walked solemnly and silently, not a word or gaze passing from any one to the other.

"We made you to aid us. You were to produce the air we need, to cultivate and nurture the earth above us so that we may thrive below. But," the voice adopted the smallest bit of sadness, "we made you in our image. For that, we must apologize. It is not your fault that you are so flawed, it is only natural.

"But, General..." A fountain of shining, molten silver liquid rose before them. The general lifted a hand to shield himself from the blistering heat, straining and peering as bubbles burst and shattered against the onyx pavement. The fountain parted into multiple currents, byways of glistening silver splitting beneath shimmering onyx brickways.

"There is good news."

The general stopped, looking upward to his benevolent captors in hope. Their smiles unnerved him, filling him with all the dread-laden anxiety of a looming storm.

"You will be part of what comes next." They were beautiful. Wide grins of straight, white teeth. Eyes the size of fists, brown-yellow and knowing. "You may walk the earth yet. A better earth of better creatures."

An arm as long as he was tall motioned, and the general followed.

The long walk was quiet. The molten silver coursed beneath his feet, the black Machu Picchu falling behind as they walked toward the surface of a writhing lake. In the red light, it seemed filled with fat, fighting worms.

"I've walked the earth long enough. I just want to rest."

The figures did not reply as the lake grew larger and closer. The worms made the soft, crying screams of angry infants.

"Then, General, might you consent to a sacrifice for your children? The children men deserve?"

The general had given up his will, approaching a set of shining steps. He looked forward to rest, to the long silence. To an end.

He stood above the lake, looking down on the new children of men. They had no arms for spears, no legs for riding horses. Only long, writhing bodies, needle-sharp teeth, and innocent infant faces. All they would need for when they broke the surface and rectified an unforgivable mistake.

He smiled in peace, raising his eyes to the other end of the lake.

His eyes rested on a solitary figure, a young woman whose face and eyes he recognized despite all the distance between them.

A giant hand pushed him forward.

He fell, screaming her name.

Author's Notes: I hesitate to call "Volver Al Monte" a horror story. There is no single protagonist, no good person to cheer on. General Alfonsín Santos is a monster, inspired by too many real war criminals who become heroes because they save their nations. And yet he is no mustache-twirling super villain. His motives make sense. He's not repentant and would very likely do the same thing again. Rosalinda makes the story tragic. The inevitable tendency of strong children to become similar-though-different adults when compared to their parents. The two were on a collision course from the moment she was born, and by refusing to acknowledge this the general pays a price far greater than any death.

This story was written shortly after "Cabras," conceived of an examination of civil war through different perspectives. While there are many similarities between "Volver Al Monte" and "Cabras," the two differ in theme and focus. "Cabras" told the story of a guerilla, "Volver" of a military officer. There are two more stories planned, one about a paramilitary and the other about a noncombatant.

It was written for Martian Migraine Press' *Chthonic: Tales of Weird Inner Earth*.

A few final notes on the inspiration of this story: "*Volver Al Monte*" is a phrase used by former *paramilitarios* and guerillas in Colombia, a phrase which literally means "to return to the mountain." However, it contextually translates as "a return to war." "*Tuta Puriq*" is a Quechua term from the highlands and was the name that the indigenous population of Peru gave *Sendero Luminoso* (Shining Path) fighters.

Whiskey and Memory

JOHN PUT THE paper bag to his lips. The whiskey was smooth, tinged with the sweetness of burnt honey and oak. Warm as a mother's love.

The cold December air seeped each of his senses. The city was painted in blacker shades, darkness creeping from the sky and spilling onto every surface save for those covered in snow. The streetlamps cast everything in a bloated, sickly orange light that perversely reminded him of Halloween. If not for the biting frost which ate its way between the holes of his clothes or the snow which held down the steadiness of his step, he would expect laughing children in costumes.

But as it was, the city was only an echo of his mind. In the bleak loneliness of a winter Monday night, it was as quiet and hateful as the stirrings of his heart; as much a chasm as he was.

So he sought to fill it with all the familiar weight of his paper bag.

Taking the whiskey to his lips again, he smiled out of reflex. His face tingled as if from an unexpected but welcome kiss.

He had to keep moving. The impulse welled up from the back of his mind, the part that somehow stayed sober despite his best efforts. To linger in the past for too long was to fall prey to all of the demons who lived there. He shook his head, mustering just enough clarity to keep walking, and tucked the bottle back into a coat pocket.

He had walked in the city long enough, alone enough, to not be afraid of it anymore. Ashley had never liked it, him wandering away in the middle of the night for long walks into the parts of town made famous by crime reports. He knew it was stupid and cruel, but a part of his soul truly enjoyed how much it bothered her, how much it hurt her. Another part, more familiar and nurtured, felt closer to home in the danger.

His formative years had been ones of not knowing what would happen each day, of not knowing who was behind each corner.

Of not knowing what *they would do to him.*

He collided into something, and stumbling back from the other warm body sent him reeling from his thoughts. His feet became unsure before his knees finally buckled. A soft and exaggerated "Oof" came from above him as the cold, wet snow soaked itself into his jackets. He cursed mildly, his anger overtaking his drunkenness as he tried to get up. He pushed himself with one arm and heard the slinking sound of shattered glass rubbing against itself. A wetness from the inside of his coat spread across his layers.

"Shit!"

He was standing now, oblivious to everything other than the liquor sliding down his left leg. He did not know how he was going to get more, and the thought of sobering up was less welcome than the thought of dying. The soft humming of his buzz flew away, replaced with the high-pitched whine of stress and dizziness.

"I'm so sorry!"

The voice gave him an object to direct his panic and anger towards. But looking at her, he hesitated. She stood under the same orange streetlight that he did, in the same wide and empty street where he could see the letters on signs and numbers on doors.

Yet she was a shadow. Something obscured her features, leaving only the silhouette of a woman standing before him. She was almost as tall as he was, maybe an inch shorter, with long and wild hair of an indeterminate color. Whatever clothes she wore were pulled tightly across her curves, long legs and vital youth. He believed that, should the light fall on her, she would be shatteringly beautiful.

However, a sense of dread soaked into these thoughts. Looking at her, he felt as if he was gazing into a slightly open door, watching something he should not see. There was a *wrongness* about the shadow woman, the sort that spooked horses and made dogs howl in empty rooms.

John gathered himself, letting his instinctual anger overtake him.

"You stupid bitch," he muttered with the same venom that usually reduced Ashley to a heaving mound of tears. "You broke it."

"What did I break, cutie?"

Her voice didn't waver. By brushing off his insult she only made him angrier.

"My fucking *whiskey!* And that was the last of it."

She laughed. There was a lightness to it, the kind he had heard from his mother's tinging wind-chimes. But there was also a hollowness, a sound that echoed in dark and empty waves. The flesh along his spine shivered as he involuntarily recoiled from her.

"It just so happens," she pronounced her words with all the deliberateness of a snake, "that I have some that I could give you."

She reached into a dark bag at her side, something which he had not noticed until she reached for it. She seemed to whisper to herself, the syllabus of an indistinct and haunting song. He became transfixed, ensnared as she withdrew a sloshing bottle.

She extended it to him, and he only reluctantly took it in his hand.

It was like touching a stove. He bit his lip as heat burned through his glove. The pain jolted up the nerves of his arm, into a pulsing knot in his shoulder. He would have cried out had it lasted for anything longer than a fourth of a second. But the pain became a phantom, and once it was gone his curiosity returned.

He held the bottle up to the streetlight. It was large, a wide curve at its bottom smoothed towards a very long and narrow neck. It had a black label, decorated with bursting white roses. On the largest rose a tiny devil sat, his pitchfork intersecting the words of a label he couldn't read. There was something written beneath it, something that was in a language that wasn't English. Italian maybe. He wasn't sure why, but the thing unnerved him.

"I've never seen this before," he muttered.

The shadow nodded.

"It's a very rare whiskey. But fair is fair. Everything has its cost, its price, and I'll pay mine."

"And what, exactly, do *I* have to pay?" he asked, not losing the venom in his voice.

Though he could not see it, he felt the force of her smile.

"Nothing but a favor."

A long finger reached from the shadow to touch his chest. When she withdrew it he jumped back, frantically patting the touched spot with his free hand. The same intense, brief pain now moved spider-like across his torso in all directions. He slipped on loose ice, lifting the bottle above him to save it from cracking.

The voice spoke:

"Drink it all."

When he got up, she was gone.

People on the streets could be cruel. They could also be enigmatic, with cloudy and unknown designs unfit for the daylight. In his lonely walks he had come across more than a few monsters and more than a few shades. He dusted the snow from his pants and muttered obscenities about the woman. Unnecessarily and obnoxiously strange, he thought.

Then, armed once more against the all-too-real prospects of sobriety, he took a long drink.

II

His mother had just told his father that she was leaving him. He wasn't supposed to be up that late, but escalating whispers alerted him that something was wrong downstairs. Leaving the dark, cool sanctuary of his room, he crept down to watch the unavoidable trap of his parent's fight.

"What did you say?"

They had just gotten back from a date, a futile attempt at the reconciliation which they both desperately wanted, if not for themselves, then for the simple maintenance of a status-quo which they had become comfortable with.

"You heard me, Tom!" his mother spat between bared teeth.

She was in her white dress, a good piece of clothing which her father had given her for her last birthday. Matching thick and fake pearls hung around her neck while sparkling diamond earrings glinted in the soft lamplight.

John could only see his father's back, clad in a black sports jacket and slacks. But the way his father stood, so still and so resolute, gave John a dark and terrible feeling, the foreboding came with silent winds before onslaught-storms.

His mother did not seem unnerved by the same superstitious fear. She continued, proudly standing her ground against a gathering wave.

"What you said tonight only confirms what I should have known about you. You *enjoy* making your snide remarks, you *enjoy* insulting me."

His father's voice responded with an icy-stillness:

"You make it all too easy, dear."

She paused. John was sure she hadn't seen him sitting on the top of the stairs. Her face was too concentrated on his father, her grey eyes pointing daggers meant to rend and tear. And he saw her hands, clenched so tightly in fists aimed not at hitting, but at self-restraint.

But his mother, for all her faults, was intelligent. Even as a child, John knew that she was *far* smarter than his father. It was probably what caused his father, a man so bound to the pride of his war wounds and small income, to nurture his carefully tended grudge against her.

John's father married up, and every day was a resentful reminder of the unavoidable fact that he lived with his better.

What she said next was nothing short of a reminder of this superiority. A short laugh, a shake of her head, a hand to her eyes. She looked back at him, her hands unclenched and spread wide apart to make an obvious point.

"You know...all of 'our,'" she said this mockingly and could not help but laugh again, "all of *our* friends have been talking to me for some time now, Thomas. And...good God, you really don't know this. Looking at you, with that *idiot* and *hurt* look on your face, I can tell you *really don't*. I'd call you 'poor,' I'd call you 'pathetic,' but the truth is that you are *neither* of these things."

As she continued, John's stomach fell. He knew he shouldn't be hearing these things, each insult a nail in the coffin of any admiration or love he would ever have for his father. And despite all of his efforts after, he would never be able to forget what she said next.

"They *hate* you, you know? Even your 'army buddies.' You brag about that mark on your cheek, but they know how you got it. That poor man, begging for his life, surrendering. And you, bearing down on him with a knife. I wonder if you were smiling, as he finally realized what you were and so desperately tried to fight you off him. You're ignorant and stupid, that's one reason no one can stand you. And I loved you despite it, out of all the delusion that the beautiful boy I fell in love with could afford to be stupid and ignorant. But...Tom, you're *evil.* And after I'm gone, there'll be no one left to stop you from ending it."

That was when the conversation ended.

His father was fast, knocking his mother to the ground and kneeling above her. He didn't say anything, merely raised his elbows above and behind his shoulders without hesitation. She screamed, both in fear and surprise. There was first a loud *thwack*, and then the wetter thuds of fists against blood.

Her high-heeled foot went to his groin.

Without a sound, his father went down.

His mother wept frantically, clawing her way across the floor. She reached the front door and stood up. She didn't look back, didn't see her terrified child watching her leave.

Too late his father realized what was happening. He recovered from his pain with uneasy steps and forced himself into a grunting sprint.

But his mother was out the door. Her screams were brief, cut short by the screeching of tires.

His father stood at the door frame. Minutes passed, sobs coming in from the open door with frantic shouts and prayers. Someone yelled that they were sorry. Another, clearer than the rest and yet more quiet, reached John's ears:

"Oh dear God, she's dead."

His father's back seemed to sigh, his head hung.

Then his father turned around and saw John sitting on the steps.

III

The memory was unwelcome. It had overpowered him, drowned him in sadness and renewed hurt. With a start, he realized he had blacked out.

The snow was falling quickly, biting into his exposed flesh and tearing it red. The street was darker, as heavy gusts dimmed the lamps. From the empty buildings only a more thorough blackness shone through. The only light came from a red neon sign.

He put a hand above his eyes to protect his vision from the snow, peering to see if he could recognize the sign. He walked forward, hoping that as he approached it the sign would become more distinct.

But he only recognized one word on the sign: "Circle."

He was indignant at the sign's red glow, furious at its gothic font and foreign name. His mind swirled with snow, searching for reasons and explanations as to how and why he could have not known about this place. After glaring at the sign, his attention drifted to the bar itself.

The whole building looked as if it had suffered minor fire damage. The outside walls were streaked with what looked like large swaths of charcoal, black-grey spots indicating that blasts of fire had forever seared the building's coarse concrete sides. There were no windows to speak of, so he could not guess as to what was inside.

But it was the door that seemed the most out of place. The thing appalled and intrigued him, a wooden, medieval monstrosity. The door was wide and tall, made of boards tightly put together. It looked heavy, and placing his hand on it he felt the absurd weight of the thing, something which belonged on a fortress rather than a bar.

The door had a simple rod-iron handle and a black door knocker. The knocker was a single large iron ring held in the mouth of a gleaming, obsidian demon. The thing had large eyes, burning with anger and suffering. Its mouth held two fangs which extended over the metal ring in the awful curves of twin scythes. And there was something about the shape of its vaguely ovular head, something about the lumpy mass that invoked a reflexive nausea in him. It seemed sick and infected, with a temple that bulged out well beyond its miserable, furious eyes.

John's curiosity overtook his revulsion, and he reached for the knocker.

The sound was louder than he thought it would be, slamming against the massive wooden door and resounding into what sounded like a cavern. He knocked again, and only silence answered him.

He shrugged, and grabbed the surprisingly warm handle, pushing open the door and stepping inside.

The place was indeed a bar. And it was certainly empty.

Smoky air assailed and enveloped him. He breathed in heavily, forcing a coughing fit that scraped and tore at his lungs as it climbed up a scratched windpipe. His eyes darted for a trash can, finding one to the right of the door. Once again the phlegm shot out of his mouth, and once again he was disgusted at his own weakness.

The door closed behind him with a loud, definitive *bang*. Immediately he was assailed by a rank humidity that made his stomach even queasier as he adjusted from the outside air.

Looking up from the trashcan, he saw he was alone in the bar. He removed one jacket, tying it around his waist as he surveyed his surroundings. The soft yellow lights were barely on, forcing John to squint and strain to make out the details of the room. The dim, wood-paneled walls were decorated with various newspaper articles hung in black and red plastic frames. A pool table sat barren across from him, a thick layer of grey-white dust settled just above its green felt. Various booths and tables were also covered in the same ashen dust.

Behind the bar were several shelves of bottles, each of them without labels, and each a shade of one of five colors: Red, Orange, Yellow, Brown, and Black.

Walking along the walls, he looked more closely at the framed newspaper stories. Above one table was a headline which read, "Wife kills man for infidelity"; another, "Five killed in grocery store robbery"; and, "Senator convicted of assaulting mistress." Other articles being of the same criminal vein.

John shook his head and sighed. He had no idea what sort of place he had walked into, but he was not ready to go back outside. He took the paper bag out of his pocket and raised it to his lips.

All it took was one sip. It was smooth, a taste of sugary oak and gentle, playful fire. He closed his eyes and braced for another cough.

"Hey there, son."

He choked, his internal organs going through all the motions of vomiting. He thrust a hand to his chest, breathing flutteringly to calm his mind and body. It only barely worked, as again he darted for the trashcan to cough up something sour and hot.

"Well jeez, kid, you okay?"

The voice was deep and loud, though it had a warmth to it, a kindness that came from happy thoughts and welcome memories.

He followed the voice to the old man who stood behind the bar.

An old man who only moments ago had not been there.

His face was worn with wrinkles, running starch-like across his forehead and cheeks. His nose came forward, hooked and wide with flaring nostrils above a small smile full of white teeth. Green eyes shone out from thick glasses, while above them a thick ring of grey hair stopped well before the crown of his head.

John almost smiled to himself, thinking that the man looked something like a monk. But then he looked again.

Despite all of the friendliness written into the man's expression, a wail echoed through John's drunken mind. There was something about him, something that John thought he could see through. He battled reactions of fear and hatred. He walked toward the door.

"Wait, wait! Are you okay?"

The tenderness of the old man dampened any irrational impulse he had to run.

"You just scared the shit out of me, is all," John admitted.

"Aw hell." The bartender shook his head apologetically. "I'm sorry. I was down below when you came in." He motioned to a closed door in the corner of the room.

"Damn, I guess I didn't hear that door."

"Most don't," the bartender replied curtly.

"Well, listen," he continued. "At the very least it only seems right that you get a drink. On the house." He patted his hands against the sides of his legs, affirming to himself and John that he felt good about his decision. "And I'll even let you keep the one you've got in your hand."

John balked. He looked at the paper bag, clenched tightly in his right hand.

"That's...kind of you."

"Why don't you have a seat. Let me pour you something?"

The man pointed to a bar stool immediately in front of him. Like the rest of the bar, it was fairly standard, a red felt circle connected to a black, four-legged thing straight out of a TV sitcom. It, like everything else in the bar, was covered in dust.

John walked over, swept away the dust with an open hand, and gave an uneasy smile. The bartender beamed back, handing him a mug of yellow-brown, fizzing, frothing liquid. Its strong smell seemed to permeate through the entire bar, and it made John's nose burn and ache in anticipation. He picked up the beer, and let the cold slowly turn into warmth in his stomach.

He sighed, his cold anger disarmed by the kindness of a stranger.

"I suppose you won't be getting it too much anymore," the old man responded to his gulps.

"What?"

"Kindness."

John was lost for words.

The man continued, "People are uglier these days. More violence, heavier traffic, it's a cruel dark world out there." He made a gesture to the door. John reached for the paper bag. The whiskey tasted a little better now, less strong and more mellow.

He took a sip, mingling the bitter of the beer and the smoke of the whiskey.

He looked towards the door. It *had been* dark outside, a darkness which seemed to silently and intensely claw at the walls of the cozy little bar. Though he could not see it, he felt it. A dark full of a malignant hatred that would somehow reach inside and devour the world of the kind, tender bar.

IV

His father looked up at him from the floor.

His face was swollen and bloodied, eyes already welling shut and purple, sweat pouring down his forehead in glistening undulations. He gasped, panted, and tried to raise himself from the ground. But he was too drunk, too surprised, and too pathetic to pick himself up. Around him the house was in shambles, lined with dusty furniture, broken chairs, and empty bottles that stood as rows of silent observers. A ceiling fan hung low, burning with a soft and dying light that made his father more a shadow than a man.

John was hot, his head pounding with the frenzied beating of blood, his fists pulled so tight that they pulsated with a sharp and biting pain. He shook, every part of him ready to once again leap upon the bitter old man.

It was the first time that he realized he could hit back. The first time he realized that his father was old, bitter, and drunk; that he was not the tall monster who would tower over him and attack him with insults and blows. He didn't have to run anymore, didn't need to bob and weave between chairs and tables in the hopes of reaching his bedroom door and locking it before his father could grab his ankles.

Now he could answer his father's abuse in kind.

From the floor, the sagging shape of a man laughed.

"About time, you little coward."

The voice was low, painful, and full of venom. He was incapable of saying anything without mocking, without slipping the blade of his words into the softest and most vulnerable place in a soul. It was why John's uncle didn't visit, why his father's own brother tried so hard before he died to take John away from him. It was why John's own maternal grandfather also tried, and was likewise beat down by cancer before anyone could rescue him.

John knew that his father was pathetic, that he had no friends to speak of. He was no authority on anything. But John could not discount the truth of his father's insults, allowing his father to hurt him, time and time again.

John sat down at a table, clearing away space for his elbows and placing his chin squarely in his hands. His father hadn't been able to land a single blow. John wondered how long he had been uselessly letting him hit him. Could he have ended this at fourteen? Twelve? Why only now, at sixteen years old, had he chosen to stand up for himself?

"You don't have shit to say, do you?"

The man wallowed on the floor. He was stinking, the familiar and acrid smell of a drunk who had lost the control of his body.

John merely stared at him. His muscles uncoiled. He searched for an appropriate thing to say, but his mind offered him nothing more than images of his father's face battered and bloodied.

"Mommy's little bastard."

That was his father's favorite name for him. It didn't take long after her death for his father to turn undue anger and hatred towards John. *She left you too. Never even mentioned you before she ran out that door. Selfish bitch.* John lost count of the horrible things his father had said about him, about his mother.

"Shut up," was all John could think to say.

"Make me." The response came raspy and weak.

John looked down at him. From beneath the swelling red mounds he could see the faint glint of his father's green eyes, focused and gleaming. His features, obscured by swelling and blood, made him seem more demonic than human.

His father looked at him with an animal hatred, and despite himself John felt cold and weak.

"Make it to where I shut up forever."

"No."

His father laughed again.

"That's what I thought, you little fuckin' pussy. You can't do what it takes. They'd eat you alive out there...in war...in the world. You're not a hard man."

"That's not why."

"Oh?"

The reality of the situation had sobered John, swept aside the fleeting anger and pounding adrenaline. He remembered what his mother said to his father, what had so angered him to the point that he chased her right to her death. But now his father couldn't chase him, couldn't stop him from saying his piece.

He began forming the words that would hurt his father more than death ever could.

"You've *earned* your way to hell. I'm not going to help you get there. If you want it to end so badly, you'll have to do it yourself."

The ceiling fan hissed rhythmically. Outside, cars passed silently and sparingly, dull knives cutting through the quiet of a winter night.

"You'll have to sleep sometime, kiddo."

The proclamation made John sick. Even sicker now because John did not know what his father was capable of. He had only beaten John before. John never forgot the horrifying day that he came home from school to find his father ready, running at him with a belt and clenched fists. He ran to his room, only to find that the lock had been removed.

He didn't want to be ready to move shelves, to force his weight against the door like he had been doing for years since. Now, humiliated, he didn't want the possibility of his father smothering him in his sleep.

He walked to a chair, turning it over on its side. He looked at his father, who still had a confident and evil smirk on his face. John turned back to the chair, carefully bringing his foot down on one of the legs.

It came off with a loud snap. He picked up the broken-off leg, grabbing it with both hands. He looked back toward his father, the smirk replaced with wide eyes that shined out from his swollen face.

"What are you doing?" his father asked in a toneless whisper.

John lifted the chair leg above his head.

"Kid?" The condescending tone evaporated, leaving only a scared and fluttering ghost.

He brought the chair leg down on his father's knees, making sure he would never climb the stairs again.

V

John gasped to stifle his scream.

He was sweating, moisture covering him like a fine amphibian-slime. He shook his head, finding he was covered in a grey dust that stuck to his face in muddy clumps. He wiped his eyes and forehead, relieved to find that he was still in "The Circle," but unnerved by the sudden changes that took place during his blackout. Already he was aware of a cacophonous medley of music, laughter, and screams that overpowered the space of the formerly quiet bar.

Before John was a plastic cup, clear and brimming with ice and inviting condensation. He grabbed it and took a deep swallow, relieved to find that it was only water.

"You'll need that," the bartender said from behind the counter.

The bartender seemed younger, the hair on his head both higher and darker than John remembered it. A buzzing numbness slipped through his mind, and he accepted that the bartender had always looked this way. Maybe it was a trick of the light, or more likely the booze, that had previously dimmed and distorted the man's appearance. There weren't that many wrinkles on his face, only one smudge-like streak on his forehead. Maybe that had thrown off his perceptions, in turn obscuring the brightness of the man's green eyes and the scimitar-cruelness of his shining smile.

John tried to put words together, but it was hard to think with music coming from blaring, unseen speakers. The beats and sounds made him nauseous, falling somewhere between a track of screams and the erratic beating of drums and metal.

It was the sort of sounds that someone would make from the dying dungeon walls.

Or from the inside of a furnace.

"How long was I out?" he shouted over the music.

"You never left."

The bad joke made John groan and turn away from the bartender.

The bar was full of bodies, dancing and laughing wildly in flashing red and orange lights. In moments where the lights were bright enough he saw their faces, gleaming smiles flashing savage-sharp teeth in the crimson light. Everywhere there were women dressed in red or black, seductive women with eyes so alive, taunting and inviting as they danced together in sporadic rhythm. All of them were covered in red sweat, all were laughing or screaming as they mindlessly contorted their bodies in serpentine patterns.

A few men were among the crowd, walking between the women or slowly dancing back and forth out of touch with the awful music. But they seemed out of place, walking with the stride and power of a corrupt cop, smiling as they stalked across the floor, clapping their fists together quietly as hungry, lupine eyes surveyed women's open backs.

"Where'd all these people come from?" he asked, mustering his strength for small talk.

The bartender chuckled.

"Son, they're always here. This place is never on short supply of bodies, I'll tell you that."

He motioned to John's paper bag and the mouth of the bottle inside it.

"Some people tried to grab a bit of that while you were conked out. I stopped them though, told them it wasn't right to take a man's good whiskey."

"You know what it is?" John asked.

The bartender nodded slowly, his smile growing wider and wilder.

"Oh yeah."

"What is it?"

"The best drink you'll ever have."

It was the old drinker's maxim, that the best drink was the one in your hand. John shrugged, already tired of cryptic bullshit. Tired of the hot, crowded bar.

He'd try somewhere else.

"Welp." He stood from the stool, sliding as the world shifted beneath him. He grabbed onto the bar to steady himself, burping something stale and thick to keep from vomiting. He grabbed the bottle, slipping it back into his coat pocket.

"Thank you for the...'kindness,' but I'm gonna head out."

"Good luck with that," was all the man behind the counter said.

John frowned, wanting to tell the man to go fuck himself. He turned away from the bar and walked towards the door.

The bodies across the bar were packed tightly together, rubbing and jumping against each other in a wall of shifting hot flesh and tight clothing. Their stink wiped against him, loud laughter hurting his ears. He tried pushing, shoving, and elbowing his way through the floor, but the bodies only closed tighter around him.

He almost threw a punch when he heard a familiar laugh.

The music dimmed, the laughter subsided, just long enough for him to hear her:

"I'll just be right back."

Through the cleared crowd he saw her dark silhouette again, long legs and big hair moving swiftly in shadows before she walked into the women's restroom.

"Hey!" he called out. But the music picked up again, the dancing more frantic and tidal than before.

He squirmed his way through the bodies, arriving before the bathroom doors. He flattened himself against a wall between the men's and women's rooms, folding his arms and staring hatefully at the women's door.

He hated waiting for women, but he didn't want to let her get away again. He didn't know what he would say, but he was tired and wanted to yell at someone. The way she left him out in the cold, that was enough to set him off. Enough for him to lose his cool.

Every part of him began to itch. Pulsating aches shot up and down his calves. He strummed both sets of fingers across his arms. Then, looking at the men's room, he realized that he needed to pee.

The room was about as grimy as he expected, the sterile ammonia smell of piss made his mouth twist. He pissed with his hand against the wall, paying no attention to his aim. He smiled, not bothering to flush as he spun around to see the mirror.

There was a pale man with John's clothes. The face in the mirror had a heavy robber-mask around his eyes. It was thinner, jaw bones almost jutting out from a layer of paper white flesh which covered the too-obvious skull beneath. John's hands shook as they rose to touch his face. The nails of the creature in the mirror had grown long, and yet John did not feel them as they scraped against his face. The thing in the mirror, cut by his nails, began to bleed black blood out of his cheek and exposed rotten green-yellow tissue.

John rubbed his hands against his cheeks; no blood appeared on his hands.

A sick smell, something that was not the contents of his voided stomach, began to permeate throughout the room. He became uneasy, running towards a bathroom stall and kneeling over the rim of an open toilet.

He whispered to himself, "It's okay, you've had too much."

Outside, the bar crowd continued to rage and laugh.

When he repeated the magic phrase enough times, he lifted himself from the toilet, still unsure if he was truly well.

But that was another dark thought to keep at bay.

He took the paper bag from his coat and brought the rim of the bottle to his lips. The whiskey burned down his throat, hitting an empty stomach and shooting tears into his eyes. He doubled over, coughing until he vomited on the floor.

That was it. He needed to leave. Fuck the girl and her shadows, fuck the cryptic bartender. He wouldn't be caught puking on himself.

Not here.

He stood fully and looked back into the mirror.

Ashley stood behind him.

"Johnny, you need to stop drinking, *please*," she whispered without any strength.

A noose pulled tightly around her neck.

VI

"Johnny, baby, you should really stop drinking," a timid voice told him from behind his recliner. Sometimes when he turned his face away from her long enough, he could imagine he was alone. He was the king of his castle until she spoke. Then all illusions of vastness, of wealth, were shattered and he became reminded of all the things he hadn't given her. Of all the things he didn't have.

He gave a long, exaggerated sigh for her to linger on.

Her voice had grown weaker and weaker as their marriage dragged on. Their honeymoon years were wonderful; he really did love her then (and still did, in a way he couldn't understand or define). But she tried so hard to please him, so hard to make herself perfect and loving. He couldn't stand the submissiveness, though he wanted nothing more than for their marriage to either get on track or end.

He placed his cup down onto the nightstand. Purposely avoiding a coaster, he turned to face her. She had a cute, mousey face. Small nose, red lips pulled tightly in a frown against pale flesh. Her blonde hair was disheveled by stress, falling in tangles to the end of her neck. She was trembling as if this was a final stand, as if she was surrounded on all sides.

Jeez.

"I'll stop when I damn well please." He turned back to the television.

"Well I just think...since we may one day have a family?"

"Ashley, you're barren, we both know that." He took a sip of his drink.

"We...could adopt."

"Yeah," John snorted, "and add children to this perpetual unhappiness."

The silence was like a dull, rusty butcher's knife; in the past it had been threatening and awkward, but by now it was a daily routine. Her voice would begin to waiver soon.

"W-why do you blame me?"

John took a sip of his drink. "Because it's the goddamn truth."

"That's easy for you to say." She began to choke between sobs. "You haven't touched me in *months*!"

"Yeah, well, get someone to do that for you."

"... Is that what *you've* been doing?" she asked in horror and hurt.

"And is that any of your damned business?" John responded coldly.

"I'm your wife!"

"Yeah...for how much longer?" John heard his father in that question.

But he wasn't his father.

He would *never* hit her.

"OUT! I WANT YOU OUT!"

He laughed as he got out of the chair. He looked at her; she was shaking all over, tears streaming down her once beautiful face, her teeth chattering in frustration. And yet, he felt nothing. Well, that wasn't true. Deep down, in the darkest sanctuaries of his mind, there was a child angrily railing against the mother who left him.

Now he would do the most damage, inserting sarcastic compliments, reminding her that he used to be so sweet, so loving to her, and that she *used* to be beautiful. With these fake compliments he salted her emotional wounds.

"And how long should I stay gone *this* time, lovely wife?"

"LEAVE *FOREVER!* I NEVER WANT TO SEE YOU AGAIN!"

John laughed as he grabbed his coat and stepped out the door.

"Alright, honey, see you later."

When he came back later that evening, he didn't think anything would be different. She would be weeping in bed, and he would tenderly put his arm over her. He would hold her wordlessly, and in the morning she would brim with the small hope that this show of love provided her.

But there was something in the apartment's air. A *knowing.*

He stepped into their bedroom and found her above the bed.

In the stillness of their room, she hung lonely and quietly, her face purpled by the rope around her neck. How many times had he found her looking at the beams above their bed? How long had she been planning this?

He looked around for a note but didn't find one.

That was okay. He didn't need an explanation.

He walked up to her, holding her hand and surveying the yellow-band wedding ring. She wouldn't be taking it with her. But it was the last bit of love he had for her that let her keep it on her finger.

He walked out of the bedroom and shut the door.

The police would come eventually, but she deserved her rest.

Paper bag in his hand, he walked back out into the winter night.

VII

In the mirror, his eyes met hers.

Ashley's eyes were grey and milky now, lacking the blue shimmer they had in life. Her hair was longer and whiter, falling down well below her shoulders to a place he could not see.

Her pale, greening naked flesh brushed up against him. She was cold, icy and bloated.

"Please," she whispered. Her voice was weak, tightened into gasps by the noose around her neck. Against his cheek her breath wafted in waves of road-kill rottenness.

He choked down a sob.

He could not turn away from the mirror. If he turned around and she was *really there*, it would be the end of him.

The reflection behind him placed its fingers on the back of his neck, fat worms writhing across him in spider-touches. Her face came even closer to his, and he could feel her closeness without seeing it.

He couldn't hold back his sob, but was far too afraid to run.

Her face became sympathetic and sad. She shushed him, wrapping lithe, skeletal arms around him.

"Please, Johnny...all you have to do is *stop*."

A dry, fetid finger came to touch his trembling lips.

He screamed, swatting her from him and bursting through the bathroom door.

The bar was quiet. The lights pulsed blinding red, the air full of stifling steam and smoke. The crowd waited for him, bodies of concrete hurtled against him, legions of hands pulling and shoving him as he fought his way towards the door. A hand wrapped itself around his leg, an arm around his torso. He fought for breath, tears searing his face as the panic ate him from the inside. Succumbing to his animal fear, he began biting and clawing into sour and bitter tasting things. He spat out rancid, unknown matter as he caught rotten shards of flesh in his nails.

He finally reached the exit.

Panting and aching, he reached for the door handle.

The heat seared across his hand, scalding knives tearing across his palm. He recoiled, and through blinking tears he could see a dark-red patch of scarred tissue giving birth to searing, wet blisters and permanently charred flesh. He collapsed against the door, weeping frantically and clutching his charred hand in confusion and desperation.

The shadows only stood by, curious and bemused. Some of them wore clear smiles, others laughed without enthusiasm as if at a too-obvious irony.

"What's going on? What's going on?" John repeated to himself. "What is this place?" The question escaped his lips once. Then again. Then, finally rising into a maddened scream:

"What the hell is this place!?"

The red light grew bright, no longer dim enough for shadows.

His screams drowned his thoughts.

A leathery, clawed hand forced a bottle to his mouth.

VIII

In the bright light, John recognized the bartender.

Across the counter stood a man with slightly balding black-grey hair, green and cruel eyes, and patchy facial hair that did little to hide ugly scars. His was a face that John sometimes recognized in the mirror, a shadow welling up from the blood beneath his skin.

"You were always a stupid little shit," his father laughed. "Mommy's little bastard."

John remained on the floor.

The look his father gave him was exasperation, impatience. He frowned, silent until he could no longer stand it. He was impossibly tall now, growing larger and larger as the lights in the bar changed from brighter to darker shades of red. Less a man now, and more a giant leaning over the bar.

"Will you *please* get up here!?"

His father had two voices. One was the angry, fierce voice that his father used when he was drinking. The other was lower, a bestial growl from a wet and bloody throat.

The denizens of the club began snickering, an idiot-chirping of delight and excitement. John remained on the floor, cemented and paralyzed.

Their hands were on him, dragging and pulling him along the floor towards his father. Their faces were marked with wide eyes and sharp teeth, features contorted and pulled in sharp angles. Their claws tore and cut him through his thick coats, shredding his clothes and skin.

Strong, scaly hands came under his armpits, lifting him from the floor and onto a barstool. Another arm reached into John's coat pocket. Tree-branch limbs, red and thin, took the bottle from its paper bag. Another placed a glass in front of him, and delicately the liquid poured into the glass.

His father slid the glass closer to him.

He was younger than when John last saw him. The man behind the counter was the one who had so ruthlessly chased his wife out of her home, not the old and bitter man John had crippled. His father's shape rose, stretching almost to the ceiling.

"No...no," was all John could say.

"What...How are you here?" he finally finished.

"The same way you are, kiddo."

His father, impossibly tall and large, pointed at the glass and smirked.

"You never could control yourself. You hated me and ended up hating yourself. And you used that to justify the fact that you were broken, weak, and worthless. Now," his father took a break to shrug, "I *suppose* you could blame this on me. But the truth is, kiddo, I was *dead* when you met Ashley. I'd been dead *eight years* by then."

"I never hit her!" John said through gritted teeth.

"And what, you think that makes you *better than me*? You hounded her for the better part of two years, conned her into marrying you just so you could have some sort of lifeboat. You're just a shitty little boy trying to replace Mommy.

"But you're out of options now. You came by here the same way I did. With no one around, there was no one to stop you."

His father turned away, reaching to the bar. He poured himself a glass. His face, now the size of a small car door, lowered to meet John's. He raised the glass to his arm-sized lips, licking them mockingly.

"You're where you belong. Where men like me and you *always* go. Cheers."

Somewhere behind the chant began. "Drink...drink." A soft whisper became a grating, howling chant; the sounds of the tortured and torturer alike.

"No...please."

He looked down at his hand in horror, his mind sending every impulse to his arm to stay still. But the hand was no longer his. It reached for the glass, for the very last drop. He tried to pray, but couldn't remember the words. The tears began to claw their way down his face, using his one hand to stop the other.

But his drinking arm was stronger, lifting the glass closer and closer to his face. It smelled of fire and brimstone.

The burnt hand came to the glass, steam and sweet-pork smoke spilling from the palm that closed around it.

"Cheers," his father said as their glasses came mockingly together.

"Drink, drink, drink!" the voices behind him shouted. He cried, but their voices were too loud. Too strong.

The glass came to his lips.

He gave up fighting.

The best drink he ever had.

Author's Notes: This is the oldest story in this collection. I wrote the first draft my senior year of high school, when I had been reading Dante's *Inferno*. I got feedback from a great teacher and it went through rewrite upon rewrite. It is the longest story in this collection, and as I transitioned back into writing for publication, I knew I would have to try to get this one ready. That it had to be the centerpiece of a collection.

The first version of this story came at a time when the idea of alcohol scared me, the idea of losing yourself to something that could very well remake you for the worse. The abuse angle came later, when the idea of abusive love became terrifying to me. Abuse runs deep in this story and the cycle of violence becomes a spiral. One could make the argument that there's fate in this story, but I think that's a crock of crap. John had his chance and he didn't take it.

As the story advanced and morphed over the years, it came to take on a few more influences. I recommend giving a listen to Johnny Cash's "Delia's Gone" and Kris Kristofferson's "How to Beat the Devil."

This is its first time appearing in print.

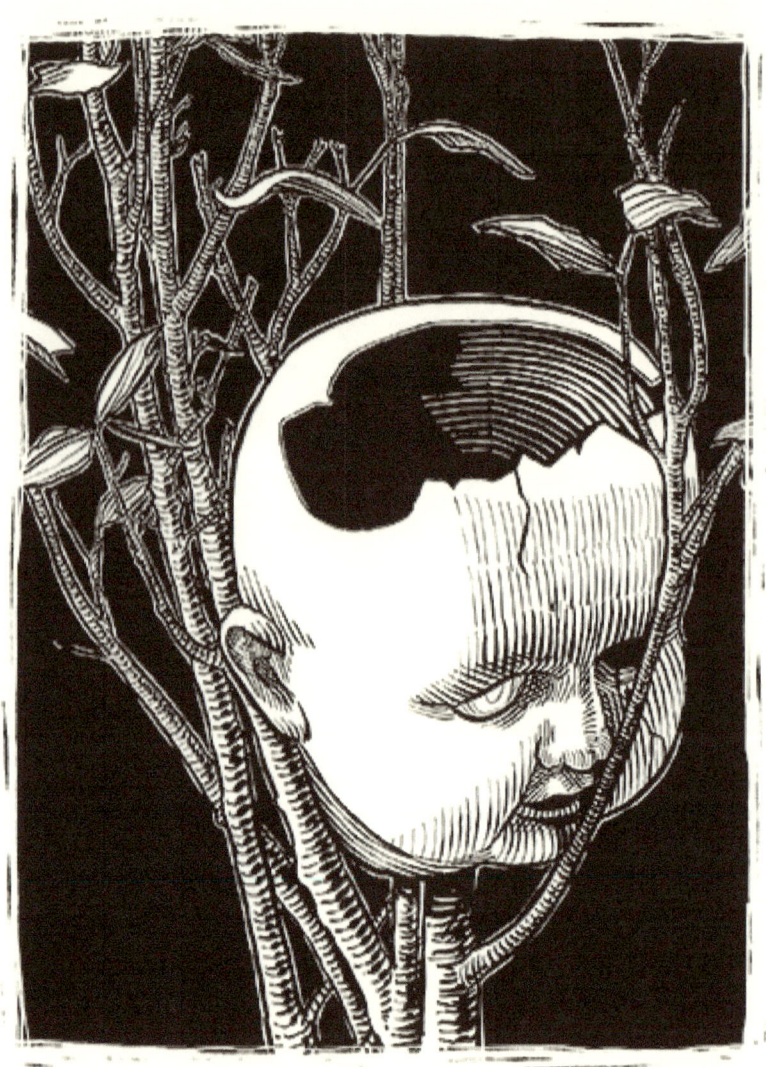

Monstruos de Agua

STORIES KEEP THIS city going.

Mexico City is an engine of hauntings, every gothic church filled with the cries of suffering brides and every alley a mouth that swallows people whole. The streets leave shoes behind without their owners. The canals, the sewers and the lakes drag the lost down into the waters far below. Rain carries their screams to the black water beneath the city, reservoirs that run teeming with blood and teeth from long and brutal wars.

Stories keep the city going, so before you hang the doll from the branch you smash its head along the tree. It splits along the wet bark, caving in a porcelain cheek and jostling loose its marble eyes. You work a twig through its blonde hair, purposefully mangling and marring it with wet green grass.

A new doll has no place on Isla de Muñecas.[1] A fresh plastic Barbie would stand out against the older dolls, stained and broken by decades of rain and dirt. A fresh face amongst such a legion of ruin would be a dead giveaway, something a more discerning tourist could tell apart

---

[1] An island on Xochimilco, a system of canals that make a floating city in the south of Mexico City. The story goes that Don Julian Santana Barrera, the caretaker of the island, found a young girl drowned along the shore. Shortly thereafter, he began to experience strange phenomena. To appease the spirit of the young girl, he offered her dolls. But she continued to haunt him. Upon his death in 2001, he was supposedly found in the same spot where he discovered the girl's body.

from the others. This would burden the story with doubts, ruining everything in the process.

So in the cricket-and-frog song you break your doll. You run her dress through the mud. You fill her shoes with dirt. You scratch out her smile to match her eyeless sockets.

She's scarier this way, a better sacrifice and a better story.

You take the rough twine and wrap it around her neck. Sometimes the dolls fall off the trees, sometimes the tourists steal them. Sometimes they seem to move, to change places in an unseen musical chairs. This doesn't bother or concern you. If the ghosts are real then they are only a part of this place just like you. Just as silent and just as impassive.

Xochimilco is always humid and cool, resting on the final open graveyard of Tenochtitlan's grand canal system. It's a long day to get here, to take the bus down from Condesa and pay a boat driver to take you past the fleet of colorful trajineras past the tourist-laden areas and into the deeper parts of the canal system.[2] Sometimes it takes a big tip to arrange their trip back. Not all, but many of the men are superstitious. Isla de Muñecas is, to them, a strange destination during the day, and at night far too overrun with ghosts. It's difficult to find a brave enough trajinero, but you gave your lancero a wad of pesos and promised him another if he came back.

You arrived on the island early, and had a whole day of removing dolls from your backpack and breaking them along vines and rocks. An entire day hiding from the tourists, some speaking soft Spanish and others loud, nonsensical English. Hours of darting behind trees, flattening yourself along the ground. You imagine you look close to one of the broken dolls yourself, and that will make things all the better come nightfall.

It's almost sundown now. The sky fades from bright pink to dark purple, the frogs and crickets are singing. You bite into a mustard-heavy sandwich that hits your empty stomach in painful, grateful waves. It's been a long day, and when you're not scaring tourists, you're modeling or performing, posing for photographs as a mermaid in the botanical gardens or as a skull-faced woman in Zócalo . You too try to keep

---

[2] "Trajineras" are the colorful boats that take visitors across the canals. "Lanceros" are their drivers.

yourself tired, so much so that you can't dwell on your own ghosts. But every late October you find yourself making their ofrendas, leaving them coffee and bread to entice them back into your life.

So now you throw yourself more and more into your work, scaring and entertaining tourists, bleeding the city dry of every last peso it will throw at you. In your pocket mirror you paint your face white and grey, a trickle of red running down like a melted crown from your forehead. The tourists usually come towards the end of the day, staggering and ready to prove themselves after far too many chelas. The lanceros will take them to the island's shore, but most keep their distance. But you're not here for the cowards. You're here for the people who want stories, who want something they can swear is true and turn pale over years after they leave.

There's a plop from the water and you look up from your mirror.

A black shape is writhing along the shore.

You've never seen an ajolote before, not outside of a museum or hatchery. Xochimilco is their native habitat, but they're supposed to be near extinct.[3] All the ones in pictures are cute and pink, but this one's jet black. A writhing, slick eel that thrashes weakly in the shallows. You put down your sandwich and slide down the bank.

You cup your hands. It's cold and heavy, heavier than what you'd expect for something this small. Its external gills remind you of a feathered crown.

And then, it looks at you.

Right into you.

You go still at its disturbingly distant smile, a look that suggests it knows something it has no intention of telling you. A face that seems on the verge of a low, cruel laugh.

A series of footsteps bend the grass. A breath of hurried English.

You dip your hands back into the canals.

The ajolote sits for a moment, still considering you.

"Ah fuck, this is creepy."

You turn away and throw stuff your sandwich into a dress pocket.

---

[3] Spanish for "axolotl," a near extinct amphibian and subject of a famous short story by Julio Cortázar.

"I want my doll," you cry out.

Silence.

"Oh shit, what was that?"

"I want my dolllieeeeee—"

You crash through the trees and into a wall of screams.

You've been fleeing your younger brother for what seems like eternity. Your feet are cracked and bleeding, so you shed them for plant stalks. At the sound of your brother's footsteps, you shed these stalks and grow your roots so deep in the hopes that he will not discover your entire being.

The fifth sun would not rise. The world would not begin. Ehecatl said that the world needed what all others did before, blood to sink into its soil. To water its life and fill its lakes. So your younger brother, as decisive and commanding as the winds at his power, took his spear in his hand and slit the throat of your twin the feathered serpent.

Mighty Quetzalcoatl, who gave himself all too willingly to die for the world. His emerald feathers falling away, heavy with glittering scarlet pearls of blood. At the sight you wept profusely, so much that your eyes fell from your face. Eyeless but not blinded, you watched as the other gods lined up, ready to sacrifice themselves for the greater good that would come next.

But you do not understand. Of course you want the world to begin, but you want *to* live *in it too! Why should* you *have to die for it? You, who have already given so much. You, who command lightning, who know death all too well. You, who have kept the fourth sun safe from the darkness of the underworld, and who returned fire so that mankind could continue to live in light even as their sun rested. You, who kept the world alive with the help of your feathered twin.*

Giving so much, you are unwilling to give any more because you do not know what sort of death will exist under the fifth sun, nor if any sort of life is worth it. No life without him *is worth it, not without your beloved twin.*

You shed your roots and rise to the surface. Your new body is slick and small, a thing that will stay in the water, out of sight from your vigilant brother. But a hand breaks the surface and rips you out from the cool, calm dark.

Your younger brother is monstrous. You have always feared him. He was made far too strong, far too wild. He is nearly formless, a shifting, writhing thing of whirling winds and four faces. Only one face faces you, and at the sight of it your slick skin goes cold with sweat.

Your darling twin. His beautiful feathers and scales sawed off with a stone spear and tied to a bleeding storm.

You scream, because as strong as you are, as afraid as you are, you are not willing to strike him back. Not when he wears that face.

The pain as he crushes you is worse than any hell you've ever known.

You wake up shouting and panting wildly. Your eyes move across the familiar apartment, bare white walls absent of pictures and art. Grey morning air comes through your window, still wet from last night's storm. October in Condesa, cold mornings and long evening storms.

If Mamá were still with you, she would have something to say about your dreams. Mamá, who had a palm reader, a tarot reader, and a psychic in her cell phone and consulted them with more regularity than any doctor. Mamá, who could only justify her existence with someone else's. Who took you and Marí down from Oaxaca to the capital, fleeing some unknown family strife, only to meet some man from the city who consumed every part of her. Mamá, full of ridiculous stories and destructive fancies that allowed her to dismiss anything truly important for fleeting, twinkling daydreams of fairytale happiness and grief. You look out your window to the building across the way, colorful clothes hanging in the grey air, and wonder (not for the first morning) if she is still alive or if that man (or another) killed her.

You remember her telling you the story, of Quetzalcoatl and his dark twin Xolotl. Of the death god's murder at the hands of his dual-faced brother Ehecatl, who slaughtered the gods to give life to the world. How Xolotl ran, transforming himself into maize, maguey, and finally an axolotl to hide from his bloodthirsty brother. Mamá would joke sometimes, saying that you were like Xolotl and Marí like Quetzalcoatl.

You did not understand how cruel she was being until you went to a museum and learned that dog-faced, eyeless Xolotl was a god of deformities and diseases. A thing of contradictions, the twin of Quetzalcoatl and a guardian of the world, who was feared and hated despite his heroism.[4]

But Marí was happy and bubbly, always wearing bright colors and always singing in her soft, light hummingbird cadence. A lovely creature whose eyes took in the world and gave so much back, a being who could enter a room and make it better without ever saying a word. Who spoke in windchime laughter, who held everyone's attention at the tips of her soft hands the ends of her dimpled smile.

In contrast to your twin, you were a calm and distant child. Many times it felt as you were not living in the world, but viewing it from space. You do not gravitate towards any color and only learned you were pretty because other people told you, though you were never sure if you believed it. Unwittingly, you would detach yourself from their conversations and become impassive and apathetic. It was difficult to only stay in this world when you could make and imagine far more interesting things than banal people and their all-too-predictable, all-too banal desires.

It made you calm, distant, able to think carefully. Cautious of the men who Mamá pulled in with her force of gravity and her desire for fabricated meaning, made you wary of the alcohol, pills, and powders that she brought home and of the stories she told from all sides of her ever-moving mouth.

But Marí stayed childishly over-eager, quick to trust people and eager to try new things, unable, unwilling or uninterested in ever saying "no." Addicted first to being liked, and then to the same ghosts that Mamá so violently pursued.

After that, the city took her just as it took Mamá.

Now it's just you, with your frightened tourists and death-god dreams.

The sound of the coffee bubbling over the stove is one of your favorites, as pleasant a thing to wake to as the rain is to fall asleep to.

---

[4] This version is based on pre-Columbian myths. Ehecatl, the warrior god of the wind, has been described as an "aspect" of Quetzalcoatl.

You don't have a cup of Mamá's; virtually everything she owned was either destroyed by her or by you. But Marí once bought you a coffee cup. Your twin was never rich, but she was always kind. Always emotional. So when you bought her a matching coffee cup, right after Mamá disappeared, you hugged her tight.

Their ofrendas are more colorful than anything else in your apartment.[5] Mamá was intensely patriotic, internalizing the myths of the people and the nation. She never discussed politics, but seemed loyal to whichever party or president occupied the government, be it the PRI or the PAN.[6] You've decorated her ofrenda in the colors of the flag, making sure that even the calaveras you bought are decorated red, green, and white.

Marí was less interested in history and more in the moment. You've made her ofrenda her favorite colors, bright pink and orange, like the colors of her favorite sherbet. She has a larger serving of pan de muerto than Mamá, an account of her sweet tooth. At this time of year, she would always try and sneak sweets from the ofrendas, and cry when Mamá slapped her hand away. It was always up to you to ensure that your sister got her sweets, stealing from Mamá's meager purse so that you could buy her something from the bakery.

---

[5] "Ofrendas," feature large in popular fiction regarding the Day of the Dead. They are altars for deceased loved ones, usually consisting of a photo, candles, calaveras (candy skulls), pan de muerto (season sweet bread) and a drink or object that the deceased relative would enjoy. In this case, coffee.

[6] The Partido Revolucionario Institucional (PRI) was founded in the decades after the Mexican Revolution. It was an attempt to control remaining warlords who would occasionally rebel against the central government. The PRI was a vehicle of these remaining revolutionaries, and held on to power from 1929 to 2000. In 1990, Peruvian poet and author Mario Vargas Llosa called the PRI's rule "the perfect dictatorship." In 2000, Mexico's first democratically elected President since the revolution, Vicente Fox, took power with the Partido Acción Nacional (PAN). Other parties, notably the PRD, shot off from the PRI during the final years of its dictatorship as reform factions from within the party. Only in 2018 did the PRI-PAN competition see its first interruption in a dramatic election which brought a new political party, MORENA into a super majority.

Their faces stare out at you, smiling in a way you never could. The two of them shared a smile, some strange genetic legacy that you did not inherit. With that smile alone, people could always tell you apart.

Most of the time, you're angry with them. For being so glib and so irresponsible to leave you alone, paying no mind to how hurtful their absences would be. But you can't deny that the idea of their ghosts visiting you is pleasant, and pouring them coffee is as close to closure as you ever expect to have. Mamá took hers black. Marí with sugar. A *lot* of sugar.

Your phone pings and you turn away from their smiling faces.

The travel agency says their clients reported unusual, frightening activity on Isla de Muñecas. They were chased, they explained, by a pale ghostly woman crashing through the trees and screaming in a "goddamn banshee wail."

Your phone pings again.

Scaring tourists is a good way to make money.

With your sister's face smiling at you from her ofrenda, you paint yourself in the mirror once more. It's careful work, first a layer of white before returning to blacken and lace your eyes. A streaking red smile stitched to look like skull teeth. You style your hair, curly and long and dark. The dress you choose is something Marí and Mamá both would have loved, a bright red-white-and-green thing with padded shoulders. The leggings underneath have pockets, and you make sure to have your phone, your keys, and a small knife on you.

Lest the city try to take you too.

Zócalo is already full of people.[7] Whole family stores splayed out on carpets, children selling chips and women selling magazines. Men in black aprons and white shirts carefully apply strands of al pastor to their trompos, igniting flames and slowly rotating the still-pink meat. Other

---

[7] The Zócalo (sometimes called "Centro Historico") houses countless museums, among them the Templo Mayor, the last remnants of the most holy sites in Tenochtitlan and the Palacio Nacional, at the time of writing the current Presidential residence and seat of government. The Spanish wanted the capital of New Spain to resemble Rome, but also brought their own Iberian style to the city center. The Catedral Metropolitanica is one such example, a massive gothic cathedral that sits directly across from the Templo Mayor. The Catedral is currently sinking, a consequence of Mexico City being built over a system of lakes.

performers are already setting up.[8] Children painted black and white like skeletons, men covered in feathers and gold. People approach them and hand them golden pesos, paying for an Aztec cleanse of smoke and fire.[9]

The long rows of European buildings always remind you of postcards from Paris, a reminder that Mexico City is an impossibly old city, interchangeable for any European capital if not for the open wound that is Templo Mayor.

You try not to look at it, but you feel the presence of the templo behind you. The open-air ruins will be busier in the afternoon. Now only a few foreigners, norteamericanos visiting for conferences or studies, walk along the perimeter to peer into the massive crater. Under the grey sky they'll see the splayed ruins of the temple spread out like a skeleton, piles of stairs made from volcanic rock with a few statues of fallen gods between them.

When Mamá took you to the templo, you and Marí were sixteen. Fifteen minutes into your walk, Mamá cried. She fell to her knees and threw herself at the bricks, slamming her fists against the ground until they became mashed, pink and red. Marí was inconsolable, screaming as you tried to lift Mamá off the ground by her shoulders. But Mamá didn't listen, and tried to climb into the pit and run towards a monument of stone skulls. When the police removed her, when you and Marí followed them outside, you could only watch as she scratched at her face until it bled.

That was the day that you began to understand. Mamá was not just "strange." She paid no mind to how Marí cried, nor to your hateful glare. She stormed off into the crowds and left you and Marí to take the bus home by yourselves. That was the day you learned that your mother was so impulsive that she would never be able to understand how her actions hurt others. The day you learned that as much as Mamá loved you, she would *always* hurt you.

---

[8] "Trompo" is the word used to refer to the skewer of al pastor.
[9] A traditional Pre-Columbian ritual in which smoke is run across the body. This ritual has both spiritual and sanitary significances, and is still practiced in the Centro Historico.

You have no interest in returning to Templo Mayor.

You already know the sad stories, sung into so many songs and written into the very DNA of the city and every person living in it. There's no need to revisit the tragedy, no need to be reminded of the things that hurt.

You set up your space in front of Catedral Metropolitana, the massive black-grey church still looming over the square despite sinking slowly every year. The faces on the statues are either stern or naïve, men and cherubs staring down from their tall spires and onto the growing throngs of families gathering beneath. The faces of the Spanish men on that building remain the same as when they first arrived to Mexico, curious, disgusted, afraid. It is no coincidence, you realized, long ago, that they stand directly across from the ruins of the Aztec's most holy sites. Rising despite sinking, while Templo Mayor is ground down in the open air by winds and storms.

You remove a long streamer from your bag, a banner of colorful skulls and eagles. You begin to dance slowly. Years of lessons (Mamá always loved her little dancing dolls, one of the few things she was always willing to spend money on) have given you careful control of your body. You sway your shoulders and wrists, feeling so much like calm-running water. You breathe carefully, catching the smoke from the other performers and letting your lungs vibrate and thrum with the rhythm of your movements.

The first coins fall into your bag. You hum louder and pound the bottoms of your ribs with hard, clenched fists. You twirl, letting your long dress whip a wide circle around you. Someone begins to clap a rhythm for you. A feathered man beats his drum. Sweat slicks your forehead.

You let your streamer fly and enter into a fury. You move faster now, burning alive with that passionate suffering that you let build up at the bottom of your diaphragm. Your breathing is still careful but sharp, rising above the pounding of drums and the beating of your heart.

Your humming turns into wailing. Your screeching turns primal. Someone whistles. Another cheers. So much of life is the celebration of pain, finding solace in solidarity. Out of the corner of your eye, green and pink bills fall into your bag. You sweat and you cry, throwing up your anguish into your song. Into your movements.

You blink through your tears and find your face smiling back at you.

Your heart stops. The whole world turns cold and quiet.

You recognize your eyes, your hair and the shape of your nose.

Her smile breaks, and she reveals white teeth. Above the noise and clapping, you hear her windchime laugh.

You break past your crowd, knocking over your bag and letting the bills fall. You're shoving people aside, darting between the feathered dancers and coughing up their smoke. The stones beneath you are spinning, the sky above shaking. You run past the security guards and underground into the Templo Mayor.

She's still in front of you, darting between the mounds of stone stairs and fallen statues.

You're screaming now. Howling and begging for her to stop from a wheezing, scraping esophagus.

When the police grab your shoulders you jolt back to attention. You turn from them, hoping to see where she went.

But the woman with your face is gone.

Getting home is an ordeal. You manage to convince the police that you were confused when you jumped the gate, that you thought you saw your missing sister running into Templo Mayor. They ask you if you are hydrated. If you are high on something. You lie, and say that you have not had a lot of water today, that you feel faint and just want to rest. Finally they let you go, shaking their heads and swearing loudly.

You don't like spending money on the Uber, especially when you come back to find your bag of profits is now empty. But you're tired, and if you're going to recover before night, you need to sleep. The ride is thankfully short, and after you turn the lock three times you finally swing open your apartment door.

Shattered glass crunches under your foot. Your apartment is a mess of shredded cloth, paper and ruined porcelain.

Coffee stains the floor around Marí's ruined ofrenda. Someone has destroyed her favorite cup, has crumbled her pan de muerto into crumbs. The calaveras you had so carefully placed around her photo are on the floor, smashed like so many doll heads. The pink-and-orange construction paper is ripped, and the tablecloth looks like it has been torn apart with claws.

At the sight of Marí's ripped picture your stomach hurts. You pick it up its pieces gingerly and try to piece it back together. But the pieces fall from your hands like ash.

Soon shock and hurt gives way to terror. Someone must be here. The door had been locked when you came in, but you notice water on the floor.

You call the police, the second time you've dealt with them today. You watch them slowly step through your apartment door with their clubs drawn, trembling and reaching for the knife in your pocket.

They emerge long minutes later, saying that they found no signs of forced entry, though one window was open. You follow them back to the window, scanning for missing items. But everything is where you left it. In front of the window is a puddle of water, though the evening storms haven't started yet.

You circle back again.

Mamá's ofrenda is untouched. Her smile still fresh, still wild. Her calaveras and pan de muerto right where they should be.

The officers ask if you are all right.

You're *tired.*

A cat must have gotten in, one of them offers meekly.

You just nod.

When they leave you throw yourself on the couch, too exhausted to weep but feeling the pressure well up just behind your eyes.

From the red water you see the world that Ehecatl's sacrifice birthed.

This world tastes of salt and copper as the feathered men take their knives to each other. They build their temples on mounds of bones, countless skulls with wide-open eye sockets that you are forced to swim through. They are marvels, these feathered men. Far stronger, far wiser than those who came before. They build an empire to end all others, to conquer the world and build on burnt sacrifices and splintered bones.

But then others come.

The moment you see them, you want to scream out. In their eyes you see the shadow of the sixth sun, the terrible thing soon to rise and never set. A burning crimson light that will not be satiated in one sacrifice, but will continue lapping up the blood of centuries for as long as it may.

They are not marvels. They are nightmares. Pale things of metal, fire, famine and disease.

As strong as the feathered men are, they are not prepared.

They are slaughtered in their feast, by the pale men and the legions of other enemies the feathered men have made in their long and brutal wars under the fifth sun. The feathered men are tortured routinely, flayed and spread for the foundation of what will come next. You watch their young emperor, defiant and hateful, accept his fate-worse-than-death on the condition that his people live. You watch them take coals to his feet, and you gasp from beneath the water at his courage.[10]

What could Ehecatl have expected? How was this world any different from what you worried would come? How could a thing fed on bones and blood not hunger for more? Demand *more?*

A pale man walks the ruins of the great city. From the water you see his eyes, and in them the light of the sixth sun burns brighter than anywhere

---

[10] The final tlatoani (ruler of Tenochtitlan) was not Moctezuma II, who has been popularized by media and stories, but Cuauhtémoc, who ascended the throne at the age of 25 after the slaughter at the great temple. Cuauhtémoc did not rule Tenochtitlan long, surrendering to Cortés in order to save his people. Accounts have that Cuauhtémoc asked for death, but was denied and instead tortured in 1521.

Cuauhtémoc would die four years later, hanged by Cortés during an expedition to Honduras. According to conquistador Bernal Díaz del Castillo, the young emperor gave these dying words to Cortés: "Now I understand your false promises and the kind of death you have had in store for me. For you are killing me unjustly. May God demand justice from you, as it was taken from me when I entrusted myself to you in my city of Mexico."

else. In that light you see further slaughter, further war. You see empires and republics fall, heroes and monsters throwing themselves against each other until the end of time.

The pale man stops. He sees something.

He reaches into the water and removes your twin's face.

You bark ineffectively.

That does not belong to him! He is not your twin!

But the pale man attaches it to himself with such ferocity, such force that for centuries the sixth world will believe he was the feathered serpent.[11]

And then he sees you.

His eyes, so much like Ehecatl's, burn into you.

You wake too suddenly.

These dreams are no coincidence. You saw the ajolote in Xochimilco, which first set you thinking about Xolotl and Quetzalcoatl. Then you ran through the Templo Mayor, which made you think of the final days of Tenochtitlan. There is no mystical significance, nothing to parse out from tarot cards or divinations.

But you turn to the ruins of Marí's ofrenda and remember the woman in Centro Historico.

You bite your tongue.

There are few explanations. The first is that you left a window open, letting a cat in. It had happened before, and cats could be nasty

---

[11] Many myths have persisted regarding the fall of Tenochtitlan and the end of the Aztec Empire. Two of which I want to address here: (1) the Spanish did not conquer the Aztecs alone. Rather, the Aztec Empire had subjugated many smaller tribes to its rule. Hernán Cortés formed coalitions with these tribes, who made up the vast majority of the army that destroyed the empire. (2) A common myth is that the Aztecs believed Cortés was the reincarnation of Quetzalcoatl, but this story has only been offered by Cortés himself, who bragged about how naïve the Aztecs were to the king of Spain. However, many historians and anthropologists have argued that it was quite unlikely that the Aztecs believed any such thing.

and destructive things. It destroyed Marí's ofrenda and not Mamá's because it was an angry animal, needing no more reason than that.

The woman, though...this worries you, because there are no good possibilities. If your sister is alive, then she is torturing you. The thought of her purposefully hurting you seems unlikely, but the idea hurts worse than if she were dead. Because in death she could not hurt you more. If your sister is dead, then you are seeing a ghost. Mamá fully believed in ghosts, that they were portends and harbingers of worse things to come. And if you're not seeing a ghost, your sister is dead and you are losing your mind.

Just as Mamá did.

This is the most terrifying possibility, that you'll let yourself disappear just like she did.

In an effort to put these thoughts aside, you change your dress for black pants and a sweater. You smear your skull paint, keeping white-grey streaks the color of war. For what you have to do now, this makeup will more than work.

It's not an easy location to reach. The bike ride takes you almost an hour, moving through the city as it lurches towards the end of the weekend. You pass through the first two sections of Parque Chapultepec, weaving between tourists for an hour before you reach the third section, where some of the wealthier residents of the city live.[12]

You hide your bike thick bushes and continue on foot.

An agency has contracted you to scare locals this time, kids looking for the Casa of Tía Toña.[13] As one of the more popular urban legends in the city, it's always safe to assume that you could find some agency with

---

[12] Parque Chapultepec was one of my favorite places in Mexico City. It is a massive park in the center of the city, with several interesting museums, lakes, and live performers. Of particular interest are the Museo Nacional de Historia, the Museo Nacional de Antropologia, and Los Pinos, the former Presidential compound.

[13] This is a particularly brutal urban legend in Mexico City. According to it, Tía Toña was a kind old woman who took children in from the streets and into her home. But the children were ungrateful, and would play pranks on her. In a fit of rage and exhaustion, Toña killed the children and hid their bodies in a nearby creek. Currently, Tia Toña's house appears to be a private residence, perhaps of someone quite important given the police presence around it. In 2009, 23 people fell 30 meters while attempting to see the house.

clients who want to go close to the mansion where Tía Toña killed all her foster children, finally driven mad by their cruelty and lack of gratitude. You go deeper into the woods, snapping twigs underneath your feet. You imagine that this is what hunting must be like, quietly waiting for the right animal to come along. You hunker down across a worn bridge and wait for night to come.

When the first kids come along, no older than sixteen, you don't even need to say anything. The slight crunching sound you make when you move through the brush is enough to send them screaming. It's hours of walking before you find a new group, one that looks roughly your own age.

"Ungrateful," you mutter.

A man with a flashlight turns towards you.

You don't know what he sees in your face, but it's enough to make him drop his flashlight and run. The others call out after him, crying to the point of weeping behind him.

It's enough to make you laugh, and despite yourself, you smile.

"Ungrateful," The voice comes from behind you.

In the fallen flashlight beam, Mamá's face is wet. Her hair is dark and slick, her skin pale and glistening. Her smile works its way into your stomach, the same smile she would give you and Marí when she used to tease you both.

"I know a secret," she says. The same thing she would say to you and Marí on your birthdays. On Christmases.

She stands there, wet and smiling, pleased with herself and her great surprise.

"I…" you finally say.

A group of tourists scream behind you.

Mamá fades away, stepping backwards into the darkness of the jungle.

You abandon Parque Chapultepec, get on your bike and pedal furiously as the storms begin.

You now understand what Ehecatl could never have known. He crushed you in his hands and yet you live. The pale men came, bearing their instruments of torture. They take their tongues to your stories, remaking you and your brothers into demons or monsters. And yet, you still live.

You were always different than your brothers; you realize this now. Having traveled the underworld, it cannot hold you long. Having commanded death, it cannot keep you still no matter how much you wish it would.

You do not know if it is possible to kill a death god, but you know you have lived through so much. Too much.

You finally accept it, that you have been made to bear witness to it all.

You rise from the red water.

The new city has been built on the bones of the old. Its lakes have been drained, exposing dry roads that will become the veins of a new empire under this sixth sun. In the ash and fire you weep ceaselessly, as you did when Ehecatl first slaughtered your brothers. You alone are left to watch the temples fall, to watch their children whither.

In your long walks you learn the new stories they tell about you. A crying goddess, a thing of wrath and fear. You never stray far from the water, but when you look to its surface you see a face that you don't recognize, something that does not at all resemble your beautiful twin. All traces of him have rotted away, leaving behind only a white skull, long dark hair, and a thin black robe that clings to you as a dark, shifting fog.

In time, you are given a new twin. Another thing of beauty. The people love Her more than they ever loved Quetzalcoatl. They affix Her likeness to their flags, painting Her soft face above their banners of war. Your new twin sways over Her people in silence, smiling and praying for them as they prepare to take part in the long ritual set in motion by Ehecatl all those eons ago.[14]

---

[14] The appearance and myth of the Virgin of Guadalupe is perhaps the most important cultural moment in Mexico's history. For one thing, the Virgin appeared to an indigenous man, Juan Diego, not a Spaniard. The Virgin herself was not white, as depicted in Spanish icons at the time, but indigenous. Also of note is that according to the story she spoke to Juan Diego in Nahuatl, the Aztec language.

Mamá is in the apartment.

You don't know how, because you locked all the doors and windows. You had no one to call, or you would have slept somewhere else. You fought sleep hard, but woke up on your couch nonetheless.

Your mother's hair drapes over you, her face just inches from yours. Her eyes are milky and yellow white, her lips painted black like a calavera.

"Your mother is not alive," she begins. Her voice is patient and low. She drips over you, each drop of water burning like fire.

You cannot move, though you feel your jaw trembling.

"Your mother is not dead," she adds.

Something is along your throat, but you don't see a hand.

From just out of sight you hear Marí's laugh.

"Life and death? How naïve. How senseless."

Your mother leans into you. Her breath is cold and dank along your ears.

"You're ungrateful, Moni. You never understood what I gave you. The gifts that are in your blood. How can a thing outside of life and death be subject to its rules? A petty, irrelevant concept designed to scare and subjugate children. Another way to justify cruelty."

"Y-you," you stutter.

"Yes, mija?"

While early Catholic authorities used the Virgin to recruit converts, she also took on a nationalist, revolutionary context. The Virgin featured heavily in the propaganda of Father Miguel Hidalgo's rebellion , a representation (for followers) that God favored the Mexicans over Europeans.

She remains perhaps the most prominent national icon.

Origins for "Santa Muerte," however, are far less clear and far less documented. Current scholarship suggests she is a continuation of Pre-Columbian death worship, referred to as "the sacred death." Worship of her has been condemned by the Catholic Church, and she is not officially recognized as a Saint. She is, notably, the only documented female death saint. Worship of her has grown since 2000, perhaps a response to rising internal violence and popular fiction.

"You're hurting me!"

Your voice seems weak, dying. Your mother's white eyes widen, taken aback by your honestly, wounded by the accusation. But then she laughs, so loud that the couch beneath you shakes.

"I've never done anything the world wouldn't do worse. I left the way open for you. Marí saw it and you didn't. There's so much you could do if you would just let go of your anger and blame. Your hate and your burdens weigh you down. You're still tethered to this place, and if you're not careful it will eat you alive."

"Give her back," you manage to growl.

"I'm not anyone's to give," Marí whispers softly from the corner, just out of sight. "I'm *fine*, Moni. No need to worry. No need to worry at all."

"Please—"

"No," Marí cries. "No, there's no reason to be here! The people just hurt you. They just use you. There's a way out of it, and I want you to come with us! Please, Moní. All you are is trapped in the same damn cycle. And all I want is for you to be happy. Can you do that? Can you be happy with us? Please?"

She steps into your view. Behind your mother she is not smiling. Tears are streaming down her cheeks, choking you as they drip onto your throat. She looks more whole when you last saw her, her cheeks full and fleshy, her hair combed and neat. But there's a pain there that you've never seen there before. It's breaking your heart. Snapping your ribs.

"Marí?" you mutter.

Your sister takes your hand in hers. Like your mother, she is cold. Her smile isn't carefree. It's heavy and desperate.

"Marí...she'll always hurt you."

And at this your sister breaks. Her face contorts into a mask, a thing of raw animal pain and hurt. She walks away from you, but not before casting one look back. Not before twisting that knife in your heart.

You're alone with your mother.

"I never stopped loving you, Monika." Her voice is quieter now, subdued and humbled. "I'll never stop loving you. But...I need to accept that you are doomed. Dedicated to chasing this sixth, ceaseless sun."

There's a burst of thunder, loud enough to shake everything around you. The rain pounds hard, so many drums banging against the roof and windows.

Your mother's lips tremble. Salty tears pepper her face.

When she takes your hand, you feel a slight presence of warmth beneath a layer of slick rainwater. She rubs her other hand along your face, just as gingerly as when you were a scared little girl.

"Maybe one day you'll stop hurting. Then maybe...then maybe you can come with us."

Lightning strikes the street just outside the window. The world around you goes white, brilliant and screeching.

When your sight returns, Mamá is gone. You leap up, running to the open window, slipping on the wet floor and crashing into a wall. You bleed and cry, calling back for Marí through the roaring downpour.

Outside, the city cries back.

Author's Notes: This story was written during October 2019, while I was staying in Mexico City. There are many misconceptions in the United States about our southern neighbor. There may, justifiably, be reservations about a white author from the United States telling these stories. To concerned readers, all I can offer is that I lived in the city for three months. I was welcomed and well-received. Mexico is an extremely proud nation, with a history of profound culture and innovation. For this reason, I cannot recommend enough that travelers consider forsaking the resort towns and traveling to Mexico City and visit its museums, the canals of Xochimilco and all of the beautiful castles of Parque Chapultepec. Such visits, instead of wild spring breaks in Cozumel or Cancún, might do much for common understandings between our two countries. It is my deeply held belief that a strong, prosperous, and secure Mexico would only benefit the United States.

This story is dedicated to the wonderful people who made my stay so fun. To my friends Cass and Adolfo, who took me in. To the good folks at Cervercería Monstruo de Agua, who gave me the idea of the title. To the caretakers of the Museums in Parque Chapultepec, and to Mexico City itself.

A colorful, vibrant and wonderful place unlike any other, but a place of ghosts nonetheless. A place where La Llorona stalks the canals of Xochimilco, where screams can be heard from the Templo Mayor. Where on a clear night you can hear children crying from Tía Toña's House. Where the histories of so many wars and revolutions are written into street names and murals, and where the past is never too many steps behind you.

The Last Dream of a Dying Highwayman

I

THE HIGHWAYMAN REMEMBERS the rope.

The fiery scratching along his neck. The snapping weight and searing pain that broke his spine.

The Highwayman remembers the bright green grass the day he died, the distant white mountain and the cold breeze of an untroubled, early spring. Sometimes he dreams of it, vaguely discomforted by these ghosts of indistinct, flittering memories. Brief revelations of the man he was before he came to the Dreamlands.

After all this time, he feels no closer to understanding.

He has walked amongst the will-o-wisps, battled the monstrous Gugs and chased away wave after wave of cavern-eyed ghoul. Even in this place-after-death, he has killed. Even here he hungers, going weeks without eating until raising enough gold or jewels to treat himself to a shower and meal. And even here, in the higher-towered and gold-domed cities, he finds himself lonely and wanting. Here, he imagines that, for all the splendors of this dream-after-death, he must have been a lonely man in life too. A lonely man, who probably died as quietly as he ever lived.

He sits in the tavern, only occasionally paying attention to what the Merchant tells him. Around them the mystics debate with each other, fair and clear-skinned men and women who seem to shimmer in the dying light. Scrolls along the wall dance and glow in living orange cadence with conversations, symbols and sigils springing to life as they emit a sweet, calming smoke. The patrons drink beer, sweet wine, and even whiskey that has somehow seeped its way into the Dreamlands from the Waking World.

The Merchant has routinely bought the Highwayman's services. He is a wealthy, cowardly man who has wronged far too many daemons and men to expect to live much longer without purchased pistols, swords, and men to wield them. For all of his fear, the Merchant lives comfortably in this certainty that he may die at any moment. He eats to excess, letting gristle and wine run down into his well-combed, copper-red beard. He dresses lavishly, a robe of gilded red silk hiding his protruding gut.

The Highwayman has little to say as the Merchant says his piece, and brings his bitter beer to his lips as he waits for the end of a long, drawn-out story.

"I apologize, my man!" The merchant's voice is unduly angry. "Do I bore you? Do I *bore* you with stories from the Shifting Wood? From reports of savage, angry Zoogs eating travelers alive?"

The Highwayman sighs.

"Merchant," he sights, "this is only a place of the same stories. Angry monsters. Evil gods. Travelling warlocks, kidnappers and ritual sacrifices. You learn to live with the stories."

"Then," the Merchant laughs incredulously, "you are aware of the Crawling Chaos? The Cult of the Greater Dreamer? That they have been reported to be in this very town?"

The Highwayman reaches into his coat and pulls out a long, ornate knife. The blade is silver, gleaming orange in tavern-torch light. It is an impractical, serpent-curved weapon, designed only to inspire fear in the ignorant. Its black leather handle ends in an emblem, the face of the great-dragon dreamer, tentacles falling off in silver streams beneath it.

"For all the Cult's bluster, 'the Greater Dream' is only made of men. Men who think they're right, that they've got *power*. But Merchant, if they ever had power, *they've got less of it now*. Got into a bit of a scuffle with three of them. They wanted my life, but I wanted it more."

The Merchant's eyes go wide as he runs his fingers along the blade. No doubt he already has an offer, a buyer in mind.

"What can I offer you for this, Warrior?"

The Highwayman shakes his head. "Take it as a promise. My regular fee, maybe a bonus when we get you through the Shifting Woods."

The smile writhes across his face like so many greedy grave-worms.

The Merchant wraps his fat fingers around the blade and withdraws it into his coat. He pulls out a purple sack the size of an apple and places it gently before the Highwayman. The Highwayman lifts it into his palm and scoffs.

"For your bonus," the Merchant smiles wider, "And your loyalty."

The Highwayman waves the merchant away. "Just be ready tomorrow morning."

And the Merchant departs, retreating into the crowd, and slowly makes his way out the door. The Highwayman stays behind, watching beads of water slide down his shimmering glass. The tavern fills with finely dressed women, men and demons, winged things with cosmic glittering eyes. A young priestess raises her glass to the Crawling Chaos. A roaring affirmation follows. Some drunken prince from far away mounts his table and begins to sing. The whooping and hollering becomes too much, and the Highwayman places a large gold coin on the counter and leaves.

Outside the world is getting colder and clearer. Soft winds carry chime-laughter from open windows, thick with the scents of thousand-lilac-and-cherry perfume. Beneath bright blue stars he brings a wooden pipe to his lips. He knows he was a smoker in life, but there's no tobacco in the Dreamlands. The closest thing he can find sometimes induces a deep, untroubled sleep and smells like mountain mornings after a long storm.

"Excuse me, sir?"

The Highwayman turns and looks up.

The speaker is a tall man, with wide shoulders and a friendly, wary face. He wears plain, simple black clothing and a heavy coat for the coming cold.

"My—my name is—"

"Stop."

The Highwayman isn't sure what possesses him to help this stranger. Perhaps it's his friendly face, or perhaps the smoke still curling out from the corners of the Highwayman's mouth and the already pleasant humming in his mind.

"You must not be from here. Names have a power here. To know a man's name is to own a part of him."

"What am I to call you then, sir, if not your name?"

"Call me what I am: a highwayman."

The speaker does not change his confused look, but nods nonetheless.

"And what are you, son?"

The speaker grimaces and looks to the starry sky. "It is strange how the simplest questions can be the most challenging. I am a learned dreamer, and have been to this place before. Though, evidently not so often as to be as learned as yourself. I am a man, of this I am sure. I *do* have a trade, though I certainly do not believe it defines me. I suppose— "

"You're a *talker*," the Highwayman groans.

"I suppose I'm a 'poet.' Yes, I suppose *that* would be where most of my meaning lies."

"And can I help you with something, *Poet*?"

"I...I heard you will be traveling through the shifting woods. That you've fought off the Cult of the Greater Dreamer?"

"Eavesdropping's a dangerous habit here."

"No, I-I'm sorry." The Poet looks at the ground and gathers his thoughts. "There's somewhere I need to be. Somewhere beyond the Shifting Woods."

"There are many places 'beyond the Shifting Woods.'"

"I must beg your patience, *Highwayman*. You are correct to guess that I am not from here. I was not aware anyone could be *from* the Dreamlands. I don't know why I'm here, to be as straightforward as I may. But if you allow me to buy you another drink, I'd appreciate an opportunity to tell you my story."

The Highwayman shakes his head. "I've had my fill of drinks and stories. But if you walk with me, I might be inclined to listen."

Like so many other dreamers, the Poet does not remember how he first slipped into the Dreamlands. He had heard stories about it before, from a circle of like-minded poets and writers who probed the greater meaning of their world. He once had friends who vanished, who after smoking hashish to find this place never returned to the waking world. The Poet did not smoke, he swore, but found himself in the Dreamlands all the same. But the Poet sought out his friends, perhaps naively, announcing that he was an artist from the Waking World.

It had been a grave mistake.

"We have been aware for some time now of an organization exploiting creative minds in the Waking World. People killed, disappeared, exploited for their artistic talent to channel some fanatics' dark God into our world. At first I believed it a myth, that these violent fools were pursuing some fiction. I never imagined that this organization had an arm, a counterpart in the Dreamlands."

And by announcing himself, the Poet had made himself a target.

He found himself kidnapped, atop an altar of snakes and tentacles. The cult had burst into his rooms. Killed the attendant of the inn he was staying in and several of the guests as well. They placed a black hood over him and bound his wrists.

On that altar the emerald idol of Cthulhu seemed more terrifying, more voracious than any living monster could be. And there, the poet made his peace with death.

The poet stops his story.

"What do you know about witches?" he asks.

"Not too much," the Highwayman replies, curiosity and memory stirring in him alike. "I've fought a few. Loved a few. They're fairly common here."

And the poet smiles wistfully.

"There is nothing 'common' about this woman."

In his story the poet is saved by a maelstrom, a howling storm that raises the cultists into the air, dashing them against rocks and impaling them on trees. And from the storm descends a woman, clad in swirling darkness and stars. He trembles before her, uncertain and afraid.

But she merely smiles at him, and plants a kiss upon his forehead.

"I woke then. But she has saved me…again and again she has saved me. And now…now I cannot wake up. I sleep here, and I wake *here*. I have not returned to the Waking World, and I do not know why."

He reaches into his black coat pocket and removes a purse, thrusting it toward the Highwayman.

"I do not have much, but I will give you everything I have to cross the shifting woods. *She* must have the answers, and I must return to her."

The Highwayman considers the purse.

"You say this woman saves you, has saved you, whenever you're in danger? If you're thinking that going through the woods is going to get you into trouble and, I don't know, *summon* her—"

"I am not trying to place you in danger, sir!"

At this the Highwayman laughs. "Son, please. Cause enough trouble and you're *always* in danger."

"Will you help me, then?"

"Yes. But." The Highwayman turns away from the purse and up towards the Poet's eyes. "You've got to give something a bit more valuable than gold. There's a power in names here, and a greater power in songs. Make something up about me. Sing it in taverns. We'll call it even."

"I—"

"You'll have time to write it on the way, Poet. Just be ready tomorrow morning. I'm picking the merchant up outside the central market. Be there and you can hitch a ride too."

The Poet offers a profuse thanks and the Highwayman, giving in to the smoke from his pipe, offers a smile before walking away.

II

The Highwayman again dreams of his noose. He dreams of angry voices and cruel laughter. He dreams of a tall white mountain and a green field of grass. He dreams of a fear, not for himself but for someone else. And in the dream, he seems sure, certain that dying will be worth it.

When he wakes the world is quiet. From his tower room the pre-dawn world wafts in an unkind cold. He moves to his baths, and wipes away the thick, frosty sweat from his nightmares. He does not always remember. Does not always *dream*. But sleeping often makes him more tired, more exhausted than living ever could.

Cleaned to his satisfaction, he dons his coat. Then his saber and pistols.

Completely dressed, he readies his caravan. Two sleek-black horses whom he has never named. A covered wagon and two trunks of food and clothing. He mounts the front and takes the reins in his hands, gently guiding his horses through the sleeping city and toward the main street.

The Merchant and the Poet both await him. The Merchant seems impatient, arms crossed across flowing yellow robes and face contorted into a sour-worm frown. The Poet seems nervous, his eyes drawn to a rifle slung across the Highwayman's back.

"I thought you said this journey would be safe, Highwayman," the Poet protests, somewhat meekly.

"And *I* had thought our journey would be a *quiet* one," the Merchant retorts, not waiting for a reply as he climbs into the back of the wagon.

"The Cult may kill you in the city, or the Zoogs may kill you in the woods. Either is *possible*," the Highwayman muses out loud. "Best to be prepared."

The Poet does not consider this for long, and scrambles after the Merchant into the covered wagon.

It is not long before the city fades behind them and the pink-red sun creeps from across the sea. The birds begin to wake and sing behind them and the looming deep greens of the forest rise before them. Beyond them rolling green-yellow fields, thick with poppies and faerie pads, shimmer in the gilded morning light.

The Highwayman relishes these moments, their quiet and their beauty. He takes a drink of cool water, and lets his mind wonder from the rolling, roaring snores of the Merchant behind him.

But the Poet seems restless, and after scratching a pen across a notepad for hours ventures to the front. There he seems to absorb the world, watching it all with an unblinking, awed gaze.

When the Poet finally speaks, his voice is low and peaceful.

"You asked me for a song. A tribute."

The Highwayman says nothing.

"I was hoping that you might tell me more of yourself. More of your *story*."

The Highwayman is not sure what to say. There is so much he does not know, or does not remember. In the Dreamlands he has been a mercenary, a bodyguard, a soldier, and a lawman. He has fought off marauding barbarians, serpent-scaled pirates from lunar shores, danced and loved with a soft-lipped incarnation of the Crawling Chaos. But none of this seems to answer the question of *who* or *what* he is.

But then, as always, the Highwayman remembers the rope.

"I am only a wraith. Just another lonely dead man."

The poet sits in silence for a moment, unsure if to press further or forget the issue entirely. Ultimately, he returns to his pen, occasionally whispering meter under his breath.

More of the world passes over them. The sun rises higher, wide and yellow behind them. The forests come closer, a thick pine-fog weaving behind stark brown-and-black trunks. The Highwayman breathes in again. The air is wet and cold, marsh and floral decay melding into the all-too familiar smell of the Shifting Woods.

The path they take was forged by learned sorcerers and dreamers, who managed to subdue the ever-changing geography of the forests with arcane symbols and enormous sacrifices. While the forest around it would change, the path should always be there, wide enough for two wagons to pass through.

The Highwayman leans back and tries to peer to the top of the trees as the sky gradually grays.

The Shifting Wood is filled of the sounds of bats, enormous crimson-winged things that sleep hanging from low branches. Birds land in the higher branches, swooping down only catch the black millipedes crawling through rotting leaves and branches. The Highwayman's eyes do not rise high from the ground. The horses have travelled this path before and are undisturbed by any change. But the Zoogs could rise from their tree-hollows at any moment. It is true that the Highwayman has made a pact with them before, that he has been in the Dreamlands long enough to know how to make his peace with them.

He moves to the back of the wagon and opens a trunk. He reaches for a long candle and a box of matches, and the Merchant remaining sleeping all the while. The Highwayman fits the candle into an ebony holder and moves back to the front. When he lights it, it emits a brilliant blue flame and the strong scent of the cool-salt ocean.

"Zoogs," he speaks out loud to the poet, "have sight and smell that far surpasses yours or mine. They'll recognize this color and smell. I got it from an elder Zoog after my last fight with them. It'll guarantee us uninterrupted passage…if they can be trusted to keep their promises."

"And if they cannot?" the Poet asks. "They're a clever, carnivorous species, not known for any kindness towards men."

The Highwayman shrugs. "Not much is clever enough to outrun a bullet."

They continue on. The Merchant has awoken behind them, shifting in the wagon and yawning loudly as he smacks his fat, wet lips.

"Where are we?" he asks.

Before the Highwayman answers, a tree snaps. A wide, thick trunk crashes to the ground across the path. The horses scream, kick up and thrash in their reins. The Highwayman draws his rifle and looks to the ground. Zoogs move slowly and carefully, but he's long known how to see them in plain sight.

Only the ground is still. The brown leaves and wet dirt are undisturbed.

Another loud snap.

The Highwayman's sights turn to the forest. At first, he sees only a cluster of pale trees and briars. A thin, skeletal cropping that had not been there only moments before. But the trees move, and the Highwayman sees it distinctly.

The monster has the frame of a man, tall, pale and frail, with sickly thinning muscle. Crouched carefully, it would blend in as a dying tree or bush if it didn't breathe. Its long fingers come up from black dirt; its chest rises from its knees. In the gray sky it sways uneasily, rising up to the middle of the highest trees. Its breath is fast, raspy and loud.

It turns its face towards them. Emaciated, sharp nose and pointed ears. Its baldness only makes its eyes more yellow and its lips more red.

The figure smiles, almost on the verge of a laugh. Rows of jagged teeth are still wet and shining with gore.

The Highwayman reaches for his gun.

The nightmare recedes back into the forest, its joints cracking and snapping with the wings as it clings so tightly to the trunks of the trees that it becomes invisible.

The Merchant sighs.

And the wagon is torn above him.

The Highwayman is launched from his seat. He lands on his back, groaning as he turns to fire up. The horses are gone, straying from the path and straight into the woods. It's not long before their screaming turns into panic, crying out so loudly as something lifts them from the ground and laughs. Their crying becomes an echo.

The wagon wood is ripped, turned into tatters and splinters by long white hands with thick yellow claws. Two of them have the merchant in their hands, as if they are children pulling at a toy.

The Merchant does not even manage a scream before the monsters split him in pieces, taking their wet portions to their mouths and biting in deeply as if he were nothing more than fruit leather.

The Highwayman shoots once, runes along the barrel of his pistol glimmering with green fire as bullets kissed by succubae and naiads bury into a white shoulder. The wounded creature screams, howling out as a black-crimson mist spills from its body. The Highwayman shakes himself up. The Poet is beside him, stammering and frightened.

"Come now!"

He lifts the Poet up, still in a haze but sprinting forward, nonetheless. The chittering laughter of the creatures and the wet smacking of their lips grow quieter behind them. But around them all the trees seem pale, and the only sounds to rise above their own heart beats are roars and snapping trees.

For a moment the Highwayman stops, grabbing the Poet by his shoulders.

"Here!"

He reaches into a holster at his side, and thrusts another pistol, less blessed and less potent, into the Poet's shaking hands. The Poet regards the weapon with unease.

"I've never shot one of these before."

"And if you don't *now*, you're not likely to get much in the way of another chance."

The two move slower now. The ancient path is no longer viable, overwhelmed and overtaken horrors the Highwayman has never seen before. The Highwayman's heard stories before, about monks who have gone made in their efforts to map the Shifting Woods. About trees who walk. Rivers that rise up from the earth only to vanish the following day. Of carnivorous swamps with rows of jagged teeth just beneath their quicksand.

It had been easier with the Zoogs.

Behind them, a branch breaks.

The face peering through the trees is wide and pale, nearly translucent in the thick grey daylight. Bald, slicked with sweat and smiling to reveal a set of long, jagged fangs.

The monster pushes back the branches and peers down at them.

The Highwayman fires from his rifle.

A black plume of gore rises up from its eye.

Enraged, the giant swats at the ground below. The Poet fires back, aiming for the other eye. A hand comes down on the Highwayman's chest and he rises through the air. He lands against a dry tree, snapping its trunk and sailing to the dirt beneath.

His head is buzzing. His vision is blurry.

Somewhere he knows the Poet is crying out, still firing and still fighting. But there are thick splinters in the Highwayman's side. Blood is making his clothes heavy and wet.

When he sees the shadows coming down from the tops of the trees, he believes he is finally dying. That a gentler darkness than the Dreamlands has come to take him away from the memories of the noose and the distant, impassive white mountain.

But something licks his hands. Something crawls onto his chest, something warm and light. The Highwayman wipes his sweat and tears away.

The cat is green-eyed and smiling. It places a single white paw on his side, whispering magic in a sacred, secret language.

From the trees, the cats pour on to the giant, cascading from branches and leaping through the air to bury their claws into its back. The monster roars, attempting to claw at its back as the cats work their way up towards its neck. They bite in, howling and meowing as the giant crashes to the forest floor.

The cats scatter quickly once the body falls, shooting out in quick battle formation.

Somewhere in the forests, more giants are screaming.

The green-eyed cat nuzzles the Highwayman's hand, purring softly.

But above him the trees break again. Red eyes snarl down on him.

The cat is curled on his chest, oblivious to the claws coming down for it.

The Highwayman takes the cat to his chest and rolls over.

The pain along his back is blinding and searing.

III

In the dream the men with the noose ask him if he has any last words.

He spits at them.

They laugh and hit him in his stomach.

"Hurts, don't it?"

He laughs too.

"Not for much longer."

One of them smiles, leering at him through the rope's loop.

"Don't worry, we'll get her next."

The Highwayman wakes with deep, panicked breathing. The cat on his chest yowls and launches in fright, meowing off the bed and into a torch-lit hall. He looks around. Stone walls, a thick blanket above him. His side has been cleaned; his wound dressed.

His clothes are neatly folded at the foot of the bed. He dresses himself carefully, still wincing and shuddering with pain.

He follows the scent of cooking meat down the hall.

The Poet is sitting at a small table, a steaming bowl of brown soup in front of him. The cat sitting on the table is regal and long-haired, black with a streak of white from his chin to his belly. It turns to the Highwayman with stern green eyes.

"You should keep resting."

His voice is deep, but the Highwayman waves him off.

"I'm not much of one for sleeping in an unfamiliar place. Even less when I don't know who's care I've entered into."

"I am Remo," the cat responds, "Brigadier General of the seventh brigade in the army of our Ulthar Empire."

"Excuse me," the Poet interjects been slurps of soup, "but my friend tells me that there is danger in saying one's name here. That 'to know a man's name is to own a part of him.'"

Remo laughs, "And who would be brave enough to 'own' a cat? Your friend clings to an old superstition, unduly afraid of the world as all men are."

"Ulthar *Empire*?" the Highwayman responds, eager to change the subject away from himself, "Y'all expanding?"

Remo's eyes look down to the table. For a moment he seems sad, or wistful. But when his eyes turn upward again, from the Poet to the Highwayman again, they are burning.

"By *necessity*, yes. Our wars with the Zoogs were long ones, to be sure…but those creatures you saw…they've *devastated* the natural order of this place. They wiped out the Zoogs, and for a long time had no natural predators, until they expanded into the Black Mountains, the borders of Leng and the of night-gaunts and Gugs. Now Ulthar hunts down the remnants, wiping them out so they cannot further damage this world."

"What are they?" the Highwayman asks.

"Nightmares. The manifestation of some trauma in the Waking World. Tell me"—Remo turns to the poet—"how does the Waking World farc?"

"Hate. Constant disease and sickness. And war." The poet's eyes drift past the cat and towards an empty space. "A war unlike any other."

"That explains it, then," Remo nods. "These nightmares, like so many before them, will pass."

Remo turns to the Highwayman. "You're a sad man, aren't you?"

"I just don't much like cats, is all!" the Highwayman yells back. "I had *dogs* back in the Waking World. Good, loyal things that had enough goddamn sense to not sneak up on an armed man!"

"An armed man who," the cat meows, "so dislikes cats that he risks his own death for a cat whose name he never even learned?"

The Highwayman scoffs. "I've died before. Didn't take then."

"Yes...I know."

"You *know*?"

"We cats are the greatest dreamers. Are renowned for it. To save your life, one of my colonels had to commune with your own dreaming. You have...a long story."

"First I've heard of it."

"Wit will get you far. Your sword will get you farther. But only so far still. You're like so many other men. A stranger to peace. And I'm afraid that you're in for no small amount of suffering if you continue down this road without stopping and looking in."

"Horseshit."

"Shouldn't you at least hear him out?" the Poet interjects. "Not only did he save your life, but, Highwayman...if I am truly to write a song for you, it really would help if you could tell me more—"

"If you want to talk, talk to the goddamned cat! I'm going to go back to bed!"

The Highwayman turns away before either the cat or the Poet can respond. Cats *always* try to test him. He wouldn't bow or worship them like other people would, so they would just *play* with him. Poke and prod him with the knowledge that if he so much as simply hit one of them that it would be the same as declaring war with all of Ulthar.

The Ulthar *Empire.*

He is going to rest. He is going to rest and then he is going to go back to the city.

"Did you really mean it, Christopher?"

He stops.

The cat at his feet is black and white, like Remo. But his fur is smooth. His paws are white, and his voice is high and soft.

"Do you really not like cats?"

"Don't…say my name," the Highwayman growls.

"I'm sorry, Chr—sir. You saved me from the Loomers, is all. I saw into your heart, your dreams. Into your life and…well, you're a *good person*, is all."

The Highwayman considers the animal for a moment. It seems to smile at him, with wide green eyes and soft purring.

Then he keeps walking.

"You're acting like you wish you were dead," the cat sadly calls after him.

The Highwayman does not turn.

"You would be no good to her, dead."

As a thunderclap, he remembers.

He turns to this cat, bewildered. "You…have we met before?"

"Maybe, sir," the cat meekly offers. "We cats are the most prodigious of dreamers, always walking between so many lives and so many worlds. I do feel, I *do* feel that I met you before you saved my life."

The Highwayman pauses, caught off guard. Then he smiles, the lightness on his face welcome and familiar.

"No need to thank me for that, partner."

The cat offers something between a yawn and a smile, exposing the pinkness of its gums and tongue.

"'Partner,' yes, sir. Yes, I believe 'partner' sounds very familiar. Perhaps one of many names I have once wore."

"And what name do you wear here, what do they call you in Ulthar?"

"Colonel Lawrence, sir. And you may call me 'Lawrence.'"

"Well, Lawrence." The Highwayman almost finds himself chuckling, despite the anger and indignation he felt only moments ago. "I don't dislike cats all that much, no. Your…your General is right. I'm scared, is all. I'm sorry if I hurt your feelings."

"She had a cat, didn't she?"

"Yes," he softly replies. "A little man not unlike yourself. Always looked like he was dressed up, ready to go somewhere important-like."

The Highwayman stands up straight, uncomfortable and uneasy.

"I remembered her name…for the first time since I came to the Dreamlands, I remembered her name. Was that you?"

"Yes," Lawrence replies coolly. "You saved my life, sir, I only want to return your kindness as best I could. Would you…would you like to remember her more?"

"Yes. Please."

And with that the Highwayman retreats to his room, lying on a bed and petting a curled Lawrence, gently carried to sleep by purrs.

The Highwayman dreams of deep brown eyes above a wide, white smile. She has dark skin, smooth fingers that interlace with his own as they watch a dancing child. The child scoops up dandelion seeds, creating a cloud as wild and beautiful as her bouncing, curly hair. The woman at his side laughs at her daughter, who looks so much like her that the Highwayman's heart hurts from happiness and hope.

The Highwayman dreams of a witch and their Waking World. A woman who could talk to mice, who whispered good secrets to them from the foot of her bed. Good secrets, shared with friends, made the world better. This was her most potent, simplest magic. She talks with her cat too, and sometimes the Highwayman thinks that the little creature can understand him as well as his witch. It treats him as a welcome guest in their home, following from a distance until he sits down. Sometimes it even jumps on his lap, and accepts slow, tender scratches along its head.

The Highwayman dreams of many visits with the witch and her daughter. Of catching glimpses of secret lessons between mother and daughter. The art of healing. The art of whispers. The simplicity and profundity of secret, unclaimed kindness.

The Highwayman dreams of a sickness. A thing that rides the mayflies and sucks all the light from the world. The witch in the Waking World fights, but she sheds her weight as if it is being squeezed from her. She thins and flattens before him, and the Highwayman comes to believe that some invisible vampire is growing swollen and fat at her neck. The cat vanishes one day, and the witch's daughter, now a witch herself, refuses to eat.

The Highwayman dreams of a cold, trembling hand interlaced with his own. Of fading brown eyes, and a still, calm smile.

The Highwayman dreams of holding the witch's daughter, of hugging her tightly and running his fingers through her hair as she sobs. The Highwayman dreams. And it is sad, it is hard, and it is pleasant all at once.

"Was she *your* daughter?" Lawrence asks as the Highwayman stirs.

"In all but blood, yes. She was mine." The Highwayman is somber now, hurting and healing from his long remembrance sleep.

"I loved her mother, but she had that little girl before they met me. Heh." The Highwayman smiles. "Why, I reckon she ain't 'little' anymore. When I died…she had nineteen years on her. I…I died protecting her. Didn't I?"

"Yes," Lawrence answers.

"Did…was I successful? Is she—"

"I don't know, Christopher. I'm sorry. I'm so sorry."

The Highwayman sighs, lifting himself up as Lawrence scatters off his chest.

"Don't be sorry, friend. You've helped me. More than I ever thought I could be."

"You don't regret it? The knowing and hurt?"

"Nossir. No, I don't."

IV

The Highwayman and the Poet grow restless and uncomfortable in the fortress of the cats of Ulthar. Unused to being powerless, the

Highwayman only bitterly obeys General Remo's orders for bedrest after Lawrence follows with pitiful, mewling pleas.

There are other cats in the fortress, soldiers charged with beating back the Looming nightmares and restoring some tranquility to the Shifting Woods. They are proficient hunters who bring back deer meat, mice and birds for the Poet to cook. Whatever other vocations the Poet had in the Waking World, the Highwayman suspects that cook was not one of them. The meat is bland, tough and dry.

"What you need," the Highwayman tells him one day, "is a child. You can't be a bad cook, not when you've got a picky eater in the house."

"Your daughter, she was picky?"

"Oh gods, yes," the Highwayman laughs. "And her mama couldn't cook."

"Warrior, mercenary," the Poet grins, "*cook*. Is there anything else you want added to your song, Highwayman? Any title you've held that you're particularly proud of?"

The Highwayman does not hesitate. "Father."

In the long days ahead, they speak further. The Highwayman tells his stories, and the Poet writes his song. The Highwayman promises, unbidden, that he will continue on with the Poet once he is recovered. That they will reach the Poet's sorceress.

"I died once, trying to do the right thing," the Highwayman explains. "I reckon I'm up to it again."

"What does it mean?" the Poet wonders aloud, "To die here, in a place like this?"

"Probably not much. Not unless you *make* it mean something."

On the day they leave the forest, they are followed by an escort of nine cat soldiers, jumping and along the branches.

"Highwayman," General Remo calls out from above.

"You may not always like cats. We are teasing creatures, who find great amusement in playing with lesser things. But you are good, and you are kind. For this reason, know that you are always welcome in Ulthar. You need only announce that you are a friend and welcome guest of General Remo, and you shall be treated as an honored visitor in any Ulthar home."

"Maybe one day," the Highwayman calls upward, "maybe when this world is back to normal, I can get around to visiting."

"Please visit, Christopher," Lawrence pleads above. "Please remember to visit your old friend."

"Alright," the Highwayman smiles. "I promise."

They are left at the edge of the shifting woods, emerging into a plain of tall, yellow grass. Ahead of them, rising in the steep distance, are the black mountains before the plateau of Leng, onyx and gleaming with snow beneath a brilliant blue sky.

"You feel good about that?" The Highwayman motions to the gun holster the poet now wears at his side.

"No, if I'm to be honest." The Poet sighs.

"Good," the Highwayman says. "No man should get too comfortable in a habit of spending bullets. But they should be ready to."

They intend to walk to the nearest town, the nearest *human* city. There, they will inquire about the sorceress, her nature and her location. The Highwayman says he will continue on with the Poet until they find her, and reaffirms this commitment along their journey.

"But what will you do after that, Highwayman?" the Poet asks one night, as skewered and crudely seasoned rats sizzle above a crackling fire.

The stars in the Dreamlands are unlike those in the Waking World. There is more color to them, not only glimmering-diamond white but brilliant sapphire blues, ruby reds and deep amethyst purples. They cluster and swirl, forming constellations wholly different than those he once mapped out with a woman and young girl as they lay under the Rocky Mountain sky.

"I suppose," the Highwayman muses, "I'll keep living. And your sorceress." He pauses. "You think she'll send you back?"

"I…I hope so."

"If she does"—the Highwayman sits himself upright and looks intently at the Poet—"I want you to promise me something."

"Surely."

"You're from a time far ahead of the one I left, I've gathered that much already. But I want you to go back, I want you to find my daughter's grave. And…" The Highwayman swallows. "I want you scatter some dandelion seeds. Will…will you do that for me?"

The Poet nods, and through the orange fire the Highwayman can see the smoke in his eyes. "Assuredly, friend Highwayman. I promise you."

The Highwayman wakes to a pale green light.

In it he can see the Poet, alert and pistol in hand.

The Highwayman rises quickly to his feet, hand immediately on his holster.

Around them the will-o-wisps move slowly, great floating masses of light that drift as balls of swirling fog. The field in which they rested is now full of the wisps, forming a perimeter around both the Highwayman and the Poet.

"I've heard," the Poet hisses through gritted teeth, "that if a wisp passes through you, it takes a year of your life."

"I've heard that too," the Highwayman whispers back. "Fairytales, but that's not what I'm worried about.

"I've traveled a lot. Seen my share of wisps. Usually, they're aimless, drifting with the wind. I've never seen them circle anything, let alone people. And," he adds, "I've never seen them glow *green*."

The Highwayman unsheathes his sword and makes a small cut across his palm. He bloodies the blade, which sparks and hums with a deep purple light. A gift from the Crawling Chaos herself. Wetted and fed on blood, the sword can now cut beings both corporal and ethereal.

A wisp lunges at the Poet. The creature goes solid just as it rams into the Poet's chest, knocking the pistol from his hand and sending him to the ground. It expands, a murky and heavy puddle of slime, covering the Poet's arms and legs.

The Highwayman dashes through the remains of their fire, kicking up ash and embers in his wake.

The tip of the sword is enough to burn, enough to force the creature to phase back to a mist.

But only in vain.

As it rises, the Highwayman cuts upward, cleaving the wisp in two as it evaporates and whimpers into cold, falling dew.

Another charges him from behind, knocking the air from his chest as it rams into his back.

The Highwayman tastes blood just behind his teeth.

The wisp congeals around him, weighing down his wrists and legs. He feels split and burning along his ribs, the green slime twisting heavily to break him slowly.

The Poet is shooting, though the Highwayman can't tell if his timing is careful enough to wound the wisps as they turn solid.

A pop, and the Highwayman screams.

"Enough."

The voice is low and commanding. The wisp breaking the Highwayman's back becomes weightless, lifting into the air. But the Highwayman is spent. Hurt and broken. He does not know what he can and cannot move. He is far too disoriented by the pain to try.

When human hands lift him by his armpits he cries, tears stinging the corner of his eyes as they force their way out.

The Poet feels a long, curved knife at his throat. The wisps now hover above them, merging in a sick green haze that emits a foul, fetid odor. In this infected light the Highwayman can make out his sword, his pistols on the ground, and the fell figures in black cloaks around them. Their hoods down, the Highwayman sees them as they are, thin, starving, pale and cavern-eyed.

The Highwayman is not afraid. But he *is* angry.

Angry that out of all the things that could kill him, it might be these men. These foolish, craven men who paw at the end of the world, high on their hopes for an apocalypse that would have consequences well beyond themselves.

"You." The cloaked man with the knife at the Poet's throat addresses the Highwayman through filed teeth and self-mutilated tongue. "You are the one who killed our brother. I smell his death on you."

The Highwayman attempts to wheeze out a response, but a fist in his already shattered ribs sears away all thoughts and words.

He buckles to his knees.

The Poet, large and broad-shouldered himself, wrenches himself free and grabs the knife from his captor's hands. Used to slaughtering men who are drugged and subdued, the pale starving followers of the Greater Dreamer are not ready to fight two warriors, wounded and tired though they are.

But with a wet whistle, they command a sickened wisp. The creature knocks the Poet before the Highwayman and pins him down. The Poet screams as the same chorus of pain suffered by the Highwayman only moments before is visited on him.

"Yours would have been a merciful death, Soft Dreamer," the same cultist addresses the poet. "As gentle a slit-throat sleep as the one so enjoyed by the Greater Dreamer in his sunken home. But your chorus, your screams, will join this murderer's.

The Highwayman does not understand the words, the croaks emitting from the swollen throats of these frail men. Panicked and immobile, only a few reach him.

"Cthulhu."

"R'lyeh."

The Highwayman attempts to crawl, to scream and flee. But the best he can do is wiggle.

"Prostrate worm," a voice breaks from the chant. "Murderer. *Heretic*. We will send your torment to the Greater Dreamer; we will send your screams. We will send your crying. And they will be so loud, so strained that you will *wake him!*"

Perhaps it is a stone, or the handle of a blade, that comes down across the back of the Highwayman's head. All he knows is he only feels it for a moment.

Then, he is gone.

The darkness in this place is absolute.

Somewhere in the distance a cat, or some poor creature, is yowling. The scream is animal, pained, as if flesh is being pulled slowly from its bones.

When he steps, he is unsure of his direction. Is he moving flatly, across a floor? Along a wall? One moment the surface beneath him is solid and strong, then loose and liquid. He slips, his leg submerged in something unknown and frigid.

He has brought all of his hurt with him, wherever he is. He claws upward to avoid sinking into those unseen depths, breathing heavily as he shivers and weeps.

The animal screaming continues, undisturbed or uninterested in any suffering other than its own.

The Highwayman wanders, for days or for hours.

In some time he begins to see, though no light has disturbed the geography of this hell. Obscenely floating inverted ebon pyramids, looming as eyes and obelisks above him. Sheets of tearing ice as far as the eye can see. The long, pantomime scream echoing within it all.

Nothing to eat. No sleep to be had. And yet the Highwayman does not die. Nor does he even tire. He only hurts, shivering, burning, echoing, and bleeding.

But he does not stop moving. Not even when his knees lock up and he is forced to crawl.

His mind dwells on the ice beneath him, on the dark waters beneath it. He knows what is down there, what hateful God lurks beneath. And when it finally opens its eye, it burns in a color the Highwayman has never seen before. He screams then. He screams and he cannot stop.

The eye seems to consider him, perhaps angry, indifferent, or bored. Then another opens. And another. Through sheets of ice the Highwayman's whole world becomes blinded. If there was still enough of him left to form a thought, he would miss the darkness that had so cruelly blinded him when he first arrived. Now he can see everything.

And the sight is flaying him alive.

A streak of darkness, not unlike a storm-cloud trail, cuts into the light below. Then another, until stripes of merciful blackness envelop all the light below. Tendrils gently raise him from the ice, above the fading black pyramids and away from the eternal screaming below.

Somewhere he hears the desperate voice of a familiar friend.

But finally, at long last, the Highwayman is sleeping peacefully.

V

The Sorceress exacts her revenge as she rescues her Poet. She descends from the sky as a torrent of wind and black rain, cutting and rending into the cultists with such immediate and absolute savagery that the Poet must stare at her through a red cloud. Released from their hold, the wisps turn a soft white and, seemingly regretful of their actions, linger to hold vigil over the Highwayman.

In this dying light, the Poet finds him old. So much older than when they first met all those years ago. His salt-and-pepper beard seems jet white beneath the pink and red of his blood. He calls out to him, shaking his shoulders and using his name.

The Highwayman's eyes are open but quivering, focused on some far away horrors.

"They sent him to R'lyeh!" the Sorceress calls out.

From her storm-cloud robe she withdraws a gilded bag. She pours its contents on to the Highwayman's face, a thick yellow powder that cakes his frightened features.

"To call him back," she explains to her Poet, though he hadn't even thought to ask.

The Poet beholds her. Her black hair shimmers beneath the will-o-wisps, her red lips are pursed in concern. For a moment of blissful selfishness, they are the only two creatures in existence.

"Who are you?" The question wells up involuntarily from his stomach, forcing its way past his throat and lips.

The Sorceress stops for a moment, turning her green eyes to her Poet with a sad, soft smile.

"Do you really not understand? After all you have been through?"

The Highwayman groans, and the Sorceress turns her attention towards him.

"In this world and in all worlds, there are relationships such as ours. The creator and their inspiration. The inspiration, and their architect. Life and life-givers. You are my Poet, and I am your muse."

The Poet beholds his Sorceress in awe. Somehow, he finds "muse" inadequate.

But she is too occupied with the dying man beneath her to notice that the Poet has fallen in love. And the Poet, eyes falling on his dying friend, does not know that his Sorceress has already loved her Poet for such a long time and for forever still.

"It is no good," the Sorceress cries as she swats the Highwayman's cheek. "The Dreamer has claimed his life."

"There's *nothing* we can do?"

"A muse can shape and color the world, a poet can give this form and color meaning. We are," she takes his hand in hers, "a connection between our dreaming and waking worlds. A perfect, beautiful channel between the realms.

"I"—she turns to the Highwayman—"I can send one man across the channel. But only once, and only one."

And wordlessly, the Poet understands his muse.

The Highwayman wakes to the rope. It scratches and crawls along his neck, weight pulling at the top of his spine. A tall white mountain looms in the distance. Bright green grass sways under an untroubled spring wind.

The men in front of him laugh at his writhing, at his attempts to claw through the rope and rescue his throat.

"We'll get her next, you old bastard," one of them swears. "This is what you get for protecting a witch that don't mean nothin' to you."

The word splits beneath gunshots. The men in front of him buckle beneath their spilt skulls.

The rope above him snaps.

Hands are on him, pulling at the noose and moving gently through his hair.

Through his tears, the Highwayman blinks and stares into deep brown eyes beneath wild, dandelion hair.

Author's Notes: Though I never finished it, I admit to taking a lot of inspiration for this story from Philip José Farmer's "Riverworld" stories. The first release of *Whiskey and Other Unusual Ghosts* had no Lovecraftian stories, and I'm sure there will be purists who deride my version of the Dreamlands as a place whose ecosystem is intimately tied to the Waking World.

This story was written in the early days of the COVID pandemic, and there's something to be said about writing an adventure with your friends. The story features a certain talkative poet, a certain sorceress, a certain cat named "Larry" and, of course, the estimable General Remo. A big thanks to K.A. Opperman and Ashley Dioses for being part of this story, and big ones too for Matthew Bartlett and S.P. Miskowski for letting me use their cats.

I hope that this is not the last story with the Highwayman I write. I grew a certain fondness for Christopher's tenderness and his honesty. He'll be back again, and again, and again.

Afterword

WHISKEY AND OTHER Unusual Ghosts has been fomenting for years. It began with conversations with friends, those bored "What are your hopes and dreams?" on back porches. Purple Texas skies. Cold beers. It was a dream I had given up, on more than one occasion. I only kept going because there were people with me every step of the way.

At their core, these are stories about hauntings. Things that leave long and lasting scars on the characters navigating their ruthless and unfortunate world. The past, loneliness, and addiction. These are more terrifying to me than any demon or monster. They can come to define someone, to set them on a path of self-destruction that ends in one horrific moment of self-realization.

One brief revelation.

My goal for this book was to write and assemble the sorts of stories that resonate with me the most. Stories where, if you remove the supernatural, there is still a very real and potent horror story. They are stories about the sins of fathers, the looming and omniscient specter of depression, cyclical violence. Violence most of all. The intimate and personal acts of violence, and the widespread and dehumanizing violence of war.

That, over all else, is the truest horror story.

But I have been held up, surrounded by and egged on by a whole legion of people who love me. People who have coaxed me through the darkest episodes and who refused to see me give in. People who gave me their time and their patience as I went through every agonizing story pitch.

I want to start with Ed, Mike, Tighe, and Nina. Some of you were there from the beginning, on those back porches and under those Texas skies. I would not have made it here without you. Thank you.

And then there's the family. My dad, who drove me all over DFW looking for comics so he could spend time with me. Who learned all the characters' names and watched so many ghost shows with me. My grandparents, who drove me to the library almost two days a week. My loving stepparents, aunts, uncles, and cousins.

Then there is a whole slew of people in the weird community. KA Opperman, Ashley Dioses, Russell Smeaton, Jordan Kurella, John Paul Fitch, Christopher Ropes, John Linwood Grant, Duane Pesice, how many great conversations have we had? Thank you for them all. There's others still. Matthew M. Bartlett, Mer Whinery, Jonathan Raab, S.P. Miskowski, Gwendolyn Kiste, Nadia Bulkin, Brian Evenson.

Then there's Scarlett R. Algee. Scarlett, who saved this book from the dead once its former publisher went out of business. The death of this book was one of the saddest, hardest things I've went through. And I believe you saved it. Thank you so much. For everything..

And then there's Mom.

Mom and all her scary books. All her Halloweens.

Mom, and her sometimes overzealous support and confidence.

This is for you, Mom.

I love you.

And thank *you*, whoever you are, holding this book. I can't tell you how grateful I am that you gave it a chance. But I can thank you for coming all this way with me. I'll offer you one final story:

Prophecy in Brief

IN 500 YEARS, long after you are dead, it will come into Earth's orbit. Scientists will marvel at it from a distance, an unknown object of planetary size coming across the emptiness of space in order to parlay with our planet for what they believe to be a few brief minutes. Of course, the hypotheses will be plenty, and there will be the crackpot fringe theorists who predict the same end of the earth that they have been predicting since the 1800s.

The object will approach from behind the moon.

The hours of fleeting peace will be in the silence that rests on stupefied lips. Every living thing will look and wonder at the new arrival, whose orbit keeps it a sleek, black circle whose absolute darkness makes its surface invisible to even the most powerful of telescopes. But there are the few who will later claim the impossible, that they had heard screams coming from across the millions of miles before the object ceased its orbit and stayed in permanent position between the earth and the sun.

After only ten minutes the panic will begin. Even centuries from now the people who feed off fear will still be the dominant life form of Earth, they will use the eclipse as a cover for the most heinous acts that our race has ever committed. What will begin as looting will escalate to the most rapid, carnivorous genocides that our short history will ever record. In two days, after descending temperatures, all of those who could afford to leave the planet will, leaving the impoverished and hungry to die behind, under whatever sociopathic masters rise up and take reign of the dying.

What will remain of humanity in those last days is only an echo of its most primal ape-form. They will walk the freezing mausoleums of their cities, bone and club in hand as they pursue any life which might sustain their own. In their most ecstatic, elated moments they will turn to the dark circle which denies them their sunlight and they will pray, thinking it to be either God or the Devil. Life will end quickly after this, as first the forests and then even the deserts begin to freeze over.

The freeze happens more slowly than the scientists and their feeble laws would suggest, far slower than we would suspect now. In the creeping passage of time, the more murderous of our species, who will survive the longest, will begin to discern the whispering in the back of their minds as thoughts that are not their own, subconscious suggestions from a dark surface. At this final realization they will look to the sky and see the plain illuminated smile of the unknown planet beaming down at them.

And we will be able to hear its lips stretching, its teeth moving apart, as it utters the last goodbye we ever hear. Then it will descend on us, the highest form of life feeding on the second highest.

When it is finished, it will leave for greener, fatter fields.

Author's Notes: I have very vivid nightmares. This was one of them.

About the Author

S. L. Edwards is a world-traveling Texan who's finally made it home. He enjoys dark fiction, dark poetry and darker beer. He's the author of the novel *In the Devil's Cradle* and the short story collections *Whiskey and Other Unusual Ghosts* and *The Death of an Author*.

www.ingramcontent.com/pod-product-compliance
Lightning Source LLC
Chambersburg PA
CBHW020359030726
47496CB00007B/2222